REVERIE
FALLING FROM HELL
BOOK TWO

SUSAN PERSON

For all those who ever considered burning the world for their love

REVERIE

CHAPTER I
RENA

Hell's heat had nothing on the man beside me. Jax's woodsy scent wafted over me, and I rolled over to find him still asleep. Next to him, in bed, was one of my favorite places to be. I loved him, and I wasn't afraid to think it or feel it anymore. Sweet angel's ass he was handsome. His dark waves fell over his brow. The peaceful look on his chiseled face made me want to let him rest, but today was the day I handed the throne back to my father, Lucifer.

A ceremony had been planned to declare me as the heir and the crowned princess of Hell in the official capacity. After the ceremony, Jax and I would have a few months on Earth. Then, I'd return to the Underworld and begin my duties. Father and I reached a compromise because the Ascendant, Uriel's artifact that was corrupted and required me to temporarily incapacitate Father, had shortened my time in the Overworld. The events forced me to take the throne and rule Hell for a brief time, but that term was done. All we had to do was get through the next few hours, and Jax and I could disappear for a while.

I covered Jax's mouth with mine. He sighed, and wrapped his arms around my back, and a sense of safety and love enveloped me. A tingle pulsed in my chest. Euphoria from the closeness distracted me from the duties of the day. I stared into his eyes and saw happiness. His eyes hadn't turned blue like Father's after I used the ankh, the key of life, on him to return him from vampire to half demon and half human. Instead, his went from vampire red to the hazel they had been his whole life and demon red when he got angry. He looked like himself and sounded like himself and I loved all of him.

"Rena," he mumbled against my mouth and pulled back. He stroked my arms with a feathery light touch. "You know what happens when you wake me up like that."

"Mmm hmmm." I hummed against his neck and nipped just below his ear. Arousal pooled in my belly.

"Fuck." He let out a moan and flipped me onto my back. His hard length ground against my center. "I love you, Rena. Everything about you. From your silver hair to your wings so deeply purple they are almost black to your heart and soul."

Soul. A bitter taste formed on my tongue. That four-letter word would eventually separate me from Jax, but I'd do everything in my power to make sure we were together for lifetimes first. Gabriel and the other archangels had been right when they said I had one. I confirmed it with my trip to the Library of Knowledge, but I didn't know how to reconcile it with being the daughter of Lucifer and Lilith.

Jax slid his hands down my side. He stopped at my waist, his fingers tightening. I pulled him closer, wanting to feel every inch of him against me.

"How much time do we have?" he whispered in my ear, sending tingles down my spine.

A knock rapped on the door. *Seriously? They can't wait another thirty minutes? It is a special day though.*

I patted Jax's shoulder for him to let me up. "Not enough. If only we were on a deserted island."

Jax chuckled. "If only."

"Morena, are you awake? I have your gown for the ceremony." My mother's voice cut through the door with ease.

Jax's forehead fell against mine. "I can't wait for our time on Earth where I can have my wicked ways with you."

I crushed my lips against his. "Me too." I wrapped my legs around him and flipped him over. "Except I think I'll be the one doing the wicked things."

Jax laughed. "You better get the door, or she'll call the guards."

I resisted the temptation to ride him from this position and instead shifted to get off of him. As if he understood my need, he thrust his hips up. "Damn, Jax." I stifled a moan. There was never a time I didn't want him.

"I'll have to stay here for a few minutes."

I laughed and moved off him. "What if there was a grey wing at the door?"

The playfulness left Jax's face at the mention of the emotionless creatures we'd fought a few months ago. "Then I would slice its head from its shoulders."

His reaction wasn't what I expected, and I regretted how the change of subject affected his mood. He was a little off lately, and I'd chalked it up to the ceremony. The pressure was heavy to make the occasion perfect.

"Relax. Michael said they hadn't seen any in a month. He believes they have been vanquished." A part of me swallowed the guilt for that order, but they were like a plague, ready to consume anything in their path. There were no discussions with them. No reasoning with them. No capacity for compassion or love or humanity. They only understood how to do what they were created to do.

Another knock, this one harder, rattled the door. *Time to become what everyone else thinks I'm supposed to be. Except Jax. He sees me.* "On my way, Mother."

The fluffy robe I'd tossed in the chair by the bed was a little wrinkled, but it's not like I was going out in it. I threw it on and opened the door.

"Morning, Mo…" My voice trailed off when I saw three women standing behind Mother.

Mother kissed my cheek. "Good morning, dear. I've brought some help to prepare you for the ceremony. Is Jax still here?"

"Still here, Lilith," he yelled from the bedroom.

I covered my smirk with my hand. Mother was so serious I didn't think she would appreciate the humor.

"It'd be best if you got dressed if you're not already," Mother called with a smile on her face.

My face heated.

"One step ahead of you," he said.

"You're adults, Morena. There's no need to be embarrassed." She took my hand. "Now, come. We need to get you ready."

"This is a lot of pomp and circumstance for something I already declared when Father was incapacitated." I would do what needed to be done, but this grand scale for everything from the guest list to the attire to the food was…a lot.

"It is." She motioned for the three women to follow. "But the formality necessary."

I rubbed the back of my neck. The pressure of what the ceremony meant settled there, and I wondered if a similar protocol would have been required if I'd become the heir to Mother's path. *Does it hurt her I chose Hell over the Night Children?* "Do you wish I was taking your place instead, Mother?"

She sat on the couch and patted the seat next to her. I took it. "Morena, I want you to be happy. If you're not sure about succeeding your father, though, you need to tell him now."

It was too late. I'd declared it on a battlefield in front of virtually every demon and archangel. There wasn't another option, and Jax and I could be together this way.

Ruling Hell was my future and my destiny. I wasn't bitter about it, but regret gurgled in my belly for not having more time to just be with Jax before duty was a priority.

"My decision was made the moment I spoke the words, Mother. I'll not recant it now just because Father is better."

She brushed my hair back over my shoulders and rested her hands on either side of my face. "But you know he will support whatever his daughter wants."

It was tempting to explore what Mother said, but there could be a cost for it. I'd claimed the throne on a battlefield in front of the majority of demonkind. To back out would be an insult to Father, perceived as a weakness, but the biggest consequence would be the unavoidable shift in the balance. I wouldn't take that chance. "We have no idea what kind of repercussions it would cause if I changed my mind, but I'm not. I'm committed to my choice."

"I just don't want you to lament it." She folded her hands in her lap.

Her empathy tugged at my heart. "Do you have any remorse for your decision to love Father when you have to split your time?"

"Never," she said. A small smile formed on her lips. "I'd have never had you if I'd chosen differently, and you are the greatest gift I could have asked for."

I blinked back tears. "I don't regret my choice. It feels right." *Most of the time.*

"Then let's get you ready." She turned to the three

women waiting just inside my room. They were all waiting near the door, looking in different directions without looking at us. Mother trusted the ladies, or she wouldn't have spoken in front of them. Besides, anyone in such close proximity to her would have to swear the oath to her, and I recognized them from her regular team when she was in Hell, so it was no surprise to see them. "This is Frieda, Jane, and Tilly."

"Yes, I remember. It's nice to see you all again." I smiled warmly at them.

"They will do your hair and makeup, and all three of us will help you into your gown after you have your bath." She gestured to the garment bag that both Frieda and Jane held onto. There was a time when I thought of myself as a princess and wanted the fairytale life, but that wasn't what it meant to be the heir to Hell. Watching Jax die from Gabriel's sword changed my perspective. The grandness of being demon royalty wasn't nearly as important. I wanted to build a life with Jax, even if it was in Hell.

Tilly stepped forward with a wooden box. "And you will wear this today."

She opened the box to reveal a diamond-and-ruby-encrusted black tiara.

Panic laced its way through my body and wrapped around my heart. It tightened like a vise I sucked in a calming breath. *Here we go.*

CHAPTER 2
JAX

I hurried through the shower to give Rena and her mother's team room to prepare. The sweet sound of my love's voice rang through the bathroom door like the most erotic song. My dick twitched at the confidence she had. I stroked my cock once, thinking of how she handled me. I wanted her, but she was occupied. I discarded the urge to jerk off to the memories of last night given the audience in the other room. *But damn, I never get enough of her.*

Her assertiveness and strength as a leader grew every day, and I'd never understand what she saw in a half-demon, half-human, or whatever I was now. The ankh we used on her father had changed me back from a vampire to supposedly what I was before, but I didn't feel the same. I hadn't told Rena something was off. She had enough pressure without my complication adding stress. The only thing that felt the same was my deepening love for Rena. I was prepared to strike down archangels to save her, but she didn't need me to rescue her. And her independence was a turn-on.

Rena's voice drifted in again. "Stop rushing, Mother. I'll take a bath as soon as Jax is done. We have time."

For someone over two thousand years old, Lilith, Rena's mother, liked to be punctual. Lucifer walked through the Underworld as if everything was set to his schedule and as the King of Hell, it was. That luxury belonged to him, but he cut me slack there, as punctuality wasn't my strong suit.

I inhaled, preparing myself for the entourage outside. Once through the door, I took in the room to what looked like the coronation of Hell had exploded.

I found Rena's gaze, and desire rose in me. "This is — "

My love crossed the room and slipped her hand in mine. "A lot. I know. But after today, we get to go be us for a while."

Luck hadn't really been on our side, but I hoped she was right.

"Lilith." I nodded to Rena's mother.

"Jax." She smiled and sipped her tea. The Mother of Night Children started every day with tea, unlike her actual Night Children who started their day at dusk with blood. Rena didn't drink blood often as a demon but she didn't necessarily have tea for breakfast like Lilith either. Although, she enjoyed a cup of the hot liquid often. The tea service made everything seem normal, but today wasn't a normal day.

I tugged Rena toward the door with me. "Last chance to escape."

She stood on her tiptoes and slid her lips over mine in a kiss too soft for my liking. I wanted to scoop her up and carry her to bed, but that would have to wait for later.

"It will be over before we know it," she said.

I kissed the tip of her nose. "I'm holding you to that promise. I'll see you soon, my love."

"Jax, you need to be back an hour in your uniform before the ceremony to escort Morena," Lilith called from where she was fluffing a garment that looked like a massive, dark cape.

"Yes, I'm aware," I said. Lilith had reminded me of my duties for this pageantry at least a dozen times this week. She might as well have said they needed me to smile and be pretty. A quiet chuckle shook in my throat.

I excused myself and wandered down the hall. Lucifer brought electricity to Hell long before my time, but the lights were often kept to a soft glow from sconces on the grey rock walls of the passages. Carved ceilings adorned the ones Lucifer and Lilith frequented. Some soared so high they were difficult to decipher from a distance, but each held meaning to the journey Rena's parents had made.

My stomach growled. The hunger was so intense, I gripped my stomach. I headed to the kitchen, but it wasn't food I was hungry for like before I was turned vampire and back. It was blood. My midsection grumbled like starvation was imminent. The cravings ached like a part of me was still vampire, but that couldn't be. *Could it? Probably just residual effects from the process.* I'd gone through my personal stash of blood, so I detoured to the kitchen area for more. I never seemed to be satisfied, but I wasn't about to eat human flesh as the alternative either.

The other demons exited when I entered. They gave me a wide berth since my return. The high-ranking ones didn't, but the lower levels considered me a superior now. Not because of the half-demon to vampire and back to half-demon thing but because of my relationship with Rena. They assumed Lucifer would appoint me to general today, but that wasn't the plan. I'd have done it if Rena wished me to, but she wanted me to make my own decision without her influence. Lucifer gave me the choice of positions, and I chose to be at Rena's side. He could call me her personal guard or whatever he wanted, but no one was getting closer to her than me.

I surveyed the pile of blood bags in front of me. Nine. Yesterday there were seven, and the day before that there were six. My thirst for blood couldn't be sated any more than my longing for Rena. I wanted more of both of them every passing day.

The hunger waned enough I could focus on my next task. I grabbed a handful of blood bags and headed for the sparring area. Exercise took my mind off the constant craving. I could think while on the mat, but I starved from the exertion. The reprieve for an hour or so was what I was chasing to get my mind focused for the ceremony.

CHAPTER 3
RENA

Where in all that is Hell is Jax? I knew we'd had a lot on our plates, but he'd disappeared several times over the last week. I didn't think the ankh had done anything other than revert his vampirism. He was Jax, after all, but something was going on with him. *I'll ask him about it after the ceremony.* I turned back and walked the length of the room, which was a difficult task given the weight of the gown I wore.

"Stop pacing, Morena," Mother said. "He still has ten minutes. He'll be here, and you're going to wrinkle your dress."

My jaw clenched. "Well, you said I can't sit down, so either let me pace or let me sit."

"Fine. Pace," Mother said, flustered. She was stressed. I was stressed, and I'm sure Jax was stressed. The nervous energy made it impossible for me to be still.

I turned to make another lap. The door opened, and

Jax's strong frame filled the space. The tense set of his jaw lessened. Relief and desire tangled inside me. Jax made anything look incredible, and this garment looked exceptional on him. He wore the red and black uniform of Mother and Father's guards. He swore his oath to me, and I was the heir. The colors were mine too. He glanced between Mother and me as if he could read our thoughts.

"Am I late?" His brows pulled together.

"No, Jax. You're right on time," Mother said. "Morena is just nervous."

I fought the urge to roll my eyes.

He crossed the room in a swift motion and crushed his lips to mine. The metallic tang of blood mixed with mint wafted around me. It wasn't the first time this week or the last month. He'd fed a lot...more than a demon should need to.

"You okay?" I whispered against his lips, concerned he was hurt in some way. *Why else would he need to consume so much blood?*

He pulled back. "Of course."

I studied him, and he didn't appear to be in pain. He wouldn't tell me if there was anything wrong while Mother was here. My questions would have to wait until after the ceremony.

"Here." Mother shoved a tissue in front of Jax's face. "Wipe the red lipstick off your mouth. Morena, come let me fix your makeup." She did a quick touch-up.

"Sorry," I said, worry building in me.

"No apologies needed." She glanced between us. "But no more kissing until after the ceremony."

Jax's stare roamed over the massive gown. "We certainly can't do anything else until then."

I swatted his arm.

"Jax, help me attach the cape. I sent the ladies on to clear the hall." Mother held out the black cape adorned with black crystals. The detailed design was beautiful despite the weight. *One more step toward making my role official.*

Jax grabbed one side. "Where does it attach?"

"Just at the top of the shoulder."

Jax skated his hand across my collarbone. My stomach fluttered at the featherlight touch. He slipped his fingers under the fabric as he found the snaps and hooks. My core clenched from his brief touch. "This is quite complex."

"Yes." I let out a breath.

"Later, you two," Mother said.

My desire was immediately quenched.

Jax cleared his throat. "Done." He kissed my temple and stepped back, taking in the gown from the floor to my neck before settling on my lips. My desire flared again under his heated gaze. "You look breathtaking. Every bit the queen you were meant to be."

Something flashed across his face. It was almost like... pain.

A knot formed in my throat, and I swallowed hard against it.

"Are you ready?" Mother asked.

Was I? I didn't know for sure, but I was committed to this journey. I held out my hand to Jax. As long as the love of my long life was by my side, I could do this. "Yes, I'm ready."

Jax's shoulder brushed against mine, and he linked our pinkies together. His fingers threaded through mine. Mother opened the door and led us down the private corridor where the guards would meet us to walk the rest of the way to the throne room. Sweat slicked my palm, but Jax didn't pull away. I'd claimed my heirship on the battle-field and declared my intention. *So, why am I so nervous? Because there is no going back, and things will change after. I accepted it.* I stole a glance at Jax. He'd said he accepted it, too, and I'd spend our alone time showing him my appreciation. *Get this done and we will be free for a while. I'm ready to spend time alone with Jax.*

Mother went ahead of us. We waited in the side hallway so no one would see us during Mother's announcement and entrance.

Flanked by some of Father's most loyal guards, Jax and I moved to just outside the door. The lead guard rapped twice on the large, double wood panels. Both sides opened at the same time, and a horn blew.

"Her Royal Highness, the Princess Morena," the demon next to the horn blower announced.

I never allowed anyone to call me princess. I'd grown to hate the title as I got older. It always felt unnecessary and formal. *Today, that changes. My role changes. My life changes.* Fear spiked up my spine. Jax squeezed my hand before letting go and offered his arm instead. I inhaled a deep, calming breath and slipped my arm through his.

A sea of demons filled the throne room. Heads in the crowd inclined as we made our way down the black carpet. Father stood at the end with his hands clasped in front of him. Never one to apply rules to himself, he didn't wear a standard uniform like the guards or Jax. Instead, he wore a solid black uniform and a red sash adorned with ruby and black stones similar to what covered my tiara and gown. His dark hair was combed back off his face, making the streak of silver that appeared after the ankh restored him stand out.

Father's face was solemn, but a small twitch at the corner of his mouth told me he wanted to smile. He'd seated Stassi, my only human friend, in a place of honor on the front row with her vampire boyfriend. She smiled broadly at me. I'd have to thank her for coming because what human willingly goes to Hell for their friend?

A pentagram marked the end of the path. Mother stood on one side, dressed in an adorned black gown. Worry tightened her shoulders, and Father, on the other side, looked far more relaxed. Jax stopped just short of the end and turned to me. He mouthed, "I love you."

His lips grazed my knuckles, and he passed my hand over to my father. I locked in my game face. Father and I stepped into the pentagram, and it flamed to life but did not burn us. A reminder this was where I belonged.

Mother and Jax turned to face the crowd.

I inhaled slowly *One...Two...Three...* And let it out

slowly *One…Two…Three…* The calming technique Jax and I used hadn't failed me yet, but there was a first time for everything.

Father directed his gaze at me. There was pride in his eyes and love and something else that might be a touch of remorse. It gave me a boost of confidence but did not squelch my nerves. "This is your time, my dear daughter. I hope you embrace it and make it your own."

"Thank you, Father." My body shook. I worried the gown would give me away, but the weight of it hid the visible sign of my fear.

Father and I faced the crowd. Jax was too close for me to focus on him, so I stared out at the multitude of people. *Well, demons, fallen angels, a handful of vampires, and one human.* My gaze settled on Stassi. She smiled, and I was grateful we'd been able to return to friendship, best friends.

"Devoted citizens, I come to you with news about the future of our kingdom. Today, I present to you my daughter, my successor, the future queen, Morena. From here forth, she will be known as the Crown Princess Morena of Hell."

This is really it. In two, three, four. Out, two, three, four.

A breeze rushed past me, and gasps rang out around the room. Stassi's mouth gaped open. Not the reaction I expected. It took seconds for me to realize it wasn't about me. Jax lay on the floor next to me.

No. Panic shook me to the core. I dropped to the ground next to him. His eyes were closed. He looked flushed. His face and neck were a bright red. It was too reminiscent of when he went through the vampire change. My mind went down a list of what could be wrong. *Did the ankh not work? Is he turning back into a vampire? Is he hurt?* I patted my hands over him but found no injuries. "I don't see anything. What's happening to him?"

Mother knelt and touched his cheeks. "He's burning up, even for a demon."

"What is it?" I asked. Mother shook her head. I looked at Father.

His brows bunched together. "I don't know."

"We have to do something." I bit down on my wrist to give him some of my blood.

"Not here," Father said. He motioned for two demons to help. I recognized them from the attack on Gothica. *Tashara and Forest.* They were Night Children Father saved by turning into demons.

Stassi knelt beside me. "They need to move him, Morena."

I nodded my head in agreement with Father. Stassi slipped her hand under my elbow to help me to my feet.

The guards lifted Jax, and his body was lax. Too lax. I bit down on my lip to choke back a sob. Stassi wrapped a hand around my waist and guided me behind them. *I can't lose Jax. We've survived so much. This can't be it.*

Someone in the crowd took a knee, and then the entire room was on their knees in respect as the guards rushed Jax out of the room. He'd wanted respect since I'd known him. It saddened me this was what it took for the rest of Hell to show him.

We hurried back to my room. I held Jax's hand, regret flooding my chest for the pressure I'd put on him for this ceremony. He wanted to be with me, and the demands were great for our current state. This was my fault.

Worry for Jax coupled with the heaviness of my cape was smothering.

The guards put Jax on the couch with his head on a pillow, and he looked worse. He was in bad shape. *But from what?* As soon as they had Jax settled on the couch, I started fiddling with the fasteners of the mantle. *I can't move enough to help him in this thing.* "Someone get this cape off of me before I rip it off."

Mother undid the snaps and hooks quickly. The cape fell to the floor, but I still felt suffocated. My knees thumped against the ground when I dropped down beside him.

"Refael, my sister, you are needed here," Father called out.

A burst of Heavenly light blinded us before the wispy blonde appeared in her lustrous purple gown. "Brother, it has been some time."

Her voice was a sweet sound, like a gentle bird.

"It has, Sister. Too long." Father embraced her quickly. "I want to catch up with you, but I need you now."

She could sense illness. She looked from him to me. One of her eyebrows shot up. "My niece, are you unwell?"

"No, Aunt Refael." I glanced at Jax and back to her. *Can she not tell it's Jax who is sick?*

"Then who?" She looked around the room, and her gaze came to rest on Jax. She took careful steps and knelt beside the couch. "He has been through much. His life spread across multiple worlds. What a strong soul. Unfortunately, I cannot help him."

Disbelief racked my brain as I gasped for air. "What do you mean?"

"Only time and his decision will determine his future." Her tone was sympathetic.

"I don't understand." My throat ached from unshed tears.

"He is the one struck by Gabriel's blade?" Refael asked.

"Yes." I shuddered at the memory of Jax and my decision to turn him into a Night Child to save him. Everything bad that happened to him was because of me.

Refael looked at Mother. "And you saved him with your blood?"

"Yes," Mother said.

"And it was at your behest?"

"Yes." I nodded. "I made that choice."

"And now you choose to love him and he you, but it requires you to stay here. In Hell."

I didn't understand what that had to do with what was happening with Jax, and we didn't have time for archangel riddles. "How does that relate to him being sick?"

"His soul is torn. Torn between the blade of an angel,

the human realm, the Night Children's blood, and your love. Jax is all these things but none of them completely. He needs to heal, and he can't do it in Hell."

"Where do I take him, then?" I'd go anywhere to save him. The ceremony wasn't completed, but Father and Hell would understand. *Wouldn't they? Would it make me look like a weak leader if I didn't finish it?* It didn't matter. I would go where Jax needed to be to save him.

"To the human realm. His decay will slow there, but it will not stop."

Decay? That word alone drove my fear in like a spike of sadness. "For how long?"

"However long it takes him to heal," she said matter-of-factly. The irony the half-human side aged in the human world didn't escape me. "You need to give him the space and patience to do so."

I'd make sure he was somewhere safe in the human realm, even if that meant losing face with the citizens of Hell.

CHAPTER 4

JAX

My throat burned like the fires of Hell raged in it. I swallowed against the rawness, and I imagined eating sand would be easier. The hunger ached worse than I felt when I was vampire. Had the ankh failed? Voices drifted around me. *Rena. Lilith.*

There was a deep ache in my chest that spread out into my limbs. I sat up, despite my body's protests. The scent of death wafted around me, and I realized I was not in Hell. In fact, I was on the couch in Lilith's Gothica apartment. *Am I a Night Child again? No, I don't feel like it anyway. Except for the hunger. Fuck.* Light streamed through the stained-glass window that depicted Lilith and Lucifer's love. It cast a rainbow across the flow right to Rena. The concern on her face hauled all my fears for her safety to the surface. My hunger tripled, and I grabbed my throat.

Rena's eyes widened a little. She grabbed Lilith's arm as if for support.

"Mother," she whispered.

Lilith went to the refrigerator and pulled out a plastic bag. *Blood.* My stare trained on the one thing that could satiate my hunger. I salivated. She handed the bag to Rena.

Rena moved slowly toward the couch and took the seat beside me. She was cautious, as if she was afraid she would set me off, but she wouldn't. I was hungry. That was it. I didn't like seeing her worried or in fear, whichever she was. "Here. Drink this and then we need to talk."

Fuck. I didn't need to hear another word to know I wasn't going to like it. The way I arrived at Gothica was a missing memory, so the news she wanted to share would not be good. I sucked the blood down in three big gulps and braced myself. The hunger wasn't gone, but it was quieted for a few moments. "Tell me what happened. No secrets between us."

"No secrets," she said, her voice so soft I barely heard her despite my enhanced hearing. "Jax..." She trailed off and looked at her mother.

"I'll give you two some time," Lilith said, crossing the apartment swiftly and closing the door behind her.

I tucked a loose strand of silvery hair away from Rena's face and cupped the soft skin of her cheek. She closed her eyes and rested her head on my hand.

Her eyes opened and met mine. She brought her lips to my palm. My cock responded as if it was as starved as I was. She drew our hands in her lap. I wanted her, but there was a discussion needed. Sex would have to wait.

"Whatever it is, Rena, we'll tackle it together."

"I don't think we can this time, Jax." Hunger and fear spiraled through me. My stomach sank so far it felt like it landed on the floor.

"Just tell me, my love."

She inhaled a deep breath. "Your soul has been ripped. Shredded and spread into different realms."

A soul is a soul. How could it rip? "I don't understand how that is possible."

"I didn't either until Father called Aunt Refael to heal you. She was able to see the many transitions you have been through, and she could see all of it and how it tore your soul. A piece of you is scattered in the multiple realms you touched."

"Because I was demon, then vampire, then back to demon? How does that impact my soul?"

"Not just demon..." She paused. Her brows furrowed, and her face tightened as if it was painful to say the words. "You were part human too. Your soul is spread across the demon, human, and vampire realms."

"But demons don't have souls."

Her eyes met mine, and I saw the answer there. She had a soul.

My damn human side. Always making me a weak fucker. Even now. I thought I was finally a whole demon after the ankh. "Because I was part human, I had a soul, and that soul has been through its own war. How do we fix me?"

Rena wrapped my hands in hers. Concern darkened

her eyes. "That is up to you, Jax. You have to figure out who you want to be to heal."

This was a no-brainer choice for me. I'd always choose Rena. It didn't matter what the question was. She was always the solution to any equation for me. "But I know the answer. I want to be with you."

"It's not about me." Her hand rested against my chest over where my heart beat again after my return from being vampire. Her touch comforted me, but the placement was a reminder of how broken I was. "I know you love me, and I love you as you are. Any way you are. But you have to figure out what world is yours, and that can't be about me. To heal, you must pull all the pieces of your soul to you, but there must be conviction in it."

In my heart, I wanted to be wherever Rena was, but the human realm had always seemed more normal to me. The comfort I felt while on Earth was a peace I never experienced in Hell. I wanted both serenity and Rena. It'd never be a question for me. Rena was my person. I'd go where she went. *Fuck.* My throat flamed with hunger.

"I need to eat," I said. "Blood. Not human food."

She nodded. "That's going to get worse until you are better too." Rena's tone was sympathetic, but I didn't want sympathy. Not now. Not ever.

"Great." I walked to the refrigerator and grabbed a bag. Nothing else in me ached except for telltale signs of hunger. "You know how much I love feeding."

The cool metallic liquid soothed the burn in my throat. *I used to hate the taste of blood, but damn, this tastes good.*

"And what happens if I don't merge or weld or whatever my soul back together?"

"That's not an option," Rena said.

She crossed the room and leaned forward on the opposite side of the kitchen bar from me. Her entire face seemed to droop in unhappiness. It was overwhelming how it rolled off her and filled the room.

"What happens, my love?" I leaned over from the other side to be nearer to her.

"You'll die," she said. Tears brimmed in her beautiful blue eyes. "And nothing beyond that."

Fuck my human side. I jerked back and grabbed another bag of blood. The plastic ripped open easily, and the liquid slid down my throat to cool the fire in my belly. Rena looked the saddest I'd ever seen her, and it was because of me. She didn't need this shit right now. I swiped a hand over my face like that would erase the issue. I had to let her go. She couldn't watch me suffer through whatever grim deterioration was about to happen. *Damn eternity.*

CHAPTER 5

RENA

Defeat scored Jax's face, but I refused to let him give up. I might not be able to fix this, but I'd stand by him just as he stood by me to prevent hell on Earth and to save my father.

Mother knocked and came through the door with terrible timing. She assessed the situation with the deep scrutiny she used on everything. Her posture was stiff with tension, but she pushed forward. "Jax, how are you feeling?"

"Like shit, but I don't think that's going to change for the time being."

Mother squeezed his shoulder and turned to me. "Morena, we need to go back to Hell and finish your ceremony. Your Father will only be able to delay so long."

Disbelief wandered up my spine until the thoughts connected in my brain. I assumed the ceremony would be postponed, given the situation. We'd only been gone an hour, maybe two at most. "What? I'm not leaving Jax. Hell can freeze over."

"Morena," Mother chastised.

Jax took my hands in his. I saw conviction on his face. He was going to side with Mother. "She's right, Rena. Hell needs stability more than ever now that the demons have seen that Lucifer, as powerful as he is, can still be harmed. They will challenge him without a successor, and we all know how well your father will take that."

I wasn't sure if I disliked being right more or his sensibility about the situation. I stared up at the ceiling like the answer would be there and let out a calming breath. His argument was logical, but I hated it. I didn't want to leave him alone with life or death at stake, but that was exactly what Refael had said. *Alone. The ceremony didn't necessarily have to be today. It needed to be soon but soon was relative for demons.* "You're right, but I can stay for a few months and then do the ceremony."

Jax's fingertips brushed against my cheeks. "No, you can't. The only reason we were to have the three months is that your vow would be in place."

Damn it. A pit formed in my stomach and was a well of sadness. My eyes burned from the tears I held back. "I don't want to leave you here alone."

"I'll be fine. I promise I'll be here when you get back." Jax's voice was soft, almost a malleable tone like the Night Children used.

Bright white light formed in front of us. I shielded my eyes.

Jophiel. My aunt, the archangel of wisdom, arrived, and it gave me the smallest bit of hope.

"He won't be alone." She smiled at me.

I couldn't hold back the relief on my face if I wanted to. Her presence alone was assurance for me. "Aunt Jophiel, thank you for coming."

"I'm here for him," she said. "But you are welcome. Return to Hell and accomplish your duties. You have my word he will be here when you come again."

My mind raced for reasons to stay. "But isn't my help needed here?"

"It is." She shifted her focus from me to Jax. "But there is much work Jax and I can do while you take care of your Hellish business."

I trusted Aunt Jophiel, but she was about knowledge, not protection. "With the Night Children massacre that took place, there's not much defense here. We'll need to coordinate some protection for Jax."

"Morena is right," Mother said. "There aren't enough of my children left to fend off an attack. I can call some more to Gothica to help supplement."

Jax's face reddened, and he ground his teeth together. "Enough. Don't talk about me like I'm not here. I don't need protection. I'm a demon, and who is going to know I'm here, anyway?"

"You are and have always been more than a demon," I said. "Which makes you a target, whether you realize it or not." And it was because of me didn't need to be added.

The guilt of what I brought to his life gouged into my scattered thoughts.

"I have help coming. Barachiel will join me to help defend your champion. There will be no need for others."

"Champion?" Jax and I said in unison.

"Is he not your chosen mate?" Jophiel asked.

The urge to laugh was only tempered by Aunt Jophiel's seriousness. "That's kind of archaic but yes."

"Then it's settled. I'll help him find the answers he seeks, and Barachiel will help defend him," she said like we should have all come to this same conclusion at the same time. "You are able to finish your ceremony and complete your duties."

I narrowed my eyes, skeptical it was that easy. "Aunt Jophiel, why do I have a feeling there is something you are not telling me?"

"Knowledge comes in its own time, dear niece. Be patient."

Patience wasn't something I practiced or relished. "I don't like being in the dark."

"You can't know everything, Morena. Omniscience is not your gift," Mother said.

I turned to her, ready to fire a retort back.

"Rena." Jax encircled me with his arms. He placed a chaste kiss on my lips. "Go. I'll see you soon."

I leaned into him, soaking up his woodsy scent. *Damn it. I don't want to leave him.* There wasn't anything I could do for him here, but duty called in Hell. I inhaled him one last time and glanced at Jophiel. "Make sure he is safe above all else."

She nodded.

I stepped out of Jax's arms and gestured for Mother to take my wrist. The debate in my head to determine if this was the right course of action ran wild, but Aunt Jophiel and Aunt B had my trust. *If only I could be in two places at once.* I retrieved my dagger from the sheath at my back. It was the only semblance of a portal I could call, and the blade only took me to Father. I slid it across my palm. The sting evaporated into the air as we were pulled through a portal back to Hell...where Father and the rest of demonkind waited.

CHAPTER 6
JAX

I'd let Rena go again, and my chest ached. *How many times could we keep doing this? How could we be together if I was stuck here and she in Hell?* I wasn't sure if the pain around my heart was from the separation or the never-ending hunger lodged in my throat that settled in my stomach. If no amount of blood seemed to quench it, there was another alternative. I squeezed my eyes shut at the thought of eating human flesh. I'd never acquired that taste. It repulsed me when I saw other demons do it.

But it sounded appealing to me for the first time. The thought of biting down and feeling the soft tissue between my teeth made me salivate. *The skin giving as I ripped it free. Get it together, dickhead.* I swiped my hand over my face like that would wipe it all away, including the disgust I felt for myself.

"Jax?" Jophiel's voice broke through my haze.

"I'm sorry. Did you say something?" I answered, ashamed of my inability to pay attention. She was doing me a favor.

"That answers my question. We need to have you focused, and you can't be with your hunger eating at the edges of your mind," Jophiel said, but she had no idea how hungry I was or what I wanted to eat.

"It's more than the edges. It's consuming me and getting worse." The hunger trapped me in a constant state of confusion. I couldn't be fully attentive anywhere. I wasn't sure I could eat enough to be present. There would be no healing if I didn't. *No life with Rena.* My heart broke as if it wanted to shatter into pieces to match my damn soul.

"As soon as Barachiel arrives, we'll get you satiated. Then, the work begins."

I marched over to the fridge and grabbed another blood bag, unsure if it was even possible to satisfy this feeling of starvation. The last of the liquid slid down my throat, and I reached for the door to grab another one. A bright light flashed around me.

"I have arrived," Barachiel said.

"That is apparent," Jophiel said.

I snorted and turned around. "Barachiel." She wasn't the biggest archangel, but she was a warrior like Michael. Dressed in green with armor glinting like Heaven's light, she appeared with a white rose in her hand. That was normal for her. Sometimes rose petals even scattered around at her command, but she saved that for special occasions.

"Jax, you look...horrible."

"Thanks." I didn't need a reminder, but I appreciated the honesty. Barachiel was one of the few archangels I trusted or connected to, and considering she could wield lightning as a weapon, that meant something. The reason I trusted her was because she kept things real and didn't mince words. She was even good with current terminology, so the words didn't come out similar to a riddle.

"Sister, I'm sure you already have a plan. Let's hear it," Barachiel said to Jophiel. "Preferably before Jax gnaws one of our arms off."

She joked, but an arm was what I'd been daydreaming of earlier. I salivated at the thought of chewing on flesh, but I simultaneously wanted to vomit at the image it conjured in my head.

"His eyes are glossing over. Better get on with it." Barachiel winked at me.

"I'm glad you find it funny because I'm tempted to take you up on the offer of an arm. Would it grow back?"

Her smile faded. My quip had fallen flat on her usually great sense of humor. *Of course, dickhead. You just asked if you could eat her arm.* I might be worse off than I thought.

"Stop. Both of you. You're wasting time." Jophiel chastised us but her tone was kind. "I want you to deliver a small shock to him. It should reset his system for a while and give us time to work."

She wasn't laughing, but she had to be joking. A lightning bolt would fry a regular demon, and I was half human, as everyone reminded me. "I'm not Lucifer. I can't survive a lightning bolt to the heart."

"Not a lightning bolt. She just needs to do a controlled electrocution."

I backed up a step. "That doesn't sound any better."

"It's not the same as harnessing lightning like we did for Lucifer. Barachiel will place a hand on your head and send a current directly into your brain. Simple."

I took a full stride backward in the direction of the door. My intention set on running as soon as I cleared it and manufacturing a portal as I ran. "And what's to stop her from cooking my brain like burnt bacon?"

Jophiel sighed. "I understand you're concerned, but Barachiel is very skilled at this."

"My sister sings the song of my praises for something I've only done with other angels." Barachiel's voice was full of confidence, but she'd never attempted it on someone like me.

"But you have done it successfully?" I swallowed against the dryness in my throat.

"Yes, on angels. Different anatomy. Same concept."

Jophiel moved closer to Barachiel. "Not that different. Our blood is the only major variant, and I've calculated it."

Blood. I glanced at the refrigerator. My hunger gurgled in my belly. If she fried me, at least I wouldn't be starving anymore. Rena's face popped into my head, but it didn't help against the deprivation of food my body claimed. "Fine. Let's do it."

"I need you standing for it, but you will fall once the pulse enters your brain." *Won't be the first time I fell down.* A memory flashed of sparring with Rena and the look of surprise when she got me with a hip toss. I smiled and closed my eyes. *If that's my last memory, it's a good one.*

Jophiel situated me near the couch and stood on one side without touching me. Barachiel positioned a hand on top of my head, like an alien ready to suck my brains out. Her palm was warm, and the scent of freshly bloomed roses spread around me.

I inhaled deeply and let it out. *Fuck. This better work. Rena will kill me if I die like this.*

"Calm yourself," Barachiel said.

I opened my eyes, trying to find nice words when all I could think was...*How the fuck do I calm myself when she's about to fry my brain?*

"What my sister means is center your energy. Think of something that brings you peace and focus on that," Jophiel said in her angelic singsong tone.

"Yes, that's what I meant."

I closed my eyes again and imagined Rena. I envisioned her hair, soft as silk, threaded through my fingers. The fucking firey expression in her eyes when I told her to look at me while she orgasmed. The peaceful look after she comes. That sweet innocence on her face when she awoke in the morning with her hair a mess. She might be the most beautiful then.

A zipping sound shot through my head like it would split it in two. The images of Rena turned into the day we fell from Hell with Lilith's touch. I'd almost lost my grip on her hand. Dizziness clouded my senses, and I fell backward.

CHAPTER 7

RENA

The ceremony went as planned. It was exactly as it was before, right down to who attended except for the most important person to me, Jax. As soon as I could, I left the reception with Mother. She closed the door to my room behind us, but I was already working on stripping out of the dress.

"Let me help," Mother said, her voice quiet.

Every broken moment Jax and I shared played on repeat in my head and strangled me. "Just take my dagger and cut me out of it."

"I will not." Mother worked through the buttons on the back.

"Why does this have buttons instead of a zipper, anyway?"

"Because it was made from part of my gown when I pledged to help Lucifer rule."

I turned around to face her. Guilt riddled me for the remarks I'd made earlier in the day. The gown was beautiful. Just not my style. "What? Why didn't you tell me?"

Mother's face softened. "I meant to when we were dressing you, but the day was a little chaotic."

I'm such a jerk. "It really is stunning, Mother. I'm sorry I failed to show my appreciation."

"No apologies needed, Morena. I know our styles are different. Mine tends to be a little old-fashioned for you."

"Let's talk about the running shoes in your closet at Gothica. They were definitely not old-fashioned."

She smiled. "I had those placed there for you. I figured you would need them at some point during your visits to the human realm."

My heart warmed. She'd always put Father and me first, even as protective as she was of her Night Children. "Why running shoes?"

"Just a feeling," she said, keeping her voice light. "Call it a mother's intuition, if you will."

"That's very good intuition." I didn't push. It had been a tough day, and that conversation could wait for another time. Besides, all I wanted was to get back to Jax.

Mother carefully laid out the dress and cape in their bags while I changed into more Earth-appropriate clothing. Jeans, a tank, and a jacket were easy and quick and got me to Jax faster.

"Before you leave for the human realm, your father and I have something for you in his office. Shall we?" She gestured toward the door. The ceremony was a big deal, and it made sense my parents would want to mark it in some way. As big a hurry as I was in to see Jax, I needed to give my parents this moment.

"Okay...But then I have to go." I took a few steps and turned around. "It's not something weird, is it?"

Mother's forehead bunched up. "I'm not sure what you mean."

"Like you're not giving me blood or some random artifact." I had a few random artifacts in my room already, but our last run-in with the Ascendant and its mind-altering effects had me a little apprehensive around relics.

"No, nothing so formal," she said.

Mother led the way toward Father's office, and we were flanked by two guards. The presence of guards nearby had been beefed up since Father took the throne back. He was on alert, and it wasn't the first time the sight made me wonder if it was cautionary or if he knew something I didn't. Maybe that's why he wanted to see me in his office.

Another guard posted by the door opened it for us.

"My wife and my daughter." Father smiled and rose from the desk. He'd changed from his formal wear into his black tunic and pants. "I never tire of seeing you."

"You just saw us." I laughed.

"But that was formal pageantry for the masses. This is for us," he said, his voice soft like an angel and not the booming voice from the ceremony.

Mother's gaze landed on Father, and she smiled. "Your Father and I were talking about how to mark this occasion, and we decided to share a very old family heirloom with you."

Please don't let this be an artifact.

Father pulled a red velvet box from a drawer on his desk and rounded the edge toward me. He lifted my hand and placed the box in my palm. The soft container was light. "From your mother and me to mark your day, but also a reminder that your choices are yours."

I opened the box to find a silver necklace. *A very beautiful necklace encrusted with stones, similar to my ceremonial gown.* I ran my finger over it.

"It's platinum," Mother said.

Platinum, not silver. Got it. The rubies and diamonds on the front glittered. "It's breathtaking."

"It's a locket. Open it." Mother slipped her arm around Father's waist.

I opened it to find a picture of Mother and Father and an inscription. *Always our daughter, the purest form of our love.* Tears burned my eyes.

"And the back," Father said.

I flipped it over and read it out loud. "Your destiny is yours."

I looked up at them. For the first time since they told me I had to choose where I'd eventually rule, I believed my destiny might not be dictated. I might have a choice. A tear spilled down my cheek.

Father reached out and wiped it away.

"Your life is always yours, Morena, and we wanted you to have something to remind you of it every day." Mother smiled.

"Thank you." My voice was hoarse through the knot in my throat. I swallowed against it. "This is the best gift you've given me."

"Let me," Father said, taking the necklace from my hand.

I turned around and lifted my hair. "You said it's a family heirloom?"

"It's made from the rubies, diamonds, and platinum of our wedding bands," Mother said.

I hadn't even noticed they weren't wearing them. I tensed. They had never taken them off.

"Relax," Father said. "We had new ones made."

"And once you return, your father and I plan to do a vow renewal to exchange the new ones."

"I don't deserve you two." I embraced them, one arm wrapped around each of their necks.

"You deserve everything you want and more, dear daughter." Mother squeezed me tight to her.

"Now, it's time to go," Father said, letting me go. "Someone else needs you for his journey."

"Jax," I whispered. My stomach dropped with an urgency to go to him.

"Yes," Mother said. "Are you ready to fall again?"

I was ready, but I didn't want to always have to depend on others to travel. "Let me try to call a portal. I've been practicing."

Father nodded.

I made the symbols with my hands and a pinkish orange light formed. It expanded to about a foot wide and collapsed. *Damn. Why is this so hard for me?*

"I can literally do almost everything...except master the damn portals." I stepped back, my frustration showing. I didn't want them to see me like this, especially after I'd just been proclaimed heir in front of everyone. *Almost everyone.*

"It just takes time and a high level of focus." Father patted my shoulder. "And it doesn't come for everyone. You have many gifts."

"Your father is right. No one can possess every single skill. That's why we have experts."

I loved my parents, especially for how they wanted to soften things like this, but I needed to do this. "You're my parents. You have to say that."

Mother and Father both laughed.

"You should know us better than that if you thought we would spare your feelings," Mother said. "But we would do anything for you."

And they had. More than once. More than twice. So many times, I'd lost count.

"Just send me on the fall before I gag." I grinned at them. "I love you two ancient weirdos."

"We love you too." Father squeezed my hand one last time.

"Very much," Mother said, her hand connecting with my forehead.

I fell to Earth like I had when this whole journey started. I missed Jax's touch during the fall. The security of his presence was absent. Then the floor of Gothica came into view, and I landed on my feet, proud the landing wasn't on my ass.

JAX

"What did you do?" Rena's voice drifted in like the sweetest melody, but there was an edge to it. The stress in it wasn't right. I could see her face, but it was out of focus. *Am I dreaming? Must be.* I settled in for the fantasy her image conjured tonight.

"He's fine," another voice said. *Barachiel's.* No offense to them, but I wanted Rena alone in this dream.

"He doesn't look fine," Rena said, her voice full of panic.

"Give it time, Morena. It's a reset on his system." Jophiel's voice spread around me.

Reset. This isn't a dream. I need to wake up. I tried to force my eyes open, but nothing happened. Tested out a hand and a finger next. They didn't work. Agitation turned to alarm. It was like the shock paralyzed me in this in-between state. *Fuck.*

"Can you just give him another shock to wake him up?" Rena said, her voice a full octave higher than normal.

"No, it's a reset, Rena," Barachiel said. "His mind needs to do it on its own."

Except my mind didn't seem to be able to break through.

"Stop pacing, Morena. Sit with him and let your love flow into him," Jophiel said.

Her love. It is all I ever need.

The cushion beside me dipped. Her soft scent drifted around me. I breathed it in like a drug.

"Jax," Rena whispered. "I know you're in there. Give in to the reset and come back to me." Her fingers coasted over my cheek. She picked up my hand and clutched it in hers. I couldn't return the squeeze, but I felt the softness of her skin against my rough palm.

My dick twitched. *Wait...did it move? Or wishful thinking?*

Rena lifted our hands, and the suppleness of her lips met my useless mitt.

My cock bit against my zipper. *Definitely feel that. At least something is working.*

"I love you." Her breath brushed against my ear.

I focused on my hand in hers and tried to squeeze. A finger moved. A single finger. *Yes. Now more fingers before everyone realizes I'm hard for Rena.*

"Jax?"

"Did something happen?" Barachiel asked.

"His finger moved. Or at least I thought it did. Maybe I

imagined it." Rena's voice dripped with disappointment. She didn't believe it happened.

I focused everything on that appendage and gripped as tight as I could.

"Jax!" She kissed my cheek. "He squeezed my hand."

Fuck yes. Come on, brain work with me here.

"He should come around soon, then," Jophiel said. "That's a good sign."

Dampness pressed against my cheek. *Her face. Tears.* I didn't want her to cry. *Fuck this.* I forced my free arm up. The movement was like lifting it out of quicksand, but with great effort, I got it to her head. I wound my fingers in her hair.

She sobbed against my chest.

"Don't cry." My voice came out rough and not like me.

"See he's fine," Barachiel said. she patted her large palm on the top of my head like a pet. I'd have been pissed if it was anyone else, but Barachiel was one of the few archangels I'd let get away with something like that.

I worked on opening my eyes. It was like they were glued shut, but I finally got the right one to open. The left opened immediately after like it was jealous. Rena's silvery blonde hair came into focus and then those eyes so blue they were almost violet followed.

"Hey." Rena's hot tears fell freely on my face.

"Hey. Stop crying."

She leaned over and grazed her lips against mine. "You scared me."

"No need to be afraid. I'm fine." My entire body ached, but I wouldn't tell her that. She'd worried enough.

"Do you want to sit up?" Rena slid her hand under my shoulders.

"Yes," I said and tried to shift, but that didn't go well.

"Slowly." Barachiel lifted me from the other side.

I situated myself once they got me upright. "That's much better."

Jophiel scrutinized me. "Most importantly, how do you feel?"

I took inventory of my body, and nothing hurt. "Fine."

"What I mean is," she continued, "are you hungry?"

My hand instinctively found my throat, but there was no ache or burn. For the first time in months, I wasn't starving. It was like getting my freedom back, and I felt lighter. I looked at Rena and smiled. "No, not at all. I'm not hungry."

Her grin spread across her face. "That's good news."

It was good news. I didn't want to eat any appendages.

"But our task isn't done," Jophiel said. "We've only temporarily removed an obstacle. We still must stitch your soul back together."

If it took electric shock therapy to quell my hunger, what the fuck is it going to take to repair my soul? I didn't know the answer, and it scared the hell out of me. I couldn't avoid it, so best to tackle it straight on.

"What do I need to do next?" I studied Jophiel.

"We need to visit a library." She grimaced and glanced at Rena. "A special library."

I expected to have to do something much harder. A library seemed far less intimidating than the electric shock I'd taken.

"You're not thinking about taking him to the library, Sister," Barachiel said. "Are you?"

"The Library of Knowledge," Rena said, her voice so quiet it almost wasn't there. Her grasp tightened on my hand. "Jax is a demon again. He can't enter."

Tension bunched in my shoulders. Bursting into flames didn't sound like a good time to me.

"He belongs to many worlds and has a soul. He can enter," Jophiel said. "With my protection, if needed."

"Can you interfere on that level?" Lilith asked from the door and closed it behind her.

Jophiel cocked her head to the side. "There are certain situations to which I can. I believe you are familiar."

The balance. How in hell's fire can I have any impact on the balance? My gaze found Rena's. *Because if I die, Rena's path might be altered. That can't happen.* Rena was important to all the realms, whether demon, angel, or human. I couldn't be the cause of her inability to fulfill her role. *I won't.*

"I'll go with you," Rena said. "I'm familiar with the library." My tension relaxed some, knowing she would help guide me.

"I'd have expected nothing less," Jophiel said.

"Count me in," Barachiel said. I couldn't explain why, but I was glad Barachiel would be there too.

"You'll understand that I cannot go," Lilith said. Her

decision didn't surprise me. Lucifer was to her what Rena was to me.

"You can—" Barachiel's voice trailed off.

"I need to be by Lucifer's side, especially if Rena is with you all," Lilith said, her tone final on the subject.

"When do we leave?" I asked. Rena's stories of how vast the library was when she followed Gabriel's feather to the hidden artifact room intrigued me. This was my chance to see it for myself and find answers. It was a win any way I looked at it. *Unless I die trying to enter.*

"We can go now," Jophiel said.

"I can't portal us there. I've never seen it for myself." I wasn't going to be able to provide passage. One of the downsides, even with a demon skilled at calling portals, was the demon had to have seen the location to have the connection. Rena had been practicing and getting better at opening them. While she had been to the Library, her thoughts were too scattered to hold a portal open for this many beings to pass through, and that was probably my fault. Even though I thought I'd hid my inner struggles, she'd been worried about me.

"You couldn't even if you had, Jax," Jophiel said. "Barachiel and I have this covered."

Jophiel wrapped an arm around Rena's waist and tucked her close. Barachiel repeated the actions for me.

"This is awkward," I mumbled.

"For you and me both," Barachiel said, a half-smile on her face. "Hold on."

A bright light that could only come from an angelic

being wrapped around us, and we shot into the air. My stomach dropped, but I didn't vomit on Barachiel. When we landed, a massive white marble building with gold embellished doors stood in front of me. It was bigger than anything I'd seen in the Greek and Roman ruins. *Could this have been their inspiration?* Rena hadn't exaggerated the size. A current hummed from it. Or maybe that was me from Barachiel's shock earlier.

"No time to waste," Jophiel said. "Let's go in."

I marveled at the sacred Library of Knowledge's entranceway, inhaled a deep breath, hoped I didn't turn to ash when I entered, and placed one foot inside.

CHAPTER 9

RENA

*B*ack at the infernal library. The freaking maze that made the Garden of Eden look like a children's playland. I didn't have the feather to help guide us this time. The power in this place hummed so loud it vibrated the blood in my veins, and if the knowledge to help Jax was anywhere, it would be here. My agitation wasn't at the library itself. It was because trips like this to save someone I love were becoming too common. I believed Jophiel, and it gave me comfort that Aunt B traveled with us. But Jax's existence was at risk, and I would do anything to save him. Every step in this building made me uncomfortable.

The marble glistened from the sun peeking through the windows. I assumed it was a sun, but maybe it was just heavenly light. I stared at it, unsure which it was.

"Rena," Aunt B said. "Keep up. It's easy to get lost in here."

Aunt Jophiel had her elbow hooked through Jax's arm. I picked up the pace to get closer to him, but I was still several feet behind them. *A presence.* Some kind of presence felt nearby. One who was familiar. I glanced around. The hum was louder here. I gravitated toward it without looking back. The whir drew me closer and overrode my need to be near Jax. He would understand. I wound through hallways, following the attraction until I reached a dead end. A gilded door like no other I'd seen in the library stood in front of me. "Beautiful." I reached out and ran my fingers over the symbols. Some were representations of the archangels, but there were others in a language I didn't recognize.

A hand grabbed my shoulder and squeezed.

"Aaaagh!"

"It's me, Morena."

I looked up into the exquisite but pain-riddled face of my uncle. "Uriel?"

"You're not ready for this door. Let me guide you back to your group."

"You knew we were here?"

"Of course," he said. "Just as I knew when you touched that door."

I gulped. "That is so invasive."

"You get used to it after thousands of years." Uriel grinned. I didn't know what a real smile looked like on him, but that grin appeared genuine if not a bit mischievous. "This place responds to you."

"To me?"

"Yes, do you not sense the energy? It guided you to that door."

I did. It had practically hypnotized me, and I wasn't sure it was a good thing this place could lead me away from important tasks. *Or Jax.*

Yet, the urge to enter through the grand door pulled on me. I glanced around him. "What is in that room?"

"You will learn the room's secrets, niece, but not today."

"Why does everything have to be so secretive here?"

"Everything is learned at the right time. I know it is difficult for you, but you must show patience."

I sighed. "I'm not good with patience."

"Especially when it comes to helping those you love. Our loved ones deserve the opportunity for their own answers. Remember that."

If I could assuage the discomfort of the people I cared the most for in the realms, that felt like the right thing to be done. I'd trade places with Jax if I could, so he didn't have to go through the affliction of being in my circle. "I want to spare them pain."

"And you take it on for yourself. That's not healthy, Morena. All beings experience pain and grow from it."

Voices drifted down the hall. "Here we are."

I walked toward the sounds but stopped short. "Are you going to..." Uriel was gone. He brought me back to the group but didn't stay. His behavior was the definition of a grumpy old man who was a softy inside.

Aunt Jophiel leveled a stern gaze at me. "Rena, I was about to backtrack and look for you."

"I'm right here. I could hear you all and followed the sounds." A look from Aunt B told me she knew I wasn't telling the entire truth, but Jax looked happy exploring. I didn't want to disrupt that peace with the mention of Uriel. Jax might get angry, as he usually did when it came to Uriel, and the anger could trigger his hunger. The reset was temporary, and we didn't know how long it would last. He needed to remain wholly in this moment, and a hunger like he'd experienced would make that impossible. I reached for Jax's hand. Nothing would change the love I had for him. He entwined our fingers as we followed my aunts. For now, he was good, and it was my mission to keep him that way.

"We're almost there," Jophiel said. She didn't react to my comment like Aunt B's covert look.

Jophiel led us down a few more turns to a wooden door positioned in the center of one of the end caps. Three sets of sectioned shelves were on either side, and racks of books were over the door.

"Good use of space," I said.

Jax chuckled. "It is."

The wooden door struck me as out of place among the elaborate ornamentation of the others I'd seen and that we'd passed along the way. It appeared as if someone had made it look inconspicuous on purpose. The wood lacked any ornate features or any features at all really. It could be a janitor's closet if they had those in the Library of Knowledge.

Aunt Jophiel ran a hand over the wood and turned to the side. "Jax? Rena? The room requires a drop of each of our blood to enter."

I studied Jax. His eyebrows bunched together. He was as unsure as I was about the request. Blood. The sight. The smell. It could trigger his hunger, and he'd be consumed with it again.

"Many of the rooms here have special keys needed to enter them. This one requires knowing all who enter," Jophiel said.

"Jax, are you worried the blood will bring back your hunger?" Barachiel asked. "If that is why you hesitate, you need not worry. It's a drop. You should be fine."

Should. I took Jax's hand. He squeezed mine. I led us to the door. There was a small spike, similar to the one on Father's throne, at the center of the door.

"This seems less than sanitary," I said.

"It's safe." Aunt B pressed her thumb to it. Her blood was absorbed on contact. "Though it will not open until we have all participated."

I stared at it. *Fuck it.* I jabbed my thumb against it.

Jax's brows bunched together, but he forced his thumb against the spike. He lifted his thumb and watched the wound close.

I took his hand between mine. He looked fine, but his jaw was clenched like he was waiting for the hunger to hit. I mouthed, "You're okay."

He nodded and moved aside.

Jophiel went last, and the door swung open as soon as she withdrew her thumb from the spike. The room was dimmer than I expected.

"What we're looking for is this way." Jophiel pointed to a dark area.

My stomach tightened. The darkness made me feel trapped, but we needed answers.

JAX

I stepped forward with Rena's hand in mine, and a wood floor appeared in front of us. As we made our way past the shelves, different areas branched off. Some were lit well with golden light glinting off of them and others were dimmer, as if deliberately made dark.

Jophiel stopped in front of another door, but this one wasn't as plain. It was a copper color with intertwined symbols. I studied the images and quickly realized what they were. The Garden of Eden...the giant tree I'd been in awe of, and the mirror of the two versions of Eden divided by the silent room. Both sides looked the same, but one was a thing of life and beauty and the other was meant to be a prison.

"Why here?" I asked. Rena tightened her grip on my hand.

"It's the origin of the soul," Jophiel said, like I should have known the history. "All souls."

I glanced at Rena. She shrugged. It made me feel better that she didn't know either.

"Don't be so cryptic, Sister," Barachiel said. "The Garden was where the first soul was created and took human form."

"Like the Adam and Eve fable?" Rena asked, her brows scrunched together.

"Something like that." Amusement danced in Barachiel's eyes.

I failed to see anything comical about the situation.

"Shall we?" Jophiel gestured to the door. "Jax, you should lead us in since it is answers for you that we seek."

I nodded, releasing Rena's hand. It was my journey, so it was only fair I went first. A coppery brilliance glowed as I grasped the handle. The warm illumination enveloped me as I walked into the room. The glow softened but created a layer of light over the shelves. A large tree grew in the center of the area. Several small tables surrounded the center of it and half bookshelves encircled that space. The shorter shelves didn't impede the view of the bookcases on the outer walls. It was warm and inviting, but I wondered if there were any deceptions here, like in Eden.

"It's beautiful." Rena came to stand beside me.

"Where do we start?" I asked.

"Hold your hand out, Jax," Jophiel said. "Think of answers to make your soul whole. Yours specifically."

I did as she instructed and thought of finding the answers meant for me to heal. A coppery, threadlike gleam emanated from my palm. It wound a slow path around the tree to the outer side of a short bookcase. "Guess that's where we're going."

A tendril connected to a shelf and a book with golden brown leather for a cover sat at the other end. I inhaled, following the thread. The answers we received weren't always the ones we wanted. I wanted an easy solution, but little in my life had been easy...except loving Rena. To live for her, the book had to be opened.

I retrieved it from the shelf and carried it to a table everyone could gather around. I sat the bound pages in the center and stared at it like it was a bomb that would explode. Rena slid into a chair next to me, but her aunts stood on the other side.

The leather continued to glow with the coppery sheen that most things in the room did. I ran my fingers over it. *Why am I so afraid? This could tell me how to heal the part of me I didn't even know was broken.* I flipped through some pages.

"Am I supposed to read the whole book?" I asked.

"Follow your instincts," Barachiel said. "Feel the connection to the book and let it guide you."

I turned the book over so the cover was down and began to flip the pages with my thumb. The fiber of light disappeared, but a subtle vibration emanated from the book. *Show me the answers. Help me heal myself.*

The book lifted from the table and my grasp. Pages turned on their own accord until they stopped about three-quarters of the way through the book. It floated back down to the table and came to rest in front of me.

I picked it up and read the passage. I cleared my throat and re-read it. *The balance cannot exist without the scale nor the scale without the balance. The two are entwined, forever longing for the other when apart and never fulfilled until they are together. The scale will perpetually wander for answers, while the balance is steadfast. The scale weighs the world for worthiness and decides the fate of the balance. Bound for eternity they will be.*

"This doesn't apply to me." I spun the book toward Jophiel and Barachiel.

"What does it say?" Rena asked.

"The truth," Jophiel said.

"It's not the truth," I said, my voice low to keep my anger reined in. I knew it wasn't. Rena and I loved each other. We weren't forced together by some ancient scribblings.

"Let me see, Jax." Rena slipped her hand over mine and reached for the book.

No way could that be true. "Lucifer would have told me."

Rena gasped. "Jax…"

"It's not true," I said.

"But it is." Barachiel gestured to the book now in Rena's hands. "We see it here."

"So, we didn't have a say in our destinies?" The pain in Rena's eyes told me she believed it. Another piece inside me broke.

I refused to take that news as the truth. "We always have a choice."

"You had a choice, yes, but you found each other," Jophiel said. "And now you will lead all realms as one."

"Jax wandering the realms and me ruling Hell? But then we'll be apart, not together," Rena whispered. "Like my parents."

That would never happen as long as my existence continued. Maybe even after it ended if I had a say in it.

"Possibly," Jophiel said.

I knew then there was more than what was written on the page. More than what the face value of these words appeared to be.

Rena passed the book back to me and pointed to a particular line directly below the passage I'd read.

Though their love will heal a family and the world, the battle for balance will never end. Eternity will require them to steady the scales of time.

"What the fuck does that mean?"

"Language, Jax," Jophiel said. "It means the balance was never just about Rena. It was about both of you."

"But I'm the son of a human and a demon. How do I impact the balance in any way?"

"You became vampire and returned to your original state. No other, not even Lilith herself, has been able to reverse the curse."

Rena cringed at the reference to the Night Children being a curse. As someone who had been one for a brief time, it hit me like an insult. I set the book down and tugged her to my side.

"There's power in being the first." Barachiel picked up

where Jophiel left off. "There's power in a being one who walks in many worlds. There's power in you, Jax."

Pressure radiated out from my heart. I grabbed my chest. If demons could have heart attacks, I was convinced I was having one. I'd been turned into a Night Child and back to a half-demon, half-human, and a stupid verse was what would take me out. *Fucking angels and their fucked-up prophecies.*

CHAPTER II
RENA

Jax doubled over. Panic spiked in me, and I rubbed his back. "Are you okay?"

He didn't respond.

"We need to go," Aunt B said. "Being here affects him differently than the rest of us."

"Barachiel, you take them back. I need to visit with a friend."

I shot Aunt Jophiel a look, but she breezed out of the room without acknowledging me.

Aunt B took my arm and wrapped the other around Jax. Bright white light engulfed us and, with a blink, we were back on the rug of Mother's apartment in Gothica. The constant hum of the library disappeared.

Jax's face was pale compared to earlier, and his eyes were unfocused. He looked like he was about to vomit. I didn't know what to do for him. Maybe he needed blood. "Better?"

He nodded but didn't say anything.

"Hungry?"

He shook his head and sucked in air. "Need a minute."

I helped him to the couch, and he dropped down on it. His breathing evened out. I rested my hand against his chest. The rhythm of his heart steadied. Relief replaced my worry as the tension left Jax's body.

"Aunt B, will he be alright?"

"Yes, he'll be fine." She smiled. Her relaxed posture should have been a relief, but Jax's color was still off.

I glanced around, expecting to see Mother, but she wasn't there. Had she gone back to Hell? "How long were we gone?"

"Not long," Barachiel said. "If it is your mother you are concerned for, she is downstairs."

"Thank you," I said.

"Jax, are you well enough to discuss now?" Barachiel perched on the arm of the sofa.

"Yes." He scooted upright on the couch. His color looked better. "I can breathe. What happened?"

"Just as Rena must decide on her primary home, you must as well one day. Being there was pressure against your shredded soul."

The reality Jax might choose to stay on Earth even after he was healed hit me hard, but I wouldn't influence his decision any more than he would mine. If we had a choice, despite what the damn book said, Jax would get that choice. I loved him too much to even try to take that freedom away from him.

"Why does it get better here?" Jax asked.

"The human realm has far fewer constraints to it than an angelic or demonic realm."

I studied her. That was uncharacteristically cryptic for Aunt B. Of all my aunts and uncles, she was the one who was least prone to talk in riddles. If she was using guarded language, there was a reason, and I tucked that away for when I could do some research alone.

The door opened, and Mother took us in. Stress bunched into the two lines between her brows. "I thought I heard an arrival."

I crossed the room and hugged her. She wrapped me up in her embrace. After reading the short entry in the book at the Library, I understood more about what she and Father had dealt with for two millennia. It wasn't what I wanted for myself, but if it was my future, I knew I could do it. I had the two best examples to follow.

She patted my arms. "Are you hurt?"

"No," I said. "I appreciate you, Mother. I should tell you more often."

"What did you find out?" she asked, her tone suspicious as I pulled back.

"I don't know where to start." I studied Jax, noting how much better he looked versus at the library. This was more his story than mine to tell.

He shrugged. "I'm some kind of unique thing."

"You're not a thing, Jax. There's a lot to you, but you're not a thing," I said.

Mother looked to Aunt B. "Can you make sense of what these two are saying?"

I took a seat beside Jax, and he rested an arm around my shoulders. In his arms was my place and where I felt most secure.

"Jax is unique because he has been part of many worlds. There are no others who can claim to have walked through so many realms and still return to their original self."

"Except I haven't returned to the original form. Have I?" Jax's voice was pitched lower. He locked on Aunt B.

My scalp prickled, and a chill ran through me at his menacing tone. "Jax, what do you mean?"

His eyes narrowed at Aunt B. "Your aunt knows what I mean."

CHAPTER 12

JAX

I'd known before I asked the question. Before I read the passage. Before we went to the library. The ankh had pulled most of the vampire tendencies out of me, but I still felt different. I thought time would fix it. *Fuck. Am I going to be able to stay with Rena like this? Will she want me knowing I'm messed up inside?*

Jophiel emerged from the bright light of Heaven in the middle of the room. Most of the archangels traveled the same way. I assumed it was like an angelic portal.

"What am I?" I glanced between Barachiel and Jophiel.

"You are you, of course," Jophiel said.

I hated the riddle shit most of the archangels used.

"I believe he's asking more specifically, Sister." Barachiel placed her hand on Jophiel's shoulder.

"The being you are most closely associated with is a jinn." Jophiel clasped her hands in front of her. I'd heard of the jinn, but I thought they were more fable than truth.

"A jinn?" Rena asked. "I thought those were stories told to human children to scare them."

"No, they once walked the Earth unseen," Lilith said. "But Jax can be seen."

"His ancestry must have been from jinn at some point, and the ankh woke it up," Barachiel said.

"Or changed him," Jophiel added.

"But the jinn died over a millennium ago when they were discovered and could no longer become invisible." Lilith's forehead wrinkled.

"So, what were the jinn?" Rena asked.

Lilith sighed. "They were a very rare demon who lived in the human realm. Very few ever visited the Underworld and chose to walk among the humans, even though they were invisible to them."

"They existed in the smoke and fire of the human realm," Jophiel said.

"Until the day a jinn fell in love with a human." Barachiel studied me. "When she wished she could be seen by him, she took on a human form."

"So what happened to the others?" The parallel of loving someone in a world you couldn't fully live in wasn't lost on me. Lilith and Lucifer had shared a similar love, and that could be the same fate for me and Rena.

"They saw her happiness and wished for the same," Jophiel said. "Unfortunately, human life is far shorter than jinn or other demons."

"So, they wished for shorter lifespans?" Rena asked.

Jophiel nodded. "Some did not wish to outlive their human loves."

"But the impact to their population was devastating," Barachiel said. "Jinn weren't a huge populous of the demon community to begin with and so many chose a human life."

"It ended their line," Lilith finished. "That doesn't explain how Jax is a jinn, though."

Barachiel and Jophiel exchanged looks. Barachiel inclined her head toward us.

Jophiel took a couple of hesitant steps forward. "The ankh doesn't just heal from random inflictions. It can return to an original source, and in Jax's case, the origination of his line was jinn."

The solution seemed simple, but no one else said it. "Then I can just wish for my soul to be glued back together."

"No, no, no," Barachiel said.

Jophiel grimaced. "That is a dangerous wish. You could break or restitch destiny."

Damn. I wouldn't chance my life with Rena by rewriting destiny. I rubbed my chin. The answer to everything was no, so what was I expected to do? I wanted to yell or take my frustration out on a Nephilim. With no Nephilim near, I packed it all away.

"Nothing can ever be easy," Rena whispered. She was what I was fighting for, and I valued every struggle that led me to or allowed me to be with her.

"No, if it was easy, it wouldn't be worth it." I leaned

over and brushed my lips against her temple. There was no answer I would accept that resulted in losing her.

She slipped her hand into mine and squeezed. "We'll figure it out."

"Wait," Lilith said, her spine straightening. "Jinn were said to have souls."

"Indeed," Jophiel said.

Barachiel tilted her head to the side. "The only demons who did."

"That's how you knew I'd be able to enter the library. My demon side wasn't a risk if it was jinn and I had a soul," I said.

"Yes," Barachiel confirmed.

One of Rena's eyebrows shot up, and it was so similar to what Lucifer did when he was in disbelief. "That was a big risk with Jax's life."

Jophiel shook her head. "No risk when we were sure."

I must have misheard her. "How sure could you have been?"

"We had no doubt in the knowledge," Jophiel said.

Rena blew out a breath. "If you had cost him his life, I would have been the one raining Hell down and not my father." Her demon voice rocked the room.

"I'm fine." I squeezed her hand. Hell fire burning up the room wouldn't be helpful. "Breathe in. Two. Three. Breath out. Two. Three."

She closed her eyes and breathed with me, but the tension in her shoulders was still heavy. "I don't really want to calm down."

I chuckled. "I can tell. But look at me. I'm uninjured."

"We knew he would be fine," Barachiel said.

"Enough focus on Jax's heritage. We need to move to the next task in determining how to repair the threads of his soul," Jophiel said. "And this might be a harder task."

"I'm ready for it," I said. The new knowledge about myself gave me confidence. I wanted to get this done so I could get on with living my life with Rena.

Jophiel frowned. "You'll have to go into a very deep meditation. One that will take you down the individual threads to repair them. Jinns were quite gifted in being able to do this when they were in the original jinn form."

I groaned. "Please tell me you are not suggesting I turn into smoke and fire."

"No, not here, but in your meditation."

Why doesn't that reassure me? Something in the way she said it made me think it wasn't as easy as she made it sound. And as Rena said earlier, nothing was ever easy for us.

"Show me what to do," I said. *This better fucking work.*

CHAPTER 13

RENA

This is the stupidest idea. I can't believe Jax agreed to it. Dream walking, the kind of meditation Aunt B and Jophiel suggested, was dangerous for a demon. Until now, I didn't know the practice had anything to do with jinn when I heard the stories. Father banned the ritual because so many demons tried it and got stuck. Father had to end them or leave them in the state for eternity. He'd chosen to end them. A pit formed in my stomach, and I swallowed hard.

"Can I talk to you for a second?" I asked. "Alone."

"Sure." Jax followed me to the bedroom he occupied when he was newly turned.

"Jax, you shouldn't do this." My heart sped up as the panic gripped me.

"I have to do it." He took my hands in his and kissed my knuckles. "Trust me."

"I do trust you. It's dream walking I don't trust."

"I've heard the stories, and I know what you're thinking. I'll be back before you know it.

His confidence should have restored mine, but it didn't. I didn't have another option for him. "You're not doing this because of me. Are you?"

"No, Rena. I'm doing this to heal myself. Heal my soul." He locked eyes with me, and I saw the fear there. The real fear a demon seldom experienced. He smiled, but it didn't reach his golden eyes. He thought he was hiding his alarm from me.

I lifted my chin. It was my turn to be strong for him. He needed my reassurance and support. His sacrifices for me were many, and my time to repay them, at least partially, was now. "You're right. You'll be back in my arms before I have time to miss you."

I slid my hands up his arms and clasped them around the back of his neck.

Jax relaxed under my touch. He leaned his forehead to mine. "The only thing that will be the death of me is you."

My heart broke because I worried he was right. Instead of letting myself feel that pain, I smothered his mouth with mine. He welcomed me with parted lips, and I plunged my tongue in to meet his. It was a fierce and needful entanglement. A shiver shot down my body to my apex. My insides ignited with desire.

Jax pulled back and sighed. His hardness ground against my stomach. "We can't do this here." His voice was like gravel. "Not with all of them on the other side of the door."

"Shit." I took a step away from him, half-embarrassed but mostly frustrated.

He grabbed my elbow and stopped me. His arms wrapped me up in a tight hug. "I love you, Rena. With everything I am. With my shredded soul. With my heart that stopped beating, only to beat again with your help. I love all of you."

I blinked back tears and mashed my lips together to hold back a sob. Letting out a breath, my voice came out shaky. "I love you, Jax. I love you so much that all our worlds seem to fall away when you're in the room."

He kissed the top of my head and held me in silence for several heartbeats. I breathed in his warm, woodsy scent. It washed over me like a comfortable blanket.

Jax pulled back and held his hand out. His jaw was set. "Let's get this over with."

I drew my shoulders back and slipped my hand in his. I tried to match his confidence with my own determination. We would survive this. He would survive this. We would have a life together when his soul was in one piece again. "Let's beat this."

He leaned over and touched his lips to my temple. "That too."

A fluttering sensation took hold in my chest and spread outward. It was hope. Hope we would be reunited at the end of his dream walking.

CHAPTER 14
JAX

Rena's kiss brought me to my knees inside. Even though I stood strong, she saw through me like only she could. It was one of the many things I loved about her. I watched her from the seated position in Lilith's throne room. There weren't many vampires here, but Lilith staged one of her guards outside the door. She stationed herself, out of caution, on the inside with us prepared to block entrance for anyone.

Barachiel sat across from me. Jophiel stood giving last-minute instructions, but my gaze kept finding its way back to Rena. Her steps over the rug were measured. I didn't know if she was even conscious of the rhythm, but she moved at a slow, calming pace.

"Pay attention, Jax," Barachiel said.

"I am."

"No, you're not. You're watching Morena pace."

Barachiel turned her head in Rena's direction. "Morena, come sit beside me if you can't control your fidgeting."

Rena narrowed her eyes at Barachiel. "Aunt B, I'm not a child you can command." Rena sat down anyway.

Barachiel smirked. "Jax, give me your hands. I'll help you relax as we get started." Her eyes closed, and she held her palms up.

I glanced at Rena, and she nodded. The fear on her face heightened mine, but I had her to come back to. Barachiel's hands were warm around mine. She began to hum an angelic song. The tune wasn't anything I knew, but it sounded so familiar. The muscles in my neck relaxed. My shoulders followed along with the rest of the muscles as if she sang to them individually.

"We are ready, Jophiel," Barachiel said, her tone still singsongy. She positioned my hands on my knees. I didn't know if I'd ever be ready, but it had to be done. I let my eyes close.

A hand smacked against my forehead, like how Lilith did for Rena when she fell from Hell the first time. I assumed this one belonged to Jophiel from her instructions earlier. A low tone filled the space around me like a lullaby.

My mind emptied and then the room was dark. Pitch black with nothing around me. Not a peek of light. I took a tentative step forward and then another. *Where the fuck am I?*

I focused on the first task Jophiel had assigned to me. Find my reflection. *How am I supposed to do that?*

"Is there a mirror anywhere out here?" I shouted like an inanimate object would answer. The floor disappeared, and I fell. My heart raced from the drop, but it was a short fall until I landed in a white room. I recognized the space. *The silent room from in between both sides of Eden.*

And there in front of the door to the secret side of the garden stood me. I stared at my identical self, right down to his clothes. He crossed his arms, and his mouth moved. No sound made it to my ears as per how the silent room functioned when I was here with Rena.

I took a step toward...me, and the other me opened the door. He held his hand out as if he was holding it open for me. Nervous excitement churned in my gut. I walked through with my soundless steps until I hit the lush, groomed grass on the other side. A sense of relief blanketed me as noise returned.

"Who are you?" I asked.

"We are the same," other me said.

"Um...I'm myself. I don't think we are."

"You have multiple parts. Yes?"

It clicked. He represented one of the shredded pieces of my soul. I must play this game with him to fix myself. "Okay. Which part of my psyche are you?"

He smiled. "That's a better question. I am the part you left in the human realm, but I am not human."

"Part of my jinn demon side."

"You have a decision to make. Do you want that part back, or do you want to let it go forever?"

His question seemed like a trick. No one prepared me

for this. *If I choose to let go of a piece like my jinn, will I die? If I don't die, will I still be me?*

"I want to be whole, so, of course, I want that part back."

His eyes danced with amusement. "Good choice. Then we play."

Fuck. Isn't that what we were already doing? "Play what?" Irritation laced my voice, and I worried what would happen with him.

"The game." He clapped his hands together. A thin veil of grey smoke surrounded us.

"How do I win?"

"Find me. Find yourself." His voice drifted away like it evaporated into the haze.

I reached out to where he stood, but grey vapor glided through my fingers. A laugh drifted from my left, and I lunged in that direction. *This isn't going to be that easy, Jax. Don't be a dipshit.*

I closed my eyes and focused. *If the other version was me, what would I do?* I hated games, so I wouldn't be doing this.

The answer was in that stupid reasoning. I understood what I needed to do. I turned toward where the door was and found my way through the smoke. When I opened the door, the variant of myself stepped through.

A smug smile appeared on other me's face. "It wasn't so hard when you remembered who you were."

"No," I said. Something had changed. "Does that mean I'm whole again?"

"Not quite, but it's a start." Other me reached out and pulled me into an awkward hug. The smoke dissipated, and he seemed to as well.

Then I realized he was being absorbed into me. *Nasty.* It was gross, but a blaze erupted through my body. The heat was gone as quickly as it came, and the chasm in my chest didn't seem as wide.

Darkness crept into my periphery. *Here it comes.* I fell again. Despite the brief drop, my heart sped up like the first time. The scent of sweet grass after a fresh rain floated in the air. I landed on my back and knew instantly where I was. This was the backyard of the house Rena's parents arranged for her to spend a year on Earth. That trip never finished and was one hundred ways to a fucked-up mess. It was also the trip where Gabriel's sword struck me, and Rena made the decision to ask Lilith to change me to a vampire to save ---y existence. I knew what this was — a reconciliation of the time I resigned myself to death and lost all my humanity.

"Hello, Jax."

I expected to see myself when I turned around, but it was a version I didn't know, an aged man with grey hair and wrinkles on his face. I wanted to reach out and touch him...me, but that seemed awkward. At least there was an old Jax. *That means I survive this.*

"Hello," I said. "You are what I would be if I were solely human."

"I am," old me said.

"What's my lesson here?"

"No lesson. You are presented with a decision. An opportunity not many are given."

It's a trick. Everything about this shit is a riddle. "I'm listening."

"You can become fully human. No more demon side. No residual vampirism. You'll be free."

Ah. There's the twist. Offering me freedom. Freedom I don't need or want. Freedom that wouldn't be real, because I wouldn't be able to be with the woman I loved. My chest constricted, and I grabbed at it.

Amusement danced across his face. "That was a quick decision. Are you sure?"

"I didn't say anything." Panic worsened the ache in my chest. *Does he know my decision? Does he understand?*

"You didn't have to speak it aloud. We are one. I know your thoughts," old me said.

"Then you know I will only ever choose a life where Rena is." My chest tightened like I was in a vise. I dropped to my knees. "Am I dying?"

"No, you are being reborn."

Older Jax tapped my head and shoved me backward. I didn't stop where the floor should be. Instead, I fell, and I kept falling for what felt like a lifetime.

CHAPTER 15

RENA

Jax had been in a meditative state for half a day. The longer he was there, the more my worry festered and exploded in me. I couldn't sit still and paced in alternating circles around Jax and Aunt B and the circumference of the room.

"Why can't I feel him?" I asked Jophiel, who stood over where Jax sat with his hands still in Barachiel's. "I've felt him as long as I can remember and even more since…"

"He's on a different plane of existence, Morena. It's not somewhere you or I can travel in the way his jinn does," Jophiel said. "It's normal you wouldn't feel him there. Barachiel is his tether and will be his guiding light back to you."

"It should have been me," I whispered, tracing my path around the larger circle. "Nothing against Aunt B, but I'm his strongest connection."

"Which is why it couldn't be you." Jophiel grabbed my

shoulder to stop me. "He needed to have space to find who he wants to be."

Jax had been the same person since we were kids. He was dependable, kind, and the best sparring partner in Hell. *Will he still be my Jax after all this?* "What if he doesn't want me when he comes back?"

Mother was at my side, hugging me to her. "That will never happen, Morena. He's loved you through everything, and he'll still love you when he returns."

I nodded against her shoulder, but the memory of him sending me away after he became a Night Child skated through my mind. Mother had turned him at my request to save his life. He would have died from the slice of Gabriel's sword if I hadn't. *What if he comes back and wants to move on without me?*

Barachiel jerked. Her grip on Jax's hands slipped, and she tightened her hold.

"What's happening?" I dropped to my knees next to them, hoping he was coming out of the dream realm.

"Barachiel's connection to him has weakened." Jophiel crouched next to her. "Sister, what's happening?"

"Falling," Aunt B gritted out. "Too long. No landing."

"He's getting lost in the space," Jophiel said. "We need to pull Barachiel out."

My stomach dropped, and fear skittered over me. "And leave Jax there? No fucking way."

"This is the risk," Jophiel said. "We'll lose them both if I don't pull Barachiel out now. She can go back in after Jax."

"Jophiel is right, Morena," Mother said. "If the tether breaks while she's in there, we might never get back to Jax."

There was only one option in my mind. I wasn't leaving him in there alone. "Send me in now. Connect me to the tether. Then you can recall Aunt B."

Mother sat on the floor next to me. "Morena, you have no experience — "

"If it was Father, you would do it."

"It takes many years to master walking in the dream plane," Jophiel cautioned.

"Fuck mastering it. I'll figure it out. If you don't send me in right now, I'll find a way to do it myself."

Jophiel shook her head. "That would be dangerous. I wouldn't have a way to pull you out if you did that."

"I'm going in one way or another." There wasn't a fucking thing they could do to stop me. I had to get to Jax.

Jophiel let out a heavy sigh. "Then we need to move the tether from Barachiel to you. Scoot as close to her as you can."

I did as she asked. I had no clue what I was walking into, but this was Jax. There was no life without him, and I would save him or die trying.

"You know it will destroy your father if you are lost, and he is forced to end you both." Mother blinked her tear-filled eyes.

"It will destroy me if I don't save him," I said. "And I'd be lost to you both then."

She nodded.

"Place your hand under Barchiel's. We'll move one and then the other. For a time, you will all three be tethered together. You will experience the fall she is in with Jax. It will be sudden, so prepare yourself."

I inhaled a deep breath and let it out slowly. My hand shook as I placed it against Barachiel's. Warmth like the light at the Library radiated from her skin.

Jophiel began to sing. The angelic softness was sad and low. Barachiel's hand loosened around Jax's. I slipped mine into place as hers inched away. Jax's hand cooled without Aunt B's contact. Barachiel's hand dropped to her knee. I grasped Jax's hand in a tight hold. The tether yanked me into the dream plane, and I fell. I tumbled into a whirl of dizziness. The fall was completely different than falling from Hell, and my stomach lurched. The landing left me close to vomiting.

"Now, the other hand." Jophiel's voice came to me in a sweet song.

I did as she said, Jax's hand locked in my grip. "You are the tether now. Find him and come home."

Her voice evaporated around me, and the air swooshed as I fell again like I'd slipped from the edge of a cliff and kept falling. Wind whipped around me until it was deafening. The painful drop made it hard to focus. I closed my eyes but lost my bearings. *Not that I have any in this dark fall anyway.*

The constant drop unnerved me, but I had a goal. *Save Jax.*

I centered myself mentally since physically wasn't an

option. *Jax. Where are you, my love?* Warmth spread around one of my hands and then the other. I opened my eyes. Jax was there. He looked unscathed from the experience. I wanted to cry out I was so relieved to see him. We were upright now but still dropping like rocks.

"How do we stop this?" I asked him, refusing to fall for all of eternity.

"I don't know." Pain flashed in his eyes. "I didn't want you to come here."

"I'm sure you didn't, but when have I ever done the expected?"

He smiled a little, and the fall slowed some. It gave me a little sliver of hope we might be able to stop. Maybe the key was helping him remember what life was like.

"Remember when we snuck into Mother's private library on my sixteenth birthday?"

He chuckled. "Yes, you wanted to get some of her romance novels that she didn't think you were old enough to read."

"I recall you blushed when I read certain chapters to you."

His expression softened, and dark red glinted in his golden eyes. "That's because I was imagining you and me doing the things in those chapters."

The fall stopped, and my feet met the ground. I huffed out a breath and nearly let go of Jax from the shock. *We did it. We stopped.* Jax's hands were in my hair and his lips on mine. He devoured every inch of my mouth. I leaned into him. Desire pooled in my lower belly, and I wanted to show him every bit of my need. His tongue tangled with mine, and my core tightened in response. I held onto the moment, willing him to feel every bit of my love. But I knew we had to get out of this state. I pushed my hands against his chest.

"We need to leave, Jax. Are you ready to go home?"

"Yes." His voice was husky, and his eyes flared full demon red.

I prepared to reach out for the thread back to Jophiel. Back to Gothica. Before I could, the dark room swirled around us, mixed with shades of orange and crimson. A very familiar shade of ruby. I held onto Jax as the room turned whirlpool-like. When it stopped, I knew exactly where we were...Hell.

CHAPTER 16

JAX

A warm, smoky smell scented the air. It was impossible. I could have brought us anywhere other than where our bodies were in meditation, but the odor was familiar. One that welcomed me every time I went home. "Are we in—"

"Hell?" Rena finished. "Yes."

"I thought we were going back to Gothica."

"So did I," Rena said, sounding a bit annoyed. "Did you want to come here? Were you thinking of Hell?"

"No, I was thinking I wanted to go home with you. That I'd go anywhere with you and make it home." She was my symbol of shelter and safety, but I didn't want her in this place.

"But it's so empty here," Rena said, confusion breaking her confidence.

The answer settled on me with a sigh. "That's because it's not real. We're still in my dream realm, which means I still have a task to do," I said, hating she was stuck here in my personal purgatory.

"There's a reason I'm here with you, Jax." She threaded her fingers through mine. "Whatever you need to do here, we do together."

The love for her grew inside me as if it would explode. Her strength was mine when I thought my purpose was to always be her stability and steadfastness. I smiled at her.

A lopsided grin of confusion settled on Rena's beautiful face. "Why are you smiling, Jax? Don't tell me you've lost it. We don't have time for that."

I chuckled and pulled her to me, not even sure she was real. She was warm in my arms and molded perfectly to me, so she had to be. "I love you, Rena. I didn't think I would ever get the chance to say it again. I love you more than Hell or Heaven or humans and definitely more than vampires."

Her laugh rumbled against my chest. "Now I know you've lost your mind, but I love you regardless."

My heart swelled. I didn't realize how much I needed to hear her say it until she did. I pressed my lips to the top of her head. "I'm ready to face whatever is here with you."

"Then let's do this and get our asses home." She placed a light kiss on my lips.

I wanted more. I always wanted more with her. But I wanted her safe more than sex.

I moved away and took her hand in mine, relishing the electrical charge before I led us forward. The walls were the same dark stone lit with the same kind of lamps on the wall. Everything looked as if it were Hell. The halls were empty, though, and I had no idea what this task was supposed to be.

"Where are we going?" Rena asked.

"That's a great question but one I don't have the answer to."

She giggled. "You sounded a lot like Aunt Jophiel then."

Her giggle did things to me like make my cock twitch. "I don't think that's a compliment, since you hate the riddles from your aunts and uncles."

I stopped in front of the throne room. The doors were shut, and that was unusual. I stared at the black metal doorknob on the grand, blackened wood door reinforced with metal forged in Hell.

"Open it," Rena said. "This is where you are meant to go."

I knew she was right. This was where my next task was. I inhaled and opened the door. The throne room here differed from the one in real Hell. A bright light shone from the ceiling over a silver throne with red cushions. No rubies. No dark metal. "I don't understand what this is."

"Sweet angel's ass," Rena said, and the pain in her voice caused me to turn. Her hand was on her shoulder near her collarbone, where her birthmark was. The mark that came to life when Nephilim were nearby. She was in danger, but that couldn't be.

"Where? They can't be here. They can't enter Hell. But this isn't real Hell." *Is it possible they can enter here?* I spun around like I would see the half angels, but none were there. My gaze found Rena, and she crouched down. I dropped to my knees in front of her. The anguish in her eyes meant there was more than one close. There had to be a lot for this effect, and I'd end every one of them for hurting her. "Tell me where."

"Gothica," she gritted out. "It has to be Gothica."

How in the fuck do we get out of here? "Can Jophiel pull us back?"

"She can only reach me as the tether. Not you."

"Then have her draw you home."

"No, you might be lost if I don't stay. There are two archangels and my mother there. They can handle it." Her voice was stronger, but her face was pale. She wore the warrior look she got when she fought through pain.

"Listen to me, Rena. I will find my way back. I promise you. But your body, the real you, is vulnerable at Gothica while you are here with me."

"We go together, or we stay," she grunted out. Her eyes glowed.

"Do not do this to me, Rena. I cannot watch you die when you could have defended yourself."

Something deep inside me guided my actions. I slapped her forehead with the palm of my hand like her mother had done when we fell from Hell. I watched her fall backward and disappear. Thank Lucifer she could fight now. The room swirled into darkness. Pitch black closed in around me and then there was nothingness.

CHAPTER 17

RENA

I scrambled to my feet. Panic pounded in my heart. In front of me was Aunt B. Her eyes blinked open. She let out a heavy sigh when she saw I was alone.

"Morena." Mother's voice was too controlled. Too soft. I turned to find her by the door, her posture rigid and still. Aunt Jophiel was next to her. "We have company."

"I know. My birthmark lit up. That's why Jax sent me back," I whispered. It flared again, and I winced, grabbing my shoulder. More must have arrived for it to keep firing off a warning. I breathed through the pain just as Jax and I practiced.

"Jax sent you here?" Aunt Jophiel asked over her shoulder. "He can't."

"Well, he did." I was pissed at him for doing it, but I was more worried than anything.

"Let's talk about that later," Aunt B said. "We have a more pressing matter."

I refocused on the Nephilim and made my way closer to Mother. "Does anyone have a plan?"

"They haven't even tried to come in here," Mother said. "Yet."

A thud shook the floor. I jumped, expecting to have to fight a Nephilim, but it wasn't them. Jax lay on the floor in the fetal position. His body wasn't in the meditative posture. He'd been knocked across the room, closer to me. My thoughts scrambled. If he could leave the dream realm, why hadn't he come here with me? *Is he actually in his body?* Only one word formed on my lips. "How?"

Jax groaned. *He is in there.*

I ran to him, trying to process he was really back. I reached for his hand, and he squeezed mine in return. *I'm not in the dream realm. Jax is here.* "Are you okay?"

His head fell back against the floor. "I finished."

I sat next to him, letting his words sink in. "You're whole again?"

He looked up at me. His eyes were the warm hazel color I loved. "Because of you."

My heart sped up, and I wanted to kiss him. A crash outside the door distracted me.

"We're going to celebrate," I said, getting to my feet. "A lot. Right after we kick some Nephilim ass."

"I was hoping you had already taken care of that, but since you haven't, I'll kick Nephilim ass all day and night for you, my love." Jax moved into a seated position with his legs bent. He took his time getting up, which meant he was either exhausted or in pain. *What happened after he sent me back?*

"It's only been a couple of minutes. I'm not that good." I hadn't even had time to ascertain how many Nephilim were in the building, but the burn from my birthmark hadn't lessened.

Jax's brows furrowed. "I thought it had been days."

"Nope." I helped him to his feet. My concern amplified. He might have to sit this one out. "Can you fight?"

"What are they doing?" Aunt B asked Mother.

"Looking for a statue." Mother jammed her ear to the door. "But I haven't heard any of them say what that statue is."

A statue? They break into the home of the Mother of Night Children for a fucking statue? "Do you know how many?"

She shook her head.

"My sister and I cannot interfere, but might I make a suggestion?" Jophiel asked.

"Yes," Mother and I said in unison.

"Maybe you should portal somewhere with less Nephilim and more Night Children or demons." Jophiel's brow arched.

I held back a giggle. She looked like she actually thought she was being discreet. "That's an excellent idea, Aunt Jophiel."

I studied Jax. His shoulders slumped, but he looked recovered. I couldn't tell if he faked being better or not. "Jax, are you strong enough to spin up a portal?"

He didn't hesitate and straightened his back. "Of course."

"Mother, where should we go?"

She gave me an apologetic look that meant I wasn't going to like the answer. "Picher."

I groaned inwardly. It was my least favorite place in the human realm, possibly all realms, to go. "I assume you remember where to bring us there, Jax?"

He frowned. "The building with the blood storage?"

"That'd be the one," I said.

"We'll meet you there," Aunt B said.

Jax made the portal symbols, and Mother and I stepped through with him. The clinical scent hit me, and I fought back vomit. This place creeped me out. I'd almost take the dream realm over it. *Almost.*

CHAPTER 18

JAX

Bile rose in my throat as soon as I looked around the blood storage room, but the weakness from the journey dissipated. My strength returned faster than I expected. Last time I was here, Rena didn't know of the dissension to come, but Lucifer had brought me and very few demons into the fold of his confidence. We'd faced an enemy from within the ranks and the havoc of the Ascendant then. I'd wanted to protect her at all costs, but she ended up saving me.

I touched Rena's arm. She jerked, still on edge, and at least part of that was my fault. "What's the pentagram say?"

She ran her hand over the collarbone where her birthmark was. "Nothing."

I let out a breath and relaxed some. "Good."

"Mother, are you okay?" she asked Lilith, who stared

out away from us. The Mother of Night Children appeared uninjured.

"Do you hear that?"

I didn't hear anything beyond the hum of the blood storage units. Rena peered at me, and we both shook our heads.

"I don't hear anything," Rena said.

Lilith slid a hand over her throat, and she lowered her voice. "It's too quiet for this time of day."

I'd lost track of the time while dream walking. It was after dark. Lilith's Night Children should be out now.

Surprise registered in Rena's eyes. "It is unnervingly quiet. Where are your children? Shouldn't they be coming to meet you?"

Worry creased Lilith's usually perfect face. "They should. The sire bond should pull them here."

"Do you sense them?" Rena hooked her arm through Lilith's.

"No..."

"Maybe I should check the tunnels." I suspected we would find a similar scene to when Gothica had been attacked, but Lilith needed to know either way.

Rena's eyes locked on mine with the fierceness that drove me insane. "You're not going alone."

"We'll all go," Lilith said.

I led the way to the mine, expecting to see piles of vampire remains along the way. There were none. No signs of the vampires who occupied Picher as their regular home. *This isn't good.* Dread slow marched up my back.

"I don't have a great feeling about this," Rena said.

"Birthmark?" I glanced at her. She had one hand on her belly, and her eyes were demon red.

"No," she said. "Just a feeling of unease in my stomach."

A demon's unease was different than a human's. Our senses picked up on subtleties a human couldn't reach with theirs. I didn't share the anxiety, but I trusted her heightened senses.

"Stay behind me," I said. "Both of you." Lilith seemed out of it, so I didn't have to worry about her. Rena was a charge-forward type of person, though, and she'd prefer to lead. That wouldn't stop me from putting myself between her and any danger.

The mine was pitch black at the entrance. Most of the lights hadn't worked since shortly after the town had been abandoned. Vampires didn't need lighting with their sight and neither did demons, but the cavern was darker than it should be. I was barely able to see. The stale, musty scent hit my nostrils. I inhaled for signs of death or recent occupation, but I received nothing in return. Despite that, I drew my swords and readied for what waited.

"No one has been here for at least a week. Maybe longer," I said, peering into the unusual murkiness.

"When was the last time you had contact with anyone here, Mother?" Rena asked.

"The week after your father woke up," Lilith said. Her voice was shaky, and that did nothing to help my resolve. "I came to check on them."

"And nothing was off?" I asked. The first steps into the mine sent a shiver through me. I held out my arm for Rena and Lilith to stay behind me.

"No, they were here and well." Lilith's voice broke as if she was afraid, and that wasn't like her. I suspected it was fear of what we would find in the tunnel.

"Stop."

My internal alarms rang and spread through my nerves, taking me from on edge to fight mode. Written on the wall was a missive. *Abominations will be cleansed.*

I didn't need a light to see the words, even though they were in dark red blood. It wasn't an accident or coincidence. Someone left a message for us to find. Someone who knew Lilith would come looking for her people.

The hairs on my arm stood up. "We need to leave. This is a trap."

"Agreed," Rena said. I would have smiled that she didn't argue if the situation were different.

"No, this was a message for me," Lilith said, her voice cracked. "I'm the original abomination in his eyes."

A sick feeling pitted in my stomach. Lilith was powerful. The Mother of Night Children. Wife to the king of Hell. Mother to the heir of Hell. If some vigilante morons thought she was an abomination, what did that make me?

"Whose eyes, Mother?" Rena rubbed Lilith's arms. "The Nephilim?"

"Adam," she whispered.

"Adam who?" I asked.

Rena conveyed the answer in a single stern but apologetic look.

"That Adam?"

"Yes," Lilith leaned into Rena. "He hated me and what I represented. I'd already met Lucifer and was in love with him, and he didn't approve of me or the relationship. He tried to kill me, but I'd become the first vampire then. Eve found out about his actions and left with their children."

Lilith and Lucifer were old. It would make sense they might know Adam and Eve, but I thought the little bit of history of Adam and Eve was just stories repeated over time. I never believed they were real people. "What happened to them?"

"She stayed in touch with me, but Adam didn't see her or the children for decades."

"Eve has been very skilled at hiding in plain sight," Rena said.

"You've met her?" I'd never met anyone named Eve in Hell, but she could have been using another name to stay hidden.

"Yes. With Mother when I came to Earth with her."

"So, she's still alive? Isn't she human?"

"Like me, she is an original," Lilith said, a hint of pride in her tone.

"The original sin, right?" I asked.

Lilith barked out a laugh. "That's a misogynistic web of lies spun by Adam and perpetuated through the churches at his direction. Eve reacted to years of bad actions from Adam when she left. Those stories of original sin were written long after their relationship ended."

"Do they live in the human realm? Both of them?"

"They do." Rena guided her mother toward the tunnel entrance. "Maybe we get out of the cave to have this discussion."

I followed but planned to come back, because trap or not, there had to be clues here on where the missing Night Children were. Better to do that on my own when Rena and Lilith were safe.

Lilith straightened when we exited the tunnel as if a weight had been lifted off of her. The air outside lightened to almost a feathery state. A change like that had to be demonic. I didn't think Nephilim were capable of such acts.

Light flashed around us, and Jophiel and Barachiel stood in our path. They were a welcome sight. I knew they would protect Rena and Lilith if something happened while I was in the tunnel.

"Let's go inside," Jophiel said.

Barachiel led the way into the blood storage building. I wanted to be anywhere but in that structure. My throat itched, and I understood my agitation. *Damn. It couldn't wait a little longer to come back?* I was hungry. No denying the sensation. It wasn't the all-consuming hunger like before, but blood wouldn't be the only thing on my mind before long. *Next is flesh. Stop thinking about it, stupid.* I opened the doors of all three units, but there was no blood to be found.

"Hungry?" Rena asked.

I nodded. "It just hit me."

"Me too," she said. "I'm guessing it's from dream walking."

Rena looked far more relaxed with her hunger than I felt. That shouldn't have surprised me. She'd always been unique and one of the many reasons I loved her.

Lilith huddled with Barachiel and Jophiel off to the side. "Adam is back."

"I suspected as much," Barachiel said, her voice grim. "Eve summoned me a few days ago and was afraid for her children with her human husband."

Hiding among the humans made sense. *Are her children in danger from Adam? Where are their children? Were they alive after all this time? Probably not. But then why are Adam and Eve still alive?* The whole scenario was a brain teaser, and my hunger grew trying to unravel it. I willed myself to listen to the conversation instead.

"He doesn't know where she is?" Lilith asked.

Barachiel shook her head. "No, at least not at the moment."

I pivoted toward Rena. She looked far less confused than me. "Did you know about all of this?"

She blinked in surprise. "That Adam was back? No."

"But you knew that the stories told about Adam and Eve were wrong?"

"Of course. You didn't?" Rena scooted up on the counter, and I leaned against the quartzite surface where our hips touched. The simple contact kept me grounded from the hunger trying to take over.

"No, I thought they were humans who died millennia ago. Are they angels?"

"Not like Barachiel and Jophiel or Michael or Gabriel, if that's what you are asking. They are celestial beings, though. Adam cannot return to Heaven until he redeems himself, and Eve prefers to live on Earth. Adam refuses to make his amends until Eve agrees to go to Heaven with him."

Adam was more than a bully. He was a fucking narcissist. "Is he trying to force her hand or something?"

"I honestly don't know. He disappeared a couple of years ago, but that isn't unusual. Mother said he had disappeared for centuries at times. I'm not sure what his end game is this time."

"He's targeting your mother and her children. That can't be good."

Rena bent forward, close to my ear. "No, it can't."

I took Rena's hand and helped her down from the counter. We crossed the room to join Lilith, Jophiel, and Barachiel.

"We need to get Eve somewhere safe," Lilith said, her voice quavering. "She will be vulnerable protecting her family."

"Agreed," Jophiel said. "She must be protected."

The concern etched on Lilith's face was deeper than what she portrayed for anyone other than Lucifer or Rena. "Why are you so concerned with them, Lilith?"

Fear flashed in her eyes as she glanced at Rena, but she didn't hesitate further. "Because Eve is my mother."

CHAPTER 19

RENA

Eve is my grandmother? What? I heard Mother's words, but I couldn't resolve them in my mind. "I'm sorry. Did you say Eve was your mother? I thought she was your friend. That's why I call her Aunt Eve."

Mother's focus dropped for a moment, but she was firm when she looked at me. "Yes, and —"

I crossed my arms, reluctant to ask the next question but needing the answer. "So, Adam who just left a message about abominations on the wall of your tunnel is my grandfather?"

An expression crossed Mother's face that looked like disgust. "No, Adam is neither your grandfather nor my father."

Tension released in my shoulders, and I hadn't even realized when it formed.

"He sent a message?" Jophiel asked, her voice full of

concern. I didn't like to ignore her, and her question was the one I should be focused on. Despite that rational thought, I needed a different answer.

"What are you saying, Mother?"

Mother smoothed down her hair, a nervous tell for her. She never had a hair out of place. "Eve left Adam and had me with a human she loved. Adam killed my father, but Eve didn't know. She thought my father was killed in a random attack. She ended up going back to Adam, and he allowed me to live with them for a period."

"Until you fell in love with Lucifer," I finished, taking in the reactions around the room. Mother was the daughter of Eve, and Jax and I were the only two surprised by the revelation. Not that I'd asked a lot of questions. I knew Father, like his siblings, was created and not born, so there wasn't a need. Mother dismissed her parentage as the past since she was remade into the original vampire. Father told me once it was difficult for her to talk about her time before, and I hadn't prodded. *How did they keep that secret for so long? I guess it isn't really a secret to our family, though. Just me.*

"Yes," Mother answered, swiping her fingers under her eyes. "Until I fell in love with your father."

"Eve is my grandmother..." I trailed off. My mind was spiraling. Jax slipped his hand into mine. I gripped it, needing his strength to reason this out, but the betrayal of it all twisted in my abdomen. "How could you lie to me about something like that, Mother?"

I wasn't using my demon voice, but it was close. Jax's

eyes widened. He positioned himself where he could step between us like he feared for Mother on some level. She might be immortal, but my temper rivaled my father's, so Jax wasn't completely off base to be concerned.

"It was for my mother's protection." Mother crumpled in a chair.

The fight died in me. I could see how it drained her to share this part of her life. She'd done things to protect the people she loved. As someone who had done the same...as her daughter, I sympathized with her. "Why does she look younger than you?"

Mother frowned. "That's a rude question, but I suppose it has to do with the fact that I only became immortal when I was thirty-five. Mother was created as she is...a celestial being."

"So, an angel." It explained what my uncles had told me, and why they were convinced I would be granted entrance into the Library of Knowledge.

"No, not an angel," Jophiel said. "Eve has a soul."

Oh. Eve has a soul. Mother has a soul. That's how they knew.

Jax slid an arm around my waist. I leaned into him. His lips came close to my ear. "Do you need some time to process this? We could go somewhere."

I looked into his eyes, and my heart warmed. The love there satiated something deep in me. To be able to portray that in a look, even at a time when the world we knew was upended again, did things to my very being. There would never be anyone else for me but Jax.

"I do," I said. "But we don't have time for that."

"You are the heir to Hell. You can do what you want when you want," Jax said as if that meant I could choose myself. I already knew what the answer would be, but I loved him more for wanting me to have options.

"Only if I want to let the world burn." I turned to my mother. Worry darkened the space under her eyes. "There's only one thing we need to do right now."

"Find Adam." Mother's eyes cast down to the floor.

"Let's start with that message he left," Aunt B said.

"I can show you," Jax said to her. "Rena and Lilith might need a few minutes alone."

Aunt B patted his cheek like he was a little kid. "I told Jophiel you were smarter than you looked."

Jax snorted. "That doesn't feel like a compliment."

"You're too good looking to be as smart as you are," she said.

"So, I can't be handsome and intelligent? Rena is beautiful and brilliant." Jax peeped at me with amusement before turning his back to Aunt B.

"But she's a woman."

I laughed then.

Jax shook his head. "That's pretty sexist for an angel."

"She's teasing you, Jax," Jophiel said. "She doesn't really think intelligence and outward appearance are linked."

"Way to ruin my fun." Aunt B flicked her eyes over Jophiel.

"Let me show you the new artwork in the tunnel." He

gave my hand a quick squeeze as he led Aunt B and Jophiel out the door to investigate.

Silence filled the space in the room, but it was anything but light. More like cinder blocks stacked up in every open space, forcing us to talk. Mother opened her mouth, and I held my hand up.

"I don't understand why you would keep this secret from me, Mother." I scooted up on the countertop. "I could have had a relationship with my grandmother, who looks like she could be my older sister, by the way."

"Adam has been unstable for more than two thousand years," she said. "We had a routine to protect her. Her immortality isn't like mine. She can be banished."

I sat up straight. "Banished? Is that why Adam is a threat at times and not others?"

"You picked up on that quickly." She paused. "I banished him once, and it lasted a few centuries. I haven't tried again."

A cold chill rushed over me. "But he can banish Eve?"

"Yes, and we're not sure how long she would be gone."

For celestial beings, including demons, banishment was like a ward the human witches used, but it was much, much stronger. The power of the banishment was directly related to the one initiating it and how long the recipient stayed was dependent on their strength. If Mother wasn't sure how long Eve would be banished, that meant either Adam had some serious power or Eve didn't. "Where do they go? Heaven?"

"Adam is jinn, so to the dream walking realm like Jax visited."

I stared at Mother in disbelief. She and my aunts allowed Jax to enter the dream realm knowing that psychopath was there. He could have killed Jax to get to her. "Are you fucking kidding me? Why did no one mention this before we sent Jax there?"

"There wasn't a choice, and we knew Adam was not in that realm."

"But he's a celestial being, not just a jinn?" I asked, connecting the unsaid implication. He could move between realms, so no realm could truly hold him.

The way Mother's mouth dropped when she peered at me was telling. I wasn't going to like the answer. Pain flashed in her eyes. "He is a celestial being, but the father of the jinn."

My chest tightened. The air was sucked out of the room. "So, Jax is related to Adam?"

"On some level, yes, but it would be so many generations ago."

"So, he's like your stepbrother?" Tears of anger pooled in my eyes. I didn't even know how to process that. Betrayal burned in my belly.

Mother's face softened with sympathy. "No, I didn't even know Jax was jinn until recently. He's no relation to me and none to you."

I grabbed my stomach. Bile gurgled in it. *I should feel relief. So why don't I? I might actually puke.*

"I can't tell him this, Mother. You kept these secrets.

You need to tell him and make it clear that we are not related." Ruling Hell and the Night Children came with secrets that could never be shared publicly, and I understood that. What I didn't understand was keeping a secret like this, where it directly involved our family.

Mother held out her hand. "Maybe we need to do it together."

I ignored her offered hand and folded mine in my lap. "No, this is your mess. Not mine. The only thing I need is somewhere to throw up."

CHAPTER 20

JAX

Rena barreled into the tunnel on a mission. If her hasty steps hadn't given her emotions away, the determined look in her eyes had. The tension wrinkles on Rena's face worried me. I kissed her stress lines. "Are you okay?"

"Yes. Well, no." She chewed on her fingernail. I'd never seen her bite on her nails before. "And you're not going to be either."

"Morena," Lilith scolded.

"Mother, just tell him," Rena retorted. "Tell him."

"Jophiel and Brachial told me Adam can be banished, if that's what you're trying to let me know."

"No, that's not it."

I leaned against the wall next to her and rested my arm behind her like a support beam. "Hey, we'll catch him. It's going to be okay."

She looked at Lilith. "Is it, Mother?"

"Jax, I'm just going to say this. Please forgive me if I do not put it as delicately as it should be."

Dread crept up my legs and around my spine until it settled in my shoulders. "I'm not following, Lilith."

Lilith swallowed hard. "Adam is a celestial being, but he is also the original jinn."

The world slowed on the last words.

I studied her, noting a hint of fear mixed with concern. "So, what does that make me?" I swallowed hard to keep my throat from closing. "To you? To Rena?"

"We're not related. I was never related to Adam, and your bloodline would be so diluted you wouldn't share much of his DNA." Her gaze flicked to Rena. "And you are in no way related to Rena."

I blew out a breath, but the release I expected never came. My chest tightened, and it was hard to breathe. The light closed in around me, and I fell.

Darkness surrounded me. This wasn't Hell. *Mother-fucker.* I was dream walking. *But how? And how do I get back to Rena?*

"Hello," a male voice echoed around me. I turned around to see other me, the one who was the closest to the real me.

"Why am I back here?" I asked.

"You broke your stitches," other me said.

"What do you mean my stitches?" I asked.

"She helped you stitch yourself together, but you were not healed completely. Something happened, and your stitches came apart. So, here you are." Other me smiled broadly like he was proud.

Or was I even here? Did this fucking place fabricate it all to keep me here?

"How do I fix it again?"

"You have to correct the source of the trauma, of course."

"I didn't have any trauma," I said. That was a lie. I had a long list of traumas, but the only thing I hadn't dealt with was the recent revelation about Adam. *But what else would have sent me here?*

"You wouldn't be here if you didn't." Other me turned around and started to skip off.

"Hey! Where are you going?" I ran after...me. But other me disappeared into the deep darkness.

A pit formed in my gut. The news about Adam and the jinn that sent me here. I was sure of it the more I thought about the scenario. Another piece of me shredded because I learned something new about myself.

I couldn't keep losing my shit every time I learned something about who I was.

"You are quite impressive, Jaxon." A man appeared in the darkness. The...jinn...wore dark jeans and a white T-shirt. He had thick, dark hair like me, but that was where the resemblance ended. I envisioned my fingers wrapping around his throat. It wouldn't kill him, but a celestial being could still feel pain.

"And you must be the infamous Adam?"

He smiled a broad, white, toothy grin. "I am. I know

you have questions, and I'll put your mind at ease. You share no blood with Lilith or Morena."

Relief washed over me like a fresh rain.

"But you do share some with me. Just a drop or two." He winked at me.

Celestial being or not, I balled my fist, ready to knock his perfect teeth down his throat. For threatening Lilith. For endangering Rena. For bringing me here.

"Check your anger, Jaxon," he said. "I can see it all over your face."

"No one calls me, Jaxon. It's Jax."

"But you're the only one who calls Morena by Rena?" He raised one cocky eyebrow as if in challenge. He was baiting me.

Not the only one, but I wasn't counting Uriel.

"What do you want, Adam?"

"To free you," he said.

"Free me of what? This place?"

"In a way." He moved closer to me but remained out of immediate striking distance. "I can free you from this place. I can remove your jinn."

"Isn't it part of me?" The way Jophiel and Barachiel explained it to me, the jinn was my demon side. I wasn't thrilled about being partially some weird, rare demon, but I wasn't ready to give up that piece of soul. It made me more like Rena. Meant I could go places with her I wouldn't be able to without a soul. My human side had part of my soul. *How would that work?*

Adam leaned back and brought a foot up against the

solid black wall. He was at ease here. "It doesn't have to be."

"So, what would I be without it?"

"Just you," he said and took another step in my direction.

He was close enough I could punch him in the face. "I'm already just me, as you put it."

"But wouldn't you like to be in Heaven with Morena one day?"

The vast darkness closed in and suffocated me, but I refused to let this freak see it. "Morena and I are both immortal beings."

"She is, but you are only half immortal. You have a human side."

My stomach tightened. It reopened a wound in me that never healed. My entire existence had been one constant reminder that I was and only ever would be half demon. I never belonged in either world. *Except when I was vampire.* I was all vampire until Rena restored me with the ankh. I didn't regret my decision to accept her help. Our lives would have repeated Lilith's and Lucifer's if I'd chosen to remain vampire. At least we had an option to live out our days in the same world as when I was in my original form.

"It bothers you," Adam said. "To walk between multiple worlds. I can fix that."

He thought I needed to be fixed, but Rena accepted me whether I was a half demon or vampire. This was a trick, but I wanted to know his end game.

"What would happen to me?"

Adam pushed off the wall and circled me. "You would live a human existence. Once that life ended, you would go to Heaven and wait for Morena."

Not happening. I turned to keep him in sight. "That would be a very long wait."

"I suspect she will want to join you sooner rather than later."

That would leave Hell vulnerable. Rena wouldn't shuck her duties. I was her weakness, though. She'd been willing to let the world burn for me, just like I had been for her.

"Am I not one of the abominations you wrote about in the tunnel?"

"Yes, but you are..." He paused. "Redeemable."

I didn't need his redemption.

CHAPTER 21

RENA

I paced in front of the stupid-ass tunnel. "I don't give a fuck what the risk is. I've been there once already. Send me to the dream realm."

"We don't have the connection, Morena," Aunt Jophiel said. "The first time there was a tether. He didn't have any kind of tie to this realm when he went this time."

I couldn't accept her answer. I wouldn't. There had to be a way, and the answer came to me as sure as if I'd seen it written in one of the books in the Library of Knowledge. "Jax and I are connected. We always have been."

"That's a different kind of bond, Morena," Mother said.

"I'm not talking about attraction," I said. "Jax and I are linked. The connection is there. I sense him before I see him. I smell him before he enters a room."

"Morena, most demons and angels can sense their mates," Aunt B said.

"It's not like that." Anger flared around my heart. The word 'mates' wasn't accurate. Jax and I were more than the word implied. I didn't have to search or seek him out. He was always there. "I feel him right now. He's worried."

Mother exchanged looks with the two angels. "They have always been drawn to each other. It could be a bond like Lucifer and I have."

"What do you mean?" I asked, surprised it hadn't occurred to me.

The way Mother's face softened as she prepared to speak about Father was endearing. "From the beginning, Lucifer and I sensed each other. Long before I became the Mother of Night Children and before he fell from Grace."

Their choices made it obvious they were unique in their relationship. *Could Jax and I be like them? Did we want to be?* I didn't want to live in two worlds like they did, but if that's where life took Jax and me, I would accept it. *But not without fighting like angels and demons to stay in one realm first.*

Mother rubbed her finger between my eyebrows. "Morena, wipe the stress from your face. Neither of you has to make the choice we did."

I sighed, and guilt ate at my gut for it. "I'm sorry. I just need to — "

"Save him. I know the feeling well." Mother caressed my cheek. A sad smile crossed her face. "Jophiel, I have an idea. Remember the jinn lullaby?"

"Yes," she said.

"If we circle Morena and the three of us sing it, it might work."

She was helping me. Helping us. Mother believed in the bond Jax and I shared. She wouldn't risk sending me alone to retrieve Jax if she didn't.

"And if it doesn't?" Barachiel touched Lilith's shoulder.

"Then at least we tried something," I said.

"Very well," Jophiel said. "But you should know that you will not be tethered here. You will have to return on your own, just as Jax will."

One thing I knew was Jax and I could do anything together. *We will return.* Our connection would lead me to him, and I didn't have a clue how, but we would both come back.

"Are you sure?" Mother said. Tears dampened the corners of her eyes.

"I'm positive," I said. "Thank you, Mother, for thinking of this."

She squeezed my shoulder. "Thank me when you find Jax and return to us."

"Sit crisscross on the floor," Barachiel said. "We'll hold hands in a circle around you." I did as she said, and Jophiel, Barachiel, and Mother moved into their positions.

Mother began to hum, and the soft sound turned into a song in a language I didn't understand. My body was languid and my eyes heavy. My lids closed, and I succumbed to the darkness and sleep.

Voices drifted in from a distance, and I opened my eyes to shadows. I didn't see the source of light in the dimness, but it was the dream walking realm. I recognized the weird, out-of-body feeling from the last time. Determined to get to Jax, I stood and followed the sound.

The voices became clearer, and I recognized Jax's. *I found him.* A little tingle of relief bloomed in my chest. I inched toward the sound. He was arguing with someone, but I didn't recognize the other man's voice.

Light cast down over them like a beacon and looked strange among the darkness here. Jax's arms were crossed, and his wrinkled forehead meant either annoyance or he was about to kick someone's ass. I assessed the distance, and although it was harder to judge here, I was sure I could get to the other guy with a drop kick before he could do anything.

Jax turned in my direction as if he sensed me. *Of course, he did.*

"Rena? What are you doing here?" he asked, his tone stern.

Ouch. Is he not happy to see me?

"I came for you, of course." I moved closer, watching the stranger, unable to shake the déjà vu sense that I knew him.

"You should go back. I've got this covered."

"Do you now?" The other man, I'm assuming a jinn, looked familiar. *A jinn. Fucking Adam.*

"Adam," I said. "How very unpleasant to meet the person who graffitied my mother's tunnel."

"Morena, you are everything I expected and more." He smiled, and it was wicked and ruthless. Bile rose up, and I wished I would vomit all over him. "I trusted you would join us to help convince Jax to take my deal."

"What deal?" I asked Adam and turned to Jax. He avoided meeting my eyes. "And I hope you said no to it."

Adam grabbed his chest like I'd wounded him. "Morena, at least hear it out before you reject me."

I looked him up and down from his shady smile to his overconfident stance. He reminded me of one of the creepy carnies at a pop-up carnival I'd visited with Mother and Alessia ten years ago.

Jax slipped his hand into mine and squeezed. It was a subtle gesture that probably looked innocent to Adam, but he'd be wrong. Jax and I were stronger together, and I understood the message meant for me. His gesture told me he had a plan.

"What if there was a way for you and Jax to live out eternity in Heaven? Wouldn't you want that?"

"Not particularly," I said. "But why would you ask?"

"If I take Jax's jinn into me, he could go to Heaven."

"Why do you want his jinn?"

"That's an excellent question, and one I would expect from Lucifer's daughter."

This dude is a douche. "I'm not sure if you're trying to flatter me or what, but I'd prefer you cut the bullshit. Why do you need Jax's jinn?"

"Jax's jinn is unique."

"How so?"

"Because he's the only jinn left, besides me, with a soul."

My gasp echoed in my ears. Jax's hand tightened around mine. "New information to you?"

"New information," he confirmed. "When the jinn lived among humans, they no longer had souls. For some reason, I'm different."

I turned to him and smiled. "We're more alike than we realized. Both one of a kind."

He smiled back. "A match."

Adam let out an overdramatic sigh. "Yes, yes. This is all very touching. He'll keep his soul. I just need his jinn."

"For? And why should he give it to you?" I asked.

Adam groaned as if I asked the stupidest question possible. "He doesn't need it to be with you, and I need it for the reaping."

"Reaping?" I didn't know what that entailed, but it sounded painful. I bit down on the inside of my mouth to keep from telling him to go fuck himself.

Adam didn't seem to notice anything but hearing his own voice. "His jinn will allow me to pass through portals at will."

"Holy...Jax, that's why you could still see the portal tracks when you were vampire."

"Precisely," Adam said.

Jax shifted next to me. "I become human if I give him my jinn by the way."

"I'd love you anyway, but fuck that," I said.

"That's why I love you," he said.

Adam barked out a laugh. "I'll just keep you here until you agree."

He can try. I'll call the fires of Hell to charbroil the demented creep.

"Can you yank on the tether or something?" Jax whispered.

"No tether this time. We used a jinn lullaby to send me. We're on our own."

"Fuck," Jax muttered under his breath.

"Yep," I said. "Looks like we'll have to kick some celestial-being ass to get home."

Adam laughed. "This is my realm. I control all that is here."

I took a step forward, and it was like stepping into a portal without the swirling energy. I moved like a chess piece back to Jax's side. *Fucking weird, psycho, ancient beings.*

"He'll let you go if I give in."

"Not happening, my love."

"You know I'd much rather fight, anyway." Backing down from a bully like Adam wasn't in my blood, and it certainly wasn't in me to walk away.

Jax chuckled. "Every part of me, including my now hard cock, wanted you to say that."

I shot him a quick smile. There would be time to satisfy other needs after we kicked jinn ass. "So, joining you in the jinn version of purgatory turns you on?"

"You turn me on just by sight, touch, and smell." Jax's voice lowered more.

"I'm going to need you to show me how once we are out of here."

"Count on it," Jax said.

"If you two are done with your sex talk, I will tell you exactly how this will work."

A zing ripped through the air, and my hands were tugged behind my back. Something hard and plastic cinched my wrists together like a zip tie. I jerked against it, and the binding cut into my flesh. *Adam will burn for this.* I peered at Jax and saw fear reflected back, but there was resolution there too. The latter scared me more than Adam, but I wasn't leaving Jax this time.

Defeating a powerful jinn wasn't going to be easy. Adam held all the cards in this realm, and I had to figure out how to play this game to get us both out of here.

CHAPTER 22
JAX

She came for me, and I'd get her out of here anyway I could. "Trust me."

"What do you mean?" Rena asked. "I always trust you."

"Just go with whatever I say," I whispered into her ear. "I love you." I brushed my lips against her cheek.

"Jax..." She studied with the fierceness that ignited me hotter than the fires of Hell. "I love you too."

"Adam, release Rena, and I will concede to your request. You can have my jinn." I didn't know what the process was for removing a jinn, but I hoped it bought enough time for Rena to get out. She was my top priority. If I had to give up my jinn in trade for her safety, so be it.

"I will release her." Adam appeared out of the darkness right in front of us. He leaned in close to my face. I opened my mouth to bite him, but I ground my jaw closed. Adam was a lunatic. I wouldn't risk her getting hurt no matter how much pain I wanted to inflict on that son of a bitch, Adam. "As soon as I have your jinn."

I roared. My patience spent, I moved my arms against the plastic holding them in place. The bindings around my wrists stretched and dug into my skin. The pain spurred me on. Adam would die, and it would be at my hands. The straps gave way.

Adam withdrew, his fear written on his face and palpable in the air. I advanced every step with him. "You will never threaten her again."

"Jax." Rena's voice drifted around me.

I closed my hands around Adam's neck, but his neck felt thinner than it looked. Adam's fingers dug into mine as he tried to break free.

"Jax." Rena's voice was rough like she struggled.

I looked over my shoulder, but she wasn't behind me. I turned back to Adam, but it wasn't Adam in my hands. *Rena. What have I done?* I let go and caught her in my arms. Guilt plunged a dagger into my heart and twisted.

"How did you get there? I attacked Adam."

"I don't know," she said, her voice hoarse.

"I'm so sorry. I..." I didn't know what to say.

"It's fine. I'm fine." She rested a hand against my cheek. "Let's just shut Adam down so we can go home."

She bounced back like a warrior. Her strength was greater than mine or Adam's. I'd make this mistake up to her when we were alone. I'd worship her body the way it should be.

I nodded. "That fucker is mine."

She raised an eyebrow and grinned. "I like it when you talk like that."

The woman in front of me inspired me. I wanted to be worthy of her in every way. "I promise you will be calling my name tonight and begging for release. But first, I have an idea of how to catch Adam with his own game."

"How?" A sparkle twinkled in her eye.

It was hard to focus when she looked like my words were magic. I wanted to find a wall to push her up against and drive into her. This was a dream world, though, where reality blended with fantasy or nightmare, in our case, and I wanted her in a real way, not a manufactured way.

"Jax?" Rena called my name. "You still here?"

"Yes, sorry. Thinking about...things."

She nodded. "Plan?"

"Yeah. Remember how you used your blood to open the cells in Hell's dungeon level?" I hated bringing that up. She still regretted the mistake, but we were working with what we knew at that time.

She winced. "Of course."

"I think if we use my blood, we can track him. We might be a shit-ton of generations removed, but he is still my relative." I'd never share that with anyone who didn't already know.

"It's pretty diluted this far down the line to scry with, but it's worth a try."

"I'm not talking about scrying." I'd never ask her to perform low-level magic. That was something humans and weak demons did, but she was ready to do it. That mattered to me.

Her head shook back and forth in slow motion. "No, Jax. We don't know what that would do here, and it would leave you vulnerable."

"I know the risk, Rena, and I want you to promise me to leave immediately if it doesn't work." There was no other way.

"I'm not cutting your gut open. So, are you going to do that yourself?" It was a question, but the defiance in her voice told me she knew the answer.

"If I have to, yes."

"We don't have anything sharp enough to do it."

I lifted her hand to my lips and kissed her fingertips. "You have these." I flattened her hand out in mine so her blood-red nails were visible. Her nails were strong and meant for tearing flesh, whether she did it or not.

"Eww. You want me to use my nails to rip open your stomach?"

"That's the idea. Then grab the liver or a kidney. Either one of those should have enough DNA." The plan was a shot in the dark, but I wouldn't show my fear to her.

Pure disgust was written on her face, and I bit back a smile.

"I'm just supposed to root around in your insides for those?" She made a gagging noise.

"The liver should be about here." I pointed to the spot. "And since you deliver painful kidney shots, I'm sure you have an idea where those are."

The look on her face was anything but amused. "This is a terrible plan, Jaxon."

"Jaxon? Are you mad at me?" She was the first to call me Jax, and I never wanted her to call me anything else. Jaxon didn't exist anymore. I was only her Jax.

"No, but I'm not happy about doing this." She took my face between her hands. "You're an idiot, but I love you."

I leaned in to kiss her, but she turned her head away. It hurt, even if she had reason. "You are mad at me."

"No, save that kiss for when you're on the other side of this stupid idea."

My heart constricted. It wasn't like Rena to withhold affection. Since we'd been together, she'd often initiated it. "I'll want more than a kiss after you dig around in me."

"And you shall have more." She smiled.

Strange choice of word for her, but we were in a weird place. "Standing up or lying down?"

"What?"

"Do you think it will be easier standing up or lying down?"

"Oh," she paused. "Upright will work best." She stalked forward with a glint in her eye.

CHAPTER 23

RENA

It was like watching a bad movie, but one I couldn't leave. Tears burned against my eyes. Jax thought he was talking to me. He couldn't see through the jinn glamour Adam was using. My stomach roiled. *Please don't let me be sick with this gag in my mouth.* I jerked my hand against the plastic cuffs. If I could just get one hand free, I could launch my dagger at Adam. The weight of the dagger confirmed it was still in the sheath at my waist, but I couldn't get it out of the sheath to free myself.

Adam was close to getting Jax in a position to take what he wanted. Panic drove me to drastic measures. My training included how to dislocate a shoulder or a hand to inflict torture. I shifted my wrist around until I heard the crunch and snap. The pain webbed out around my wrist and up my arm. I bit down on my lip and closed my eyes to hold in my scream. *Fuckity fuck fuck.*

I let out a slow breath and slipped my limp hand free.

My heart pounded in my chest. I studied Adam and Jax, and they were oblivious to my actions. They were engrossed in prepping for whatever horror Adam had planned. I backed up against the wall and turned to face away from them. I situated my dislocated wrist flat on the surface. I brought my good hand over and moved into position. I'd done this before and took a deep breath to prepare for the flash of pain. With a quick push, I reset the wrist. The pops were audible but not overly loud. The pain that followed made me deaf for a second. "Fuck," I muttered under my breath.

When I turned back to scan the area for Jax and Adam, Adam had a knife behind his back and was guiding Jax back to a wall on the other side. I fought my internal freakout and assessed my next steps. Adam's back was to me, and that gave me an element of surprise I needed. I wouldn't stab him in the back with my dagger unless I had to. Only a coward would do that if there was another way, but I would do it if it was our last resort.

I called the shadows to me and crept toward them. The distance between us dwindled. Adam was a celestial being, which meant he was immortal, but he could be injured like the rest of us. I pulled my dagger out and readied for him to notice me. He was too engrossed in what he wanted from Jax, and I made it right up behind him. He had no clue I was at his back, and the taste of freedom tickled my tongue. I could reach around and slit his throat in the most painful way. I wanted him to know it was me, though.

"Adam?" I tapped his shoulder.

He spun around so fast I had to step back to avoid his knife.

"How?" he asked.

"I'm the heir to Hell. Did you not think I'd have my own tricks?" I peered around him at Jax to make sure he was ready. He gave me a nod, and I grabbed the blade from Adam.

Jax's arm slid around Adam's neck and locked him into a chokehold. "I was being nice earlier, motherfucker, but my girlfriend has your ass in her hands now."

The color drained from Adam's face. I enjoyed his suffering more than I should, but I knew what he wanted to do to those he didn't think were worthy. I knew what Eve had suffered at his hands. I knew what he was about to do to the most important person in the world to me.

"I could send you to the dungeons of Hell for the rest of eternity. You know that, right?" I stared into his dark eyes. They were like an abyss of nothingness, much like the darkness in this realm. "I think that's too good for you, though. Instead, I'm going to take you to the aunts and let them figure out your punishment."

He laughed. Jax tightened his grip. Adam's laughter stopped. Blood trickled from his lips.

"Loosen your grip, Jax." I grabbed his arm and pulled on it, but his grip didn't seem that tight.

Adam's body convulsed, and foam formed on his lips. He reacted to a force that wasn't Jax's hold. *Poison? But from where?*

Jax dropped his arm. "What the fuck?"

Adam fell to the floor.

"Do we help him?" Jax asked.

I'd never seen an angel seize like that, but I had seen a demon who thrashed and deteriorated like Adam. *Once. A very powerful demon.*

"Step away from him," I said. "He's dissolving his connection here. He'll become acidic."

Jax knelt next to him and studied the bubbling skin.

I grabbed my idiot boyfriend under the arm and hauled him away. "What part of his turning into poison do you not understand?"

Jax's eyes were wide as he stared at the goo that was once Adam. "Why would he do that?"

"It's an old demon tactic. I've only seen one demon ever do it. I'm not even sure very many are capable of it. It's not a pleasant experience from my understanding, so Adam must have known we had him beat here. He preferred to escape versus facing the punishment of the archangels. It's certainly effective. I'll give him that."

"A jinn thing," Jax said, his voice solemn. I hoped this was one demon trick he never learned to do or had to use.

"I don't know. Maybe. The other demon was a general who tried to rebel. He did it to avoid punishment from Father. I guess he could have had jinn blood, but how would he have known to do it?"

"I've never heard that story," Jax said.

I watched Adam's body disintegrate into the dark floor. Familiarity with the memory of the first time I saw a demon perform this act melded in my mind with today. "That's because there were only two witnesses."

"You and Lucifer."

"Yep." I faced him. "His name was Asmodeus, and he hasn't been seen since."

"I don't recall hearing of him." Jax's forehead wrinkled.

"I'll tell you what I know as soon as we get out of here," I said, scanning the surrounding emptiness, trying to figure out how to send us back to our bodies. The dream realm creeped me out, and we couldn't get home fast enough. Home wasn't where we would go, though, and weariness shivered through me.

"With Adam gone, I think I can get us back," Jax said. "It's like I have a jinn instinct that was being dampened by Adam. When he disappeared, I could see lines similar to portal paths."

"Take us to Picher then." I held my hand out to him. Anywhere away from here sounded good.

Jax formed the symbols for the portal. He laced his fingers with mine. Warmth spread from the touch. He was real. My Jax. And he was alive. I let myself relax a tiny bit that he was okay.

"Picher," he said, leading us into the blue light.

Darkness encapsulated us, and we began to freefall. Riding along the portal Jax called was almost like being home. *Close enough for now.* "This better not be like before."

Jax chuckled. "It's not. We're almost there."

The floor to Picher materialized below us. I landed on my feet with my hand still in Jax's. There was comfort in our soft landing. "Nice."

Mother ran over and hugged me. I pulled back. She looked Jax over.

"We're fine, Mother," I said, unable to keep the tiredness out of my voice.

"Adam didn't hurt you? You're sure? I know how he can be." Mother wasn't the kind to ramble. She had been worried for sure.

I avoided the question. Adam hurt everyone he touched, and I didn't want to rehash what it felt like to be a prize in his shitty games. "Could Adam be Asmodeus?"

Mother exchanged knowing looks with Jophiel and Barachiel. *They all knew.*

"Stop looking at each other and answer the question," I said. "Although I can guess the truth by your lack of words."

Mother peered at me, and I saw remorse. "They are one and the same. Adam has held many names throughout his life. He wanted a fresh start when he became jinn, and your father allowed him to do so. Adam chose the name Asmodeus."

"No one thought to share this when Adam suddenly reappeared?" My anger grew and my demon voice roared. I paused to rein my outrage back in. As tired as I was, my agitation was harder to control. "Why didn't you mention Adam earlier?"

Mother reached for me but paused and dropped her hand. "It didn't seem relevant."

"Why in all that is Hell would Father have given him a new identity knowing what he had done to you?"

"Because he didn't know," Barachiel said, rubbing Mother's arm.

CHAPTER 24

JAX

"How does Lucifer not know what Adam did?" I asked, tucking Rena against my side. The heat of her body reminded me we were safe, but Adam was still out there. He was probably regrouping to come at us from another angle.

"He knew what he did to my mother, but I never told him how Adam tortured me for being an abomination in his eyes." Lilith looked away as if she were mortified. I'd never seen her carry shame, and I likened it to my own ignominy for only being half demon.

"Mother…" Rena moved to Lilith and took her hands. "You let Father give Adam a high-ranking position and didn't tell him."

"I thought I could keep an eye on him and keep him away from my mother."

"Keep your enemies closer," I said. "You wanted to protect Eve."

"Yes," Lilith said. "Morena, do you remember the day Adam, or Asmodeus then, left Hell?"

"The day he dissolved into a puddle of goop? Pretty certain I'd blocked it out of my mind until I just saw Adam do it in the dream realm."

"He'd become more and more defiant against Lucifer's rules, but Luce..." She cleared her throat. "Lucifer had enough when Adam threatened you."

Rena took a step toward me.

Rage burned into every inch of my body. I should have ripped Adam's head from his shoulders when we were dream walking. "Threatened her how?"

"He said Morena could never rule Hell because she was an abomination and should be eliminated."

"How stupid to say that to the King of Hell," I said, pulling Rena against me, her back to my front. The need to have her near me and protected overrode my good sense that we were safe here. Rena's rigid posture slackened against me, and I relished the heat of her body.

"Oh, he didn't. He said it to anyone but Lucifer who would listen, and it got back to Lucifer. And if you know Lucifer, he respects those with the courage to speak directly to him."

Barachiel leaned in closer to Lilith, but Jophiel continued, "He'd lumped Morena in with the Nephilim. They are not without their issues, but they are a product of their environment. We will change them. Morena was never part of that group. Her destiny was and is unique."

Rena trembled in my arms, and I tightened my arms

around her. "It's okay. You're fine," I whispered in her ear. She leaned back against me and relaxed some. I inhaled her scent. The mix of roses and fire calmed my temper.

"That day." Lilith swallowed hard. "Lucifer confronted him, and he didn't deny what he said. In fact, he doubled down and said both Morena and I should be eliminated to wipe our sins from existence. Lucifer moved to smite him, and he invoked an ancient custom only the most powerful jinn could perform."

"He dissolved into a blob until he disappeared," I said.

"Yes," Lilith answered. "Lucifer was in shock. Lucifer knew Adam was the original jinn, but he didn't know the pure evil in Adam."

"So why didn't he try to kill me in the dream realm?" Morena's voice shook through the question.

"Because he's still afraid of Lucifer," Barachiel answered. "He's afraid of Lucifer's wrath, and he believes you are Lucifer and Lilith's responsibility."

"So, how do I factor into this? What does my jinn give him that helps his cause?" I asked, fearing confirmation of what I suspected.

Barachiel's face softened, and I expected the worst. "Like Morena, you are unique. Born from an all but dead bloodline, you shouldn't have been possible."

"But Adam had children after he became jinn, right?"

"Yes, but they all died off. It was just him left," Jophiel said. "Until the jinn awakened in you."

"Awakened?" *Has it not always been a part of me without*

my awareness? And does it even really matter if I can't use the jinn power?

"Yes, awakened. That's why he hadn't come for you before. He didn't know you existed until—"

"The ankh." I closed my eyes and let out a breath. "The power in the ankh woke the jinn."

"Yes," Jophiel confirmed. "The ankh found the jinn in you and brought it to the surface."

"Again, why does he need my jinn?"

Jophiel and Barachiel exchanged a look like they were silently debating how to answer. Jophiel nodded to Barachiel. "He's not powerful enough on his own to defeat Lucifer, but if he had a jinn like yours, one chosen by the key of life itself, he could be his equal."

It didn't make sense why the ankh had chosen me. I wasn't powerful, and I definitely wasn't as powerful as Lucifer.

Barachiel continued as if she understood my confusion. "I know it's hard to process, but the ankh blessed your union with Morena. When the time comes for her to rule, the ankh granted her the blessing of having an equal to rule with her."

Rena craned her head back and looked up at me over her shoulder. She shot me a soft smile as if she was encouraged or pleased by the news. I would never be on her level. If she thought I was worthy to be, that was the only blessing I needed.

"So, I'm still half human and half demon, but somehow her equal?"

"It's not your parentage that makes you who you are. It's what's in here." Jophiel put her hand over her heart. "The capacity to be more, to show compassion, to show love, to grow."

But I'd been ready to burn every known realm for Rena, and I would still do that. *Am I really what they think I am? Can I ever really be Rena's equal?*

Rena moved from my arms, and the sudden movement left me cold. Her forehead creased. "Is this what you want, Jax? You still have a choice, no matter what a prophecy or the ankh said or did."

"Stop." I cupped her cheek. "I want to be with you wherever that is."

She visibly relaxed and smiled again. "Right answer."

CHAPTER 25

RENA

I'd fallen asleep on the couch with him and woke up alone. I found Jax standing out front in the sunrise. The soft pinkish glow around him was magical. He looked like an...angel, but he was a jinn. *My equal.* The thought thrilled me. After all the torment he'd suffered around his identity growing up, he had a claim. He was my match, and I was thankful the ankh had blessed us. I was curious if Father had any side effects from the ankh too. He hadn't mentioned any if he had them, and I thought he would if there had been.

I sidled up beside Jax, and he hugged me to his side. I wished we had more moments like this. "It's beautiful."

"I was hoping you would come outside this morning." He kissed my temple.

"Have you always disappeared to watch them or did you just start after..." I had a hard time finishing the sentence. He'd been a vampire because of my choices, and his jinn, which he seemed conflicted by, was brought on by our relationship. Most of his trauma in life was because of his association with me.

"Yeah. Even though I could walk in the sun because of your mother, I now realize how precious they were."

"I'm sorry, Jax. It's all because of me that you are now a target for Adam." I didn't want him to be hunted because of our connection, and it made it hard to be happy he was my equal. I wanted that for him and for us.

He adjusted his body so we were facing and slid his hands into my hair. "You're not responsible for evil Adam, but I never want you to think you have to apologize for any part of our journey. Every step we take together is ours."

Tears burned my eyes. "How are you not angry about Adam and the vampire and the ankh—"

Jax covered my mouth with his, devouring it with the passion he usually reserved for our bedroom. "I love you, Rena. Without reservation. Every part of you."

"I love you whether you're a demon, human, vampire, or jinn. I knew I loved you when I was a teenager, and it's only grown over time. All the demons risk their lives for me because I'm Lucifer's daughter. You are the only one who risked yours for me, and I will always do the same for you."

He tucked a loose strand of hair behind my ear. "Except your parents, I know demons and angels don't do the kind of wedding ceremony humans do..."

My breath caught in my throat. *Was Jax proposing? Here? In Picher? Now?*

"But once we have dealt with Adam, I fully intend to ask Lucifer and Lilith for their permission to bind myself to you. You have my oath. You have my love. But it's not enough. I want you to feel the bond with me not just when we are together, but when we are apart."

My heart melted into a gooey warmness. "You know you don't need to ask them. My permission is the only one you need when it comes to me."

He smiled that soft sweet smile that only I got to see. "Of course I do, but I want them to be part of it."

The binding ceremony had a public side and a private side. Mother and Father had told me about their public ceremony, but the tales of their private ceremony and the days after were legendary. I'd heard too much information on it, and the knowledge of what the rest of the Underworld knew about my parents' sexcapades scarred me.

"So, you are assuming I'll agree?" I asked, putting my arms around his neck.

"I thought that was a given." He leaned back and looked at me. "But if you don't want to be bound to me, we could just go our separate ways..." He looked off into the distance.

I pretended to slap the shit out of his arm. "I'll use all my resources to torture you if you walk away."

He burst into laughter. "So, that's a yes."

"It's a yes, you idiot." I laughed with him. My chest warmed with the purest happiness I'd ever experienced.

Love. It swelled and expanded around me. "My only request is that we have the private ceremony away from Hell or any prying demon ears."

His eyes widened as it clicked with him. "Oh, your parents. Demons still talk about the noises—"

"Shut up!" I clasped my hands over my ears. "There are some things even an adult child should not know about their parents."

Jax laughed so hard he grabbed his stomach. I scowled at him. But it was only on the surface. My joy broke through, and a smile spread across my face. He straightened and composed himself. "I promise we will not subject ourselves to the same scrutiny. Although, I wouldn't mind if they heard you scream my name when I make you come...on my fingers...on my cock."

I slipped my hand over the bulge in his pants. "Keep talking like that, and you'll have to show me."

He put his hand over mine and squeezed. "I don't know about you, but I could use some release."

I sucked in a breath, unable to get enough air to not sound breathless. "Follow me."

Not too far from the old town center was a run-down house I'd found wandering around Picher. I led Jax away to the home.

"What do you have in mind, Rena?" His voice was rough.

"A massage for you," I said, letting the desire drip like honey from my voice. "Close the door."

The room was almost empty of furnishings, but the space offered some privacy for what I wanted to do for Jax. I grabbed his hand and guided it over my breast. Even through the fabric, his hand caused my nipple to react.

"I like this massage," he said against my lips.

I unzipped his pants and slipped my hand in until I found the smooth skin of his hard cock. I stroked my hand over it.

A breath whistled through his teeth. "Rena..."

I liked how his voice got gravelly when he was hot for me. I slipped my fingers into the loops of his jeans and yanked them down as I dropped to my knees.

His hands went into my hair. "This is the massage of my dreams."

I ran my tongue around the tip of his dick and plunged my mouth over him.

He moaned, and the sound of his pleasure did things to me. I squeezed my thighs together as I moved my mouth up and down his shaft.

I might be a future queen, but he was the one who deserved to be worshipped. His cock throbbed in my mouth. I rubbed my tongue against the underside and sucked down hard on him. His hand fisted in the back of my hair as he thrusted deep down my throat. I purred my delight at his pursuit, opening my throat to take all of him.

"Rena..."

"Mmm. Hmm." I hummed around his dick.

"Fuck," he said, burying himself in my mouth. His cock

pulsed. Hot liquid coated my throat. I leaned back and swallowed, wiping my fingers over my lips. His salty taste still on my tongue, I became hedonistic and wanted him inside me.

Jax lifted me to my feet. His lips devoured mine, urging them apart. His tongue met mine, and dampness formed between my legs. He pulled back and looked me in the eye. His hazel eyes were tinted with a bit of demon red. "I love it when you taste like me. Here." He pressed a finger to my lips. "And here." His fingers trailed down over my breast toward my stomach.

My core tightened with anticipation. I squeezed my thighs together.

"Morena?" My mother's voice carried through the door from a distance. *Not now.*

I stepped back. "Are you kidding me?" I whispered. "We'll have to take this up later."

"I can be quick." He kissed the space below my ear that made sparks scatter over my skin.

"I don't want it to be quick."

His pants were pooled around his ankles. I met his heated stare, which was both satisfied and hungry at once. I sighed, ignoring the desire swelling in my center. "Better pull those up before she finds us."

He yanked his jeans up and fastened them. "I will show you what you mean to me later."

I leaned in to place a chaste kiss on his lips, but he palmed my breast. His thumb glided over my nipple, and it hardened against the fabric of my bra. A moan slipped from my lips. His mouth descended over mine and claimed me.

"That is my promise," he said against my lips.

"I'll hold you to that." I smiled. "Ready to face my mother?"

"No, but yes."

I giggled. "Same."

Mother was turned away from us and scanned the area back toward the blood storage building.

"Mother? What are you doing out this far?"

"Looking for you." She looked us over and smiled.

Heat crept up my cheeks. "For what?"

"Jophiel believes she has figured out what Adam's plan is."

"Oh? What is his end game?" I asked, finding it hard to shift my focus from Jax's cock in my mouth to the latest news on Adam. I didn't want to think of those two things at the same time.

Mother wore a smug grin like she knew what we'd been doing. As unembarrassed as she and Father were for people to know their sexy times, I was the exact opposite. "Let's head back to the safe house, and we can show you."

Jax slipped his hand in mine, and the three of us walked in silence back to the house. I was ready for a life with less Adam.

Jophiel and Barachiel stood over a table and a map. I expected the map to be of a city on Earth, but as I got closer, I realized it was realms. Those documents were forbidden on Earth for both angels and demons.

"Why…" I started. "How is this here?"

"I brought it from the library," Jophiel said.

"Isn't that a punishable offense?" I asked with genuine concern for my aunt. The Library of Knowledge had rules that even demons knew. Our lives were in danger just having the maps in our possession. If centurions were alerted and found us like this, not even Michael could stop them, and the centuries were part of the army he inherited.

"I'll pay the price should there be one, but this is important, and I wasn't sure all of our group would be allowed entrance to visit the building."

The only one she could be speaking of was Mother. The rest of us had been, and they believed Mother could still enter. My aunt thought Mother wouldn't go, and she wanted her to be part of the plan.

"What are we looking at here?" I could see the realms, but I'd never seen a map with so many represented.

"I think Adam is trying to merge realms," Jophiel said.

"He's been visiting all of them and luring others to the dream realm," Barachiel said.

"Is that even possible?" Merging realms would be catastrophic if it could be done.

"It shouldn't be," Jophiel answered. "But Adam is a powerful jinn. The original. With that comes some unique skills."

"Like?"

"Walking between all realms," Mother said. Jophiel pointed to the space between them on the map.

"Like a backdoor." Jax flattened his hand on the map. "Is that why he needs my power? To open those doors?"

"Yes, and you are unique like him," Aunt Jophiel said. "He can twist and manipulate the essence."

Aunt B laid her hand over Jax's. "You're likely the only one capable of stopping him."

CHAPTER 26

JAX

ow did I go from a half-human and half-demon to a jinn who has to stop another jinn? I must still be dream walking. Uncertain if I even wanted the answers to my question, I asked, "How can I stop him? He's ancient and the original jinn."

Barachiel met my gaze with the kind of knowledge swirling in her bright eyes that only living thousands of years could bring. She touched my elbow like that would soften what came next. "Because the key of life chose to restore your ancestry."

The ankh. "I thought that was to be Rena's equal."

"And as her equal, you have a destiny to protect the balance. The balance Adam threatens with his plan. The ankh empowered you with the means to do so," Jophiel said.

Fuck. I'd thought of the balance and Rena as the same since Uriel's declaration, but it was multi-faceted and existed not only in but around her. "I don't feel any different than I did. I mean, I feel like I did before I became vampire."

"That doesn't mean the power isn't within you," Barachiel said. "You have a destiny, just as Rena does. Your destinies just happen to be intertwined."

"She is the balance, and you are the scale," Jophiel said. "You can't have one without the other."

The scale...what the fuck does that mean? I looked at Rena. Her face twisted in confusion that matched what I felt on the inside. "What is the purpose of the scale?"

"Judgement," Jophiel said.

Barachiel rolled her eyes. "She's being a bit dramatic. It could be judgment, of course, but really, it's the key to balance. Without the scale, there is no balance."

I'm sure some rational answer was in there, but I was more confused. I didn't know what I was supposed to do or what impact it had on Rena and me as a unit. "Like the Ancient Egyptians believed? Where the heart and feather have to balance? That kind of scale?"

Barachiel chuckled. "Not exactly. They were wise people on many things and had knowledge of the scale. The purpose...well, they kind of missed it."

"It is judgment," Jophiel said. "That is correct. They used references that made sense to their time. That was three thousand years ago."

Lilith's cell beeped.

"Gothica?" Rena asked.

"Yes," Lilith said, her tone resolute. She studied us like she needed to see we were okay. "It's all clear there."

"We should go back. Picher gives me the creeps." Rena rolled her shoulders.

I smiled at her.

"Most of it." Her cheeks turned red.

My dick twitched, and I had to make myself refocus on the current task, so I didn't sport a hard-on in front of everyone. "Do we return there? Or back to Hell where the Nephilim can't go?" Hell was my first choice, but Gothica was less conspicuous.

"Gothica draws less attention for Jophiel and Barachiel," Lilith said.

"Agreed," Rena said.

I formed the symbols to open the portal. It spun into existence in front of us. I gestured for the others to go through first, and I followed. I'd chosen Lilith's apartment since it should be the most secure. The rug Rena said she was starting to hate came into view. I could see them all there. Lilith, Jophiel, Barachiel, and my beloved Rena were all safe. I put one foot through the opening, but something yanked me away. I spun around in freefall through flashing light and darkness until everything dimmed around me and disappeared.

RENA

"Jax!" I reached for him, but his body lurched backward into the portal. It slammed shut in front of me.

My heart constricted in my chest. I glanced around from Aunt Jophiel to Mother to Aunt B. Their faces were a mix of shock and concern. Panic expanded through my chest and into my belly. "What just happened?"

"Maybe the line wasn't strong enough for all of us." Mother's stare locked on the spot the portal dropped us.

"This is Jax we are talking about. He could still read the lines when he was a vampire." I folded my hands into fists to stop them from shaking.

Aunt B studied at the same place Mother was watching. "I think the portal might have made him vulnerable to a summons."

"What kind of summons?" Adam was a celestial being, but he wasn't like Father. He couldn't summon demons.

Or can he? Adam and Jax are both jinn. "A jinn can summon a jinn?"

"Although there is nothing documented around such power in the jinn, that would be an obvious conclusion," Aunt Jophiel said.

Panic seized my body to the point I nearly froze. "The last time Adam was near Jax, he was going to gut him. Where would he take Jax? The dream realm?"

A grave expression crossed Aunt Jophiel's perfect angelic face. "To my knowledge, the dream realm cannot be accessed by a portal."

"Then where?" I practically shouted. "Where would Adam take Jax?"

Aunt B waved a hand to get Mother's attention. "Do you think he would venture to Hell, Lilith?"

Mother's unnatural stillness unnerved me. Whatever was going on in her head, she didn't intend to share. Her mouth twisted in a grim expression. "Risk Lucifer's wrath? I can't see him doing it."

"Which is exactly why he would. It's unexpected." I pulled the dagger from its sheath and slid it across my palm. "See you there."

"Rena—" Mother's brows furrowed, and she reached for me.

The pull of the summons was already taking hold, but Mother's hand was firmly around my wrist. We were both dropped in Father's study.

"That was a strange entrance for my two loves,"

Lucifer said, pleased to see us. "What has you in such a hurry?"

Mother got to her feet first and held out a hand for me. "Adam. We think he brought Jax here."

Father laughed, but there was an edge to it, and his teeth were bared. "Adam? He wouldn't dare."

I didn't know what Adam planned to do to Jax here, but I was sure I didn't have time to coddle Father's ego. "Oh, he'd dare a lot of things from what I witnessed."

Father narrowed his eyes and glanced between Mother and me. "One of you start talking now."

Mother recounted the events that led us here for Father. I moved around the office, grabbing weapons from the various places he thought were secret stashes. There wasn't time for this discussion.

"You two can keep talking if you want, but I'm going after Jax." I hurried toward the door.

"Stop," Father said.

I froze in place and turned. "He is the love of my life. You can't tell me not to go."

"I'm not," Father said, his voice soft but firm. "But you're not going alone."

He grabbed his sword from the wall, a sword I was certain hadn't seen action in a thousand years and joined me. In the hall, he told a guard to gather more. His support meant a lot. He was going to fight for Jax, but the additional weapons concerned me. If he needed assistance to fight Adam, I underestimated Adam's strength.

"Where should we look first?" I asked.

"The throne room. Adam has always wanted his own royal seat, but that was never meant to be," Father said.

More guards filed in next to us and behind us.

At least a hundred troops had joined us by the time we reached the door to the throne room, and it had to be enough. Jax could be dying for all we knew. *No, I would know if he is. Wouldn't I?* I bulldozed through the front of the line, took a couple of steps back to build up power, and planted my foot against the seam of the doors. They sprung open wide.

Father was right. Adam was seated on the dark metal and ruby throne. Father would dismember him and scatter him among the worst parts of Hell and Earth for trying to usurp him. I scanned the room for Jax but didn't see him and swallowed down my disappointment. Light flashed in the room and thunder rolled. Michael, Uriel, and Gabriel all appeared.

"Uncles? What are you doing here?"

"Adam summoned us, Rena," Uriel said.

I knew whatever was about to happen next would tip the balance of the scales for all of us. No one had to tell me. The change in the electrical current was palpable as it coursed through the room. It wasn't like the charges between me and Jax. Power surged, building on itself like a Hell-sized bomb. And it was ready to be unleashed.

The sour taste of dread filled my mouth as I glowered at Adam. "Where is Jax?"

Adam turned to the side, but he didn't say a word. I peered in the same direction. My stomach sank. Jax stood in a cage like a zombie. He stared straight ahead with vacant eyes. A blue current buzzed around him. The ankh hung around his neck. My heart thumped hard in my chest and broke into a million pieces. I looked back at Adam and noticed the soft sheen over his skin. *The soft blue sheen.* He was siphoning power from Jax. *The jinn.*

I flipped the dagger up in my hand and readied to aim true at Adam's head.

Adam wagged a finger. "I wouldn't do that if you want your Jax to live."

I paused, the dagger still firmly in my grip.

"He is connected to me. Anything you do to me will also be done to him."

Urgh. I can't kill or even injure the bastard. I lowered the dagger and looked at Father. His anger matched my heartache. "Is it true?"

"There is a connection between them, but I do not know how deep," Father said.

I turned to my uncles. They were in their battle stances like they awaited orders. "Have any of you seen this before?"

"Yes," Michael said. "What Adam says is true. You cannot harm him without also bringing harm to Jax."

The bastard had bound himself to Jax in a way that ensured Adam got what he wanted.

Mother stepped forward, her tone harsh. "What do you want, Adam?"

I cut my gaze toward her and saw Father had done the same.

A wistful expression passed over Adam's features before he locked it down again. "A place Eve and I can live without ever being interrupted."

The disgusting piece of shit believed that could happen.

"That will never be in Hell," Father said.

My mother inched closer. "Mother is pure and full of love, Adam. She has a life on Earth."

Adam rose from the throne. "She's had many, many lives on Earth. It's my turn with her."

He sounded like a spoiled brat mixed with the most psychotic version of a narcissist to me. "How old are you?"

Michael stepped in front of me. "You must know this is wrong, Adam. This will not earn you passage to an eternity with Eve."

"Maybe not in Heaven or the angel realm, but we could here."

Why are celestial beings so damn dysfunctional? It's like they'd lived too long.

"Listen to Michael," Uriel said. "He speaks the truth."

Adam smirked. "Oh, you're awake for this, Uriel?"

Ouch. I'd made a similar jab not that long ago. Uriel's face contorted into the most demonic-looking angel face I'd seen. He took a couple of steps toward Adam.

"Don't come any closer." Adam flipped his hand, and Jax jerked.

I plunged between my father and Michael. They each grabbed one of my arms and held me in place. I struggled against them. *Jax.* I willed him to find me, but he didn't. I squeezed my eyes shut, biting back the anger and anguish rippling through me. It was dangerous for me to lose it in here with people I loved so close.

Father whispered in my ear, "The power he is channeling could obliterate you."

I studied Jax. He stared out into the room with vacant eyes in the same manner as he had when we entered the room. *Is he still in there?*

"Lucifer, this is your home. We'll defer to you," Michael said, his voice low and menacing.

Father loosened his grip on me. "I think the only thing to do now is bring Eve here."

I should protest. I wanted to. Eve had been through enough at Adam's hands. My voice didn't work, and all I could think about was freeing Jax.

"Lucifer, please don't," Mother said, her voice breaking.

Father looked at me and back to Mother as if he was deciding, and the weight of it was what I'd sensed initially. The scales were tipping. "We don't have a choice, Lilith. I'm sorry. I'll have one of the portal guards take you." He turned to Michael. "Will you go with her, Brother? I should stay with Morena."

Michael nodded and went to Mother's side. Father released me. "You must have patience, my dear daughter."

Patience and I had never been acquainted. I squeezed my eyes shut as if that would erase this scene.

CHAPTER 28
JAX

I watched everything unfold in front of me. Rena and the others were fighting for me, but I couldn't move. Not even a pinky. Adam injected me with a concoction that knocked me out, and when I came to, I was caged like an animal. He'd made me dance like a fucking puppet right into his plans, and there would be a price for what he did, whether from me or Lucifer. Lucifer's eyes hadn't stopped glowing red since Rena kicked the door in to the throne room. But neither had Rena's. I'd never seen hers so red. *If I ever get out of here, I will rip Adam apart, starting with his fingers and ending with his head, so he will feel every single ounce of pain.*

Weakness settled in my muscles and bones. The weariness wound through my body, and death sounded better. *No.* I rejected that thought, determined to hold Rena in my arms again. I didn't know how Adam had done it, but I could see the blue line connecting us. He was draining a force from me, and I assumed it was my jinn. Jinn essence was blue. *A very pretty shade of dark blue, but not as dark as navy.* My neck felt heavy, but I couldn't dip my head to see why or how it was weighed down. The pain nearly robbed me of consciousness after I woke, but it didn't hurt nearly as much now. I could drift off for a nap. A few minutes of sleep might help me.

Fight, Jax. Fight for Rena. This will break her if you don't.

My fortitude wavered against whatever spell Adam cast over me. My strength drained the harder I fought. My body tired, and I wasn't sure how much longer I'd last fighting Adam. He would have my jinn when I weakened enough, so I'd have to push back until there was nothing left.

Rena stood in my line of sight. Michael had been situated in between her and Adam, but Lucifer sent Michael and Lilith to retrieve Eve. Uriel shielded my love now, and I should be grateful, and I was. The gratitude did nothing to stop me from wanting to drop kick him through a portal anywhere but near Rena.

Fuck. There has to be a way to break this connection. To control my jinn. Think, Jax. Fucking think.

If the ankh awakened it in me, there had to be a way to control it or activate it. Maybe that's what Adam had done. He'd switched it on for his use. *How do I channel it for my use?* I tried pulling my jinn to me, but nothing happened. I didn't know how to tap into it.

The drain on me made me hungry. Bacon, blood, bone marrow...a fucking big toe...it didn't matter. All of it sounded good. The hunger distracted me from the real issue. The one I sensed deep in me. It was my essence Adam consumed. I'd be nothing when he was done. Only a shell of me would remain if that. The very thing that made me who I was died a little more every second Adam was tethered to me. I was dying and trapped in this slow death.

CHAPTER 29

RENA

I sensed his life ending in the currents of the air. Jax was dying, and each second brought him closer to death. I didn't know how long we had. Mother might not return with Eve in time, and even if she did, it might not be enough to stop Adam.

I was the balance incarnate, but what Adam did could tip the scales. *And Jax is supposed to be the scale. Is Adam trying to become the scale himself? But his destiny would be intertwined with me, not Eve.* I looked up to find Uriel watching me.

His eyes filled with sadness. A golden tear sat in the corner, and I stared at it. Uriel cried far more than his tough exterior ever showed. He knew the answer. I knew the answer. "Did you put it together, Rena?"

My heart twisted in my chest. Tears sprung to my eyes. This enchantment Adam used couldn't be broken by anyone in this room except for Adam and me, because I was the balance. "There is no saving us both. It's one... maybe both of us."

"I'm sorry." The gold tear broke loose and ran down his cheek. "We didn't see this coming."

I wiped the tear from his face. Uriel closed his eyes briefly, and I cupped his cheek with my hand. He'd given me peace once, and I wanted to return that favor. "How could you? Adam doesn't make sense half the time."

"We will find a way," Father said, sounding determined.

"Brother..." Uriel's voice trailed off.

Father's promise was the one of a father to a child. Uriel's was one of truth. One promise could not be fulfilled and the other a promise of pure vengeance.

I looked back at Uriel. His tears had stopped. A resolved look settled on his face. "If it's me or Jax, save Jax."

"I cannot swear that to you, Rena," Uriel said. I wished he had lied to me. I'd never want to be chosen over Jax. *Never.*

The look in Jax's eyes was an abyss of nothingness. His irises weren't the lovely hazel color I loved. They were obsidian black, like the ankh, and hollow.

I'll dive into the stream between Jax and Adam. It'd break the link. At least I hoped it would before it obliterated me, as Father had put it. Jax's freedom would be my victory tonight.

"Just do it," I said to myself, my voice strong, as if I'd found power inside me.

I stepped away from Father and Uriel.

"Morena," Father said with a growl. "Get back here where we can shield you."

Father's eyes were full of fear.

The guilt from the ramifications of my choice tonight bled through me. "I'm sorry."

I prepared to jump, but a blur whizzed by my periphery. I stumbled.

Mother rushed into the room with Eve behind her. She shielded Eve as if she was her child versus the other way around. Eve's long, dark, wavy hair was identical to Mother's. *Why hadn't I noticed it before? Mother hid Eve in plain sight all this time.*

"Adam." Eve's voice was rich and soft like the finest velvet. She side-stepped Mother and advanced toward Adam with no fear. I'd expected her to cower in front of him based on what Mother had said, but Eve was strong.

"Eve." Adam's voice morphed into something less crazed, almost normal. "I've missed you."

"You miss something that never was, Adam. There never was love between us. I was never enough for you. I was never what you truly wanted, and you only coveted me when I left."

"I've always loved you, Eve," Adam said like he was pleading with her. Was it an act? He was convincing.

"No, you loved the idea of me." Eve stretched her arm out, and blue light pooled at her palms. A shiver of unease slivered through me. She was going to tempt him with her essence. "Let the young man go. It's my life force you want. Not his."

Adam focused on Eve as if she was the entire universe, and he was a planet lucky enough to be part of the space she occupied. "But I can have both."

"No." Eve took a step toward him. "You can have only one." She edged forward until her hand slipped into the stream of blue between Jax and Adam. She jerked. Jax fell to the bottom of the cage. He was free. Relief mixed with guilt because Eve would pay a price that should have been mine. I moved to go to Jax, but Father held his arm out in front of me.

Adam didn't try to stop Eve. He studied her with what looked like reverence, but he didn't respect her. The evil things he'd done proved that. His face relaxed like he'd found peace. "I feel you again."

"Yes, I feel you too." Eve's dark hair streaked with grey. She'd exchanged her ethos to save Jax.

The world slowed down as the guilt of knowing the center of my universe would survive by the sacrifice of my grandmother. *Jax.* My chest ached like the pain pried it open and set fire to it.

Mother let out a sob. Father slipped a hand around her waist and held her to him. Tears stained Mother's face as she reached for Eve. Her movements lacked energy, the fight gone. Father's grip supported Mother. He didn't have to hold her back from the scene like he had me.

"All is well, daughter. It was time." Eve turned to look

at me, and I saw peace in her eyes. Her posture relaxed. "It was finally time."

Adam dropped to his knees. Eve matched his actions and wrapped her arms around his shoulders, pulling the blue light to them. Blue filled the space around us, and I shielded my eyes. When the light retreated, Adam and Eve were gone. Vanished as they stepped through a portal, but there wasn't a portal. Sadness for her sacrifice and how my mother would mourn her inched in on me, and I, too, would mourn the loss of my grandmother.

I ran to the cage where Jax lay still on the floor. I yanked the door with all my might. It took three tries, but the hinges broke free. Jax looked as if he could be asleep, but he wasn't. I dragged him out of the metal enclosure and into my lap.

Uriel, Michael, and Gabriel gathered around Mother. Uriel's hand was on Mother's shoulder. "She chose now because she knew Morena was ready."

I couldn't think about that until I knew Jax was okay. He wasn't moving, and I needed help.

"Allow me," Uriel said over my shoulder. He laid a hand over Jax's heart. "Breathe, young demon."

Jax sputtered out a cough. My breath labored with his as if I couldn't breathe without him, but he was still with me.

I buried my head in his neck. "That was too close. Much too close."

"Closer than you know," Uriel said, his tone somber. "Eve and Adam are no longer the balance and the scale.

That duty belongs to you and Jax. You will need to prepare."

I stiffened at his choice of words but didn't let go of Jax. "Prepare for what?"

Gabriel knelt beside us, and Michael joined him. "Armageddon."

"And we will be your warriors," Uriel said.

They couldn't be serious. No one in Hell believed in Armageddon. If it were real, the residents of Hell had lived it dozens, if not hundreds, of times. "Armageddon is a fable told to children to scare them similar to the..." I almost said jinn because I'd thought jinn weren't real too.

"No, Armageddon is real." Gabriel's head tilted up, and there were two things in his eyes—belief and fear. "Eve and Adam weren't able to stop it. It is now up to you and Jax."

"What's up to us?" Jax's voice came out like gravel. He struggled to sit up.

I shifted to support him. Thoughts of end times swirled in my mind. "Don't worry about it right now. I'll fill you in later."

He sat up with much effort to an upright position. His gaze locked on Uriel. "I'd rather hear it now before I start killing angels who are too close to me."

CHAPTER 30

JAX

"It looks like I owe you." I studied Uriel. His usually pensive expression turned to concern. "But I'm not sure our existence will remain intact long enough for me to repay you."

"You owe me nothing, Jax." Uriel's humbled tone surprised me. "If I hadn't slept for so long, Adam wouldn't have gotten this far."

Michael squeezed Uriel's shoulder. Despite their differences and how dysfunctional Rena thought her archangel family members were, they did support each other like a family. "He would have found a way whether you were here or not."

Uriel patted Michael's hand. "But he was my charge, Brother, and that makes his actions my failure."

"None of us are without blame," Lucifer said, his voice softer than the scowl on his face.

"Lucifer and I knew where he was most of the time. I'd

asked him to keep tabs on Adam's location to protect my mother," Lilith said, her eyes red and swollen, but she no longer sobbed. "I was too focused on Eve to think about what he could be doing."

Gabriel edged closer but didn't touch Lilith. Without looking in their direction, Lucifer reached for Lilith and held her tight against his side. He might not hold a grudge for what Gabriel had done while under the influence of the Ascendant, but he hadn't forgotten. I couldn't blame him. If it had been Rena...

I looked at Uriel, and his glacial stare returned to his face. He couldn't read my mind, but I suspected he knew what I was thinking. *Stay the fuck away from Rena.* He glanced at the heir to Hell and back to me. He gave me a single nod. I slid my arm around Rena's waist, not unlike what Lucifer had done to Lilith, and squeezed her hip.

"Are you listening, Jax?" Rena's voice drifted up to me, her eyes filled with many emotions. Worry. Grief. I'd take all her pain to free her of the memories of what she witnessed tonight.

"Sorry, my love." I tucked a loose strand of hair behind her ear. "My mind is a little distracted." My bones ached as if they were all broken into a million pieces, but it eased as time went on. I'd be fine before long.

She smashed her lips together. "You should rest. Armageddon will not happen tonight. It could be months or years..." Her beautiful mouth turned down in a frown. I ran my thumb over the corner. If we didn't have an audience, I'd kiss her until she let out one of those soft sighs that made my insides turn to lava.

"Or centuries," Lilith added.

"Or a millennium," Lucifer whispered.

I looked from Rena's parents to the archangels Gabriel, Michael, and Uriel, all still in the room, even though Adam had been neutralized. They were still in Hell. They didn't immediately retreat from here after Adam and Eve...did whatever they did.

The archangels remained in Hell for something...or someone. "Why are you three still here?" Their silence was an answer without giving one. "Are you going to follow us everywhere now?"

"What are you talking about?" Rena's eyes widened. She sucked in a breath in the silent space as we waited for answers the archangels didn't offer. "But you weren't stuck to Adam and Eve's every move."

"Armageddon would not happen as long as they were balanced, and Eve was a master at maintaining the balance despite the chaos Adam created," Gabriel said.

"We will guide the scale and the balance." Uriel lowered his head.

"And fight for it if necessary." Michael took a knee in front of us. He bowed his head.

Gabriel mimicked Michael's actions. Uriel lowered himself into the same position.

"Awkward," I said under my breath.

"Very," Rena said. "Are we supposed to tell you to rise?"

"Only if that is what you wish," Gabriel said.

"Rise." Rena motioned for them to stand. "Why is my family so damn weird? And no one answer that."

"My brothers get ahead of themselves, Morena. Relax your worries. Armageddon will not occur as long as I sit on the throne of Hell." Lucifer's tone portrayed confidence.

"You have named an heir, my brother," Uriel said. "You are no longer the sole seat of Hell. The Crown Princess of Hell is the balance, and her mate is the scale."

Mate. Of all the things he said, that word made me cringe. Rena was more to me than a mate. She was everything. The fires of Hell, the blue skies of Earth, the sweet smell at the Library of Knowledge...She was the entirety of everything good in my life, and I'd stand beside her through Armageddon if that was her choice. But she wouldn't let the destruction of the realms happen. Rena was more than the sum of these angelic beings.

"Speak plainly, Brother," Lucifer said, his stare locked on Uriel.

"Armageddon has already begun."

CHAPTER 31

RENA

Jax's expression was guarded. He'd recovered remarkably from what Adam had put him through. His color returned to his natural, olive-colored hue. He looked like my Jax, but he was tied to me in a way that couldn't be undone. I wanted to believe he was with me because he wanted to be. *Scale. Balance. Armageddon. Will we end up like Adam and Eve? No. I will not let that happen.*

As if he understood my concern, he caressed my cheek. "We'll figure it out." His voice was soft, a gentle whisper meant only for my ears, but the expert hearing of others likely invaded the private moment.

"We will." I forced a smile and faced my parents and my uncles. "I need you to tell me everything you know about Armageddon and without riddles. Why wouldn't Armageddon come while Adam and Eve were here? How do I..." I inhaled to calm my nerves. "How do we stop it?"

Jax slipped his hand in mine and squeezed. I needed his reassurance in this moment more than he could know.

"It is a battle," Gabriel said.

"But not just a battle," Michael added.

Uriel met my gaze. "It is the ultimate battle and if you lose, the end times will be upon us all."

None of us knew exactly what the end times looked like, but there were stories, which I assumed held truth since all the other fables we grew up with were real. Besides the destruction, it would mean the end of existence for the realms. All of us. That couldn't happen. Stassi was in the human realm. My family occupied others, and we saw so many realms on the maps Jophiel brought from the Library. *Are there beings in those realms too?*

"No pressure there," I said under my breath. "And this battle will take place on Earth? Not in our demon realm or the angelic realm? Why?"

"Earth, the human home, is where Armageddon begins. Then it will spread like a rampant wildfire until the human realm is consumed. Once done there, it will move through each realm until there is nothing left."

Confusion muddled the information Uriel shared. "How?"

"Armageddon is many things," Gabriel said. "But mostly it is a disease that infects everything it touches."

"So, it's a contagion?" Jax asked, his brows pinched together.

Father moved closer to me. "The end times will come

in many forms, and once it reaches a certain point, there will be no return."

Understanding centered my thoughts. The most fragile part was the one requiring the most protection. *If it falls, we all do.* "Earth. If it consumes Earth, that is the point of no return."

"Yes." Uriel closed his eyes.

Jax ran his hand through his hair. The nervous habit told me he was worried. "How do we know something is an act of Armageddon versus human-driven behavior?"

Michael regarded Jax. "You must assume everything is but only act when you are certain."

Weariness settled over me. The cost of my choices was almost too much for me to bear. I forced Father's hand on naming me heir by claiming it when he was incapacitated. I set it all in motion. I faced Jax. The heaviest weight on me was the fact Jax was in danger because of me. I took in each face, angelic, demon, and vampire. The wrong I brought upon us would be righted, even if it cost me my eternity with Jax. Tears pricked my eyes at the thought my time with Jax was short.

"Don't." Jax pulled me to him. "I know what you're thinking," he whispered in my ear. His breath tickled my lobe. "But I'm not letting you go. You're not doing this alone. You are the balance, but I am the scale. Our lives were always meant to be entwined, whether that is for a short time or beyond."

Mother cleared her throat. She rubbed her hand over my back. "I think we were seeing signs before today.

Before Adam's attempt to grab power. The signs were pushing you to this point, Morena, but it's up to you how our stories end. We trust you and will support you."

I inhaled and let my breath out slowly. Jax leaned back and placed a kiss on my forehead. I turned to the group again. Eyes full of trust and love looked back at me.

"I promise you all. I will stop this." My heart beat in a heavy, sluggish rhythm. The future wasn't avoidable, but the people in this room were too important to risk.

Jax pulled me to his side, and the others huddled up around us. It was the strangest sight, but it somehow felt normal for my crazy family.

"We'll do this together, Morena," Father said. "All of us will follow your lead and command."

It had to be hard for him to say. He was a natural leader, and I wasn't. I had the desire to be the best at everything I did, but that wasn't quite the same as being a natural at something.

"Thank you," I said. "Thank you all for your trust." I forced a smile to my face, but the rage inside me rioted against my rational thoughts. I didn't know how, but I would save my family. "Where do we start?"

"We need a command center," Jax said. "One where we can monitor the activities around the world."

"I like it." I smiled at him, and it was genuine. "We can't do that very well from Hell. Mother, can we use Gothica?"

"It's all yours," she said, her tone earnest.

It wasn't mine, though. I was the heir to Hell, not to

the Night Children or Gothica, and I no longer wondered if that played a part in the timing of Armageddon's arrival and my being named the balance. Uriel had confirmed it. My family bustled with activity as we prepared to depart for the human realm, and my thoughts drifted to the best way to keep them safe. There was only one real answer. To watch for an opportunity to do this alone and seize it.

JAX

I watched Rena filtering through the news at an accelerated pace on the computer. It only took me a day to get her command center set up at Gothica, and we were a week into our monitoring. Lilith offered up what Rena called the throne room because it had the most open space. The ground floor placement was a logical choice for the large amount of equipment I'd purchased too.

I don't think any of us could shake off the death of so many vampires here, but everyone worked the tasks Rena assigned. The archangels were out in the world while Rena, Lilith, and I filled the command center with staff. Most of them were vampires, but we brought over some demons we knew wouldn't incite panic. All in all, there were about a hundred of us, but the space could hold more if needed.

None of our leads had panned out over the week, but

everyone moved nonstop without rest. Rena worked the hardest. Others would take breaks to feed, but she didn't. She summoned Gabriel to carry messages to the other archangels, but the reports back didn't reveal anything useful.

One of the vampires Lilith brought in was skilled at using AI to data mine the news from the Web. Selene's fingers were almost as fast as her tongue was sharp. The vampire was unusual down to her scent but the top candidate to replace Alessia as Lilith's second-in-command. Her She showed great respect to Lilith and Rena, so I ignored her jabs at the demons...for now.

"Morena?" Selene called from her seat at a desk with multiple, large screen monitors and several laptops. "Come look at this."

Rena slid back from her desk and joined Selene. I slowly made my way over to them, as did Lilith.

"What did you find?" Rena asked.

Selene pointed to one of the monitors. "Look at this article dated yesterday. It's a news story from Europe. They are referring to the mass killing as ritualistic."

"Mass killing..." Rena said under her breath as if the words were painful to say. "How many?"

"They've found two hundred and fifty so far but suspect there to be more." My stomach soured. The number was large, more on the scale of natural disasters. It had to be a sign of Armageddon.

Rena nodded. "I'll send Michael to investigate."

She exited the room, and the urge to follow her pulled

like a magnet. I couldn't ignore it. She waited at the door to the apartment at the top of Gothica.

"Something told me you would be behind me." Rena's warm smile lit up the space. It was the first real smile I'd seen on her face since we established our center of operations.

I cradled her face in my hands and caressed her lips. She deepened the kiss with urgency. I groaned into her mouth, and she pulled back. A soft sigh escaped her lips.

"I'm sorry," she said. "We'll take a break this evening and do something for us."

"You don't have to explain to me." I tucked her hair behind her ears and reassured her. "I love you, and I'm here no matter what."

"Thank you," she said. "I know this isn't easy."

"If it gives us and everyone else a future, it's worth it." I kissed the tip of her nose. "Now, go call Gabriel to carry your message to Michael."

She smiled, but her smile was different this time. It didn't reach her eyes.

Her voice sang out in the melody that was for Gabriel alone. The familiar bright white light flashed, and the messenger stood in front of us. He didn't greet Rena like he had in the past, and his skin was dull. Gabriel was tired like the rest of us. We'd been going nonstop for two solid weeks.

"You found something?" he asked, stepping toward Rena.

"Maybe," Rena said, her tone dejected. "There was a mass killing in Europe on one of the ancient temple sites."

Gabriel cocked his head to the side. "Which one?"

"Hypnos," I said. "I don't know Greek mythology. Do you know what he was thought to be the god of?"

"It's no myth," Gabriel said. "Hypnos was considered the god of sleep, and he was Adam in his original jinn form."

I blinked through the information. I'd thought Greek mythology was just that...a myth. *Was everything we were taught a fable or a myth true?*

"What?" Rena's voice was almost a whisper. "Adam lived as a god among ancient people?"

I was less surprised Adam would position himself as a god. He was an opportunistic fucker.

"It wasn't uncommon for celestial beings to do so during those times. That's how most of those myths came to be. Although many are embellished."

"This was a sacrifice to him." I heard the words leave my mouth and was certain of the truth.

"It would seem so." Gabriel rubbed his chin as if he was considering the possibility.

"So, he's not dead," Rena said, her voice still low.

"A celestial being never really dies, Rena," Gabriel said.

I flinched at his use of my nickname for her. He didn't mean it any other way than as an uncle to a niece, but I didn't like it regardless. "Do you think he is hiding in Greece, then?"

"I don't know. It could be fanatics. We will not know without investigation."

"This is not a coincidence," Rena said, her tone stronger. "I'm going. Can you let Michael know to join me there? And Aunt B too?"

"That's not a good idea," I said. She hadn't rested in a week, not that demons needed much rest unless they were healing, but the dark circles under her eyes were like caverns.

"It's my decision," she said firmly. "You will not change my mind, but you are welcome should you choose to join me."

"I will be where I always am," I said, taking her hand. "At your side."

She gave me one of those small, forced smiles, and it crushed me. My heart ached to see her happy again. To see a real smile on her beautiful face.

"Go," she said to Gabriel. "You know where to find us."

Gabriel nodded and disappeared in the same warm, angelic light in which he arrived.

"We'll tell Mother and then portal there," Rena said.

"Wait," I said, pulling her back to stand in front of me. Rena's eyes weren't the brilliant blue they were when they weren't demon red. The color of her irises was a dull grey. "You need to power up before we go. We don't know what we will find, and you need to be strong."

She didn't argue with me and only shook her head. "You're right. We can stop by the main kitchen on the way to Mother."

Rena hated drinking blood, but she refused to consume flesh, and the kitchen at Gothica was full of blood. But Rena's mother still enjoyed human meals, and her followers kept the kitchen in the apartment stocked with blood and human food.

"Why don't I cook you something to eat? Would you prefer that to blood?" I brought her hand to my mouth and brushed my lips over her knuckles.

Her eyes twinkled ever so slightly. "I'd prefer a lot of things right now, but a BLT sounds great."

She loved bacon...maybe more than me.

"As you wish, my love," I said and released her hand. "Have a seat while I cook for you."

She splayed her hands out wide against the counter-top. It reminded me of while I was vampire and almost took her there. Almost bit her. I closed my eyes and tamped down the memory. My focus shifted to the frying bacon. She watched me as I prepped her sandwich.

"Mustard or mayonnaise?" I asked, knowing full well which she preferred but wanting to see her reaction.

Rena wrinkled her nose. "I hate mayonnaise. How do you not know that?"

I laughed. "I do."

She reached over the counter and slapped my arm. "You teased me like that when we were kids too."

I glanced down at my arm and back up at her. Desire heated in my core. "Careful or our trip to Greece might be delayed."

Her eyes danced as I set the plate in front of her. "I don't deserve you, Jax."

"No, you deserve infinitely more than me. More than I could ever give you." I rested on my elbows in front of her. "But I'll endeavor every day to prove my worthiness to you."

Her eyes glistened. She leaned forward and traced her fingers over my cheek. "You have sacrificed so much. For me. To be with me."

"And you fought for me more than once. It's my turn to be your champion." I turned my mouth to her palm and teased my lips against it. "Now eat."

She laughed and picked up the sandwich. Her demeanor lightened as if I'd lessened her burdens a little. *Good.* I'd carry any weight for her to make her life better.

I turned around to clean up the mess I made because I wasn't a clean-as-you-go type person.

"Jax?" Rena called.

I looked over my shoulder. "Yes?"

"Don't do anything stupid."

I chuckled. "That's not the first time you've called me stupid." The memory of the last time ached as if Gabriel's sword cut me all over again. "If you want to go to Greece, you better finish that sandwich."

The archangels named me her scale, but my life was far more fragile than hers. I couldn't afford to do anything stupid, but I would give my life in service to her if needed.

CHAPTER 33
RENA

Mother paced the floor of the side room. I was pretty sure this was one of the rooms where the vampires brought their human sources to feed on them. Blood scented the air like it was everywhere, but it wasn't visible. The room had been cleaned, because the aroma of a bleachy cleaner mixed with the metallic scent. "Rena, you two can't go alone."

"We won't be alone. Michael and Aunt B will meet us there."

"I should go with you." She made another pass across the room. "And your father."

We didn't even know if Adam was in Greece. It didn't make sense for all of us to go, and I needed someone I trusted to stay in the command center to monitor for changes or activity. "No, you need to stay here and send us any updates or clues you find through Gabriel."

Mother wrung her hands. "I'm used to leading,

Morena, not being left behind. How can I protect you from here?"

I rested my hands on Mother's shoulders. "You are leading. This team needs someone strong and decisive. That's why I want you here."

Mother's lips turned up. "And my daughter no longer needs my protection."

"I'll always need your protection, Mother. Just in different ways now." I pulled her into a hug. She held me in a tight embrace, and worry waved off her.

I understood Mother's concern. Every time we separated, there was an undercurrent that we might not see each other again. The reality that Armageddon could happen at any moment manifested in our every movement. It was like every time we caught our breath, we were pulled under again.

Jax shifted his weight from foot to foot. He sensed the change in our family, and maybe it was because he was the balance. I released Mother from my embrace.

"See you soon." I turned to Jax. "Call the portal."

"This wasn't exactly what I imagined taking you to Greece would be like." He formed the symbols to open our path.

"You thought about it?"

"When we were practicing our portal work, we used the Greek Isles to practice our hops. The beauty is something to behold but nothing compared to you," he said. The portal appeared.

"Take care of her, Jax," Mother said.

"You have my word, Lilith."

"Love you, Mom," I said.

"Love you too."

I grabbed Jax's hand, and he led us through the light.

My feet sunk into red sand. I glanced down to see my black boots swallowed up by the grains. It was metaphorical of what we faced like we were running out of time.

"Welcome to Santorini," Jax said.

"No," My gaze traveled up to the famed site I'd been drawn to in so many readings. "Welcome to Akrotiri."

"Yes, the ancient city is just over there."

"Researchers recently discovered artifacts and writings in a cave nearby that suggest it might have been a place where Hypnos's small following worshiped him. It was at the remains of the temple in front of it where the recent activities happened. We should start there."

Jax lifted his foot and shook the sand off his boot. "Don't you want to wait for Michael and Barachiel?"

"No, I want to see the site now," I said. It seemed too heartless to say the site of the mass killing, but I built my mental walls to prepare for the inevitable impact of the energy left behind from an event so terrible. Even from this distance, I felt a low vibration. Souls would be stuck and need release, but I couldn't take on their pain and maintain my strength. *I should have sent for Uriel. Forgiveness and peace are his areas of expertise.*

Jax was a few steps ahead of me as we made our way over the terrain to the cave and temple. A hum grew louder the closer we got to the location. Jax paused, and I came up beside him. Not much more than stones in a circle were left of the ancient temple, and no barricades or police tape blocked the area off, which was weird. The grass was sparse, but it didn't look trampled like it should from that big of a crowd gathering on the spot.

"Do you hear that buzzing sound?" Jax moved closer to me.

"Yes, I've been hearing it for a while, as well as a tremor of energy. We're going to encounter some lost souls that don't know they are lost, Jax. These events usually have a lot of them. Did your guard training prepare you for that?" All demons learned about it but on varying levels, depending on rank and specialty. If Jax's focus had been on portals, he might not have gotten all the information.

Jax's face fell into what looked like regret mixed with sadness. "We were required to experience it multiple times as part of our training. Plane crashes. Mass shootings. Earthquakes." He shook his head and took a step forward.

My heart ached for him. I'd been required to experience those as well, but each time, it was like the first. I never got used to it. I wasn't sure how anyone did.

"It's never easy. Is it?" My voice cracked, and I smashed my lips together to keep a sob in. This was not the time to break down. I needed to be alert for both of us.

"No," Jax said, his voice quieter than before. "Do you know if any of your choices were accepted?"

As demons, our offer to humans was a temptation to

join us in Hell. They could always choose the other after-life, though. It wasn't until I met my human friend, Stassi, that I cared what choice the humans made. The thought of tempting her into servitude of any kind made me sick. Not that some humans didn't deserve it, but not most of them. And not Stassi.

"I was told that no demon ever knows during training whether the soul accepted their offer or not. Were you allowed to know?"

"No, we were told the same, but I wondered."

"Same and often."

"We're here," Jax said. There wasn't much left of the temple in front of the cave. It must have been a smaller one to begin with, but there were only a couple of pillars with a large marble circle in the center.

"Two hundred and fifty people died here? In this small place?" I bent down and ran my hand over the polished white stone. The sun warmed it, but there were no displaced souls here. "Where are they?"

"I don't feel any of them." Jax's voice was quiet.

"Neither do I." I glanced around. "And that's strange considering it was a pagan ritual, and the article said it was a fanatic who attacked them."

I moved to the edge of the circle and grabbed a handful of dirt, letting it run through my fingers. My eyes closed as visions, snapshots really, flooded my mind. "They completed a ceremony. Once it was done, they passed around little white cups."

"A mass suicide, not a mass murder?" Jax asked.

"It would seem so," I said. "But why would the news call it a killing?" It was like someone wanted to make it sensational for the news, but a mass suicide was almost as bad. *Why twist the story?*

Bright white light flashed around us, and Michael and Barachiel appeared.

"Because whoever cleaned the area had a connection to cover it up," Barachiel said.

"Thank you for meeting us here," I said. "Even if it were a mass suicide, shouldn't we have lost souls?"

"I've never experienced one that didn't," Aunt B said. "Especially one this size."

"So, where did they go?" I reached down for another handful of dirt. The images were the same, though. "The sand doesn't hold the answer. At least for me. And you can't sense their passage?"

"I don't feel the release of any souls here. Not even one," Michael said.

"Could they have been hidden in some way?" Jax asked. His brows pinched together. "Or consumed?"

"You think Adam did this?" Michael asked. "I'm not sure he would have the power to pull this act off yet after what Eve did to him. It should take centuries to regain his strength and even then, his power might not be what it was before."

"But this could be him?" Jax asked.

"We can't rule him out yet, but that's unlikely, Jax," Barachiel said.

"Seems very coincidental that an event like this would

take place at Hypnos's temple, and Adam was Hypnos," I said, trying to put the pieces together. I was not as ready to dismiss Jax's idea as my aunt and uncle.

"I agree it is a remarkable coincidence, but I do not see how Adam would have been in any condition to be able to orchestrate something like this," Aunt B said. "I know you want answers and that seems logical, but there are other possible explanations."

"Occam's razor." I shrugged.

"Correlation does not always mean causation though, my dear niece," Michael said.

"That's strange for a warrior to say," I said.

"Not so strange if you think about a warrior's strategy," he said.

Jax stood at the edge of the opening. "Let's look in the cave since we are here."

I nodded. "Then we'll see what we can find out from the authorities." Aunt B had a way about her that made people want to open up to her. Michael? Not so much.

Jax led us down a narrow path on the side of the cave because crystal blue water flowed in the center. Gemstones were embedded every so often as if they were there to guide us. When we were far enough in that light from the outside couldn't reach us, torches lined the walls. The coolness inside made my skin crawl, and I longed for warmth to drive it away.

"Hell's fire light our way," I whispered. The torches lit like matches down either side of the tunnel. The heat from the fire didn't stop the uneasiness.

Torches weren't the only thing that changed here. The floor was covered in mosaics, and the walls were painted with bright scenes. This wasn't the work of prehistoric people, but it was ancient. I ran my hand over one of the scenes. "Beautiful."

"It's a shame that kind of workmanship is all but lost," Michael said.

"Weren't a lot of the workers then slaves? Wouldn't you kick ass at your job if your life depended on it?"

"These artists were typically commissioned even then and not slaves, but point taken," Michael said.

"How far back do you think this goes?" Jax asked from the front. The path was only wide enough for us to pass in a single file. It only gave us one way out if something happened, unless we had time to call a portal or for Aunt B and Michael to do their archangel thing. If we had to run away from a random celestial being, we were screwed.

"Hypnos was said to hide from the sun in a cave. Of course, that was Adam's excuse for disappearing," Barachiel said.

"Which angelic beings were which Greek gods?" I asked.

"That is a long story, so let's table it for another time," Aunt B said.

"Now, I'm even more curious. Which one were you Aunt B?"

"I did not play into the belief of gods and goddesses like some of my siblings and relations," she said, and I was surprised she didn't. She had the best sense of humor out of all my aunts and uncles.

"I think we're getting close to the end. The torches are spaced farther apart here, so watch your step," Jax said.

The current of the cavern river had slowed too. Jax had to be right. There didn't seem to be any celestial being activity here. The archaeological experience was magnificent but nothing that helped us to stop Armageddon. The cave was a dead end.

"Stop," Jax called.

I froze. "What's wrong?"

"It's a wall. Just a wall. Nothing is here."

A literal dead end. I inched toward him until I was close enough to see. The wall looked solid. "Is there a door somewhere? A hidden handle?"

Jax patted his hands around the stone. "I don't see one."

I studied the water and saw it bubble and swirl. "Maybe we're supposed to go under for the door. Unless you want to portal us to the other side." I had no desire to dive into the water here. There probably wasn't anything that could hurt us, but gross. Portaling was risky and not a good idea.

"We don't know what's on the other side of this rock. It could just be more stone." He sighed. "I'll go first and check it out."

He toed off his shoes and slid his socks off. Then he pulled his shirt over his head, and I took in every aspect of his muscular physique. My muscles clenched in my belly. *Later Rena. Not the right time.*

Jax kissed my cheek and dove into the water. He disappeared almost instantly with so little light back here. My heart lurched, and I grabbed my throat.

Barachiel rubbed my arm. "He'll be fine, Morena."

"I just feel so…anxious here."

"There is something about this cave," Barachiel said, glancing at Michael. "You're even quieter than usual, Brother."

"I've noticed it too. Something does feel off about this space," he said.

The uneasiness pooled around us as did my worry for Jax. I was ready to shed my clothes and follow him. It'd been long enough. He should be back now.

Water swirled, and a head popped up. *Jax.*

CHAPTER 34

JAX

I accepted Michael's outstretched hand to help me from the water. The temperature wasn't unbearable for a demon, but it was cold. "There is a room on the other side, and it does look like someone has been there recently."

"Get your strength back and then we'll all go together." Michael patted me on the shoulder. I wasn't tired. The swim was tough but easier than fighting the fucking grey wings.

Rena knelt beside me on the narrow path. She pushed my wet hair back out of my face. "Are you okay?"

"I am now that I'm looking at you again." I leaned over and kissed the end of her nose.

A flush crept across her cheeks, and I was shocked that out of all the things I'd said to her, that phrase made her blush. Although she would deny it, she was still so innocent in some ways. I loved that about her. Her casual-without-even-realizing-it innocence was one of the things about her that could make me rock hard in seconds. I inhaled a breath because wet clothes and a throbbing cock wouldn't be an appropriate look.

"I can portal us all there now that I've seen the other side." I shifted my focus from my building desire for Rena.

"That seems more efficient," Michael said.

I rolled my head until my neck popped to shake off the memory of Adam tainting the one thing that was good. I stood on the narrow path and formed the symbols of the portal. The window was open, and I held my hand behind my back for Rena.

The room on the other side appeared to have been there for centuries but had been well maintained. There was a bed, a desk, a couple of chairs, and a table. It was lit by a natural substance in the walls.

Rena let go of my hand and ran hers over the glowing minerals. "What is this?"

"Some type of fluorescent mineral I guess," I said.

"But they don't have a light source to absorb light here." She leaned in close to the wall.

Michael scraped at a piece of the glowing substance with his fingernail. "This mineral is unusual. Sister, do you know anything about it?"

"I'm afraid this is more Jophiel's area," Barachiel said.

"Someone appears to have lived here and for some time." Rena's attention turned to the furnishings. "How did they get these things in here?"

I'd wondered that too. "My guess is via a portal like we did."

"Mmm." She walked around the room, which had to be less than a thousand square feet. Rena traced her hands along the walls like she expected her touch to gain the trust of the room so it would show all its secrets. "Anyone feel a draft anywhere?"

Michael, Barachiel, and I paused our investigations. I lifted my hands and held them out to feel for blowing air, but there wasn't even a breeze.

Stillness clung in the space around my fingers. "I don't feel anything."

Michael tried the same. "Neither do I."

"Same," Brachial confirmed.

"But yet there's oxygen here..." Rena's voice trailed off.

"There could be a crack in the main wall," I offered.

"Hmmm..." Rena turned around, looking toward the ceiling. "Can someone feel around the edges and see?"

"I'll take this side," I said and moved to the left.

Michael shifted to the right. "I've got the other."

I wished I could read Rena's mind to see where her thoughts were. She was in the zone, and I didn't want to disrupt her flow. No air came through the seam on my side. "Nothing here."

"Or here," Michael said.

Barachiel had joined Rena at the back of the room. They huddled close as if they were sharing a secret.

"Did you find something?" I asked, crossing the room to join them.

"There is some sound on the other side. It could be another way in and out," Barachiel said.

Rena glanced at me with a puzzled expression. "We just have to figure out how to get over there."

"Call Hell's fire to light the wall, Rena. I have an idea."

"Of course," she said, her voice full of enthusiasm. "You're a genius, Jax." She held her hands out. "Hell's fire, show us the secrets of this wall."

The fire responded to her command and licked at the wall. It ran over it like liquid, and I saw what I needed to see. "There." I pointed to Rena. "See where the flames flicker?"

"Yes," she said and called the fire back to her. She slid her hand into the crevice. The wall creaked like an old floor. It slid open for us but not without dropping some clods of dirt on us first. A set of stairs, with no railing and carved from the same stone, stood in front of us.

I peered up and saw light. "Look."

Rena took her turn. Then Barachiel and Michael.

"I think this was a prison of some sort," I said, a sense of foreboding chilling me.

"Or a hideout," Rena countered.

Barachiel held out her arm. "We've come this far. Let's see where the stairs go."

"I second that," Michael agreed.

Rena got two steps up, and I slid by her. "I'll go first. We don't know what we're walking into."

I was her scale, and I weighed the risk and decided it should be mine.

CHAPTER 35

RENA

The stairs were slippery compared to the other walks we'd encountered. The light grew brighter the higher we climbed, and I stepped onto the dirt to a bright midday sun. One glance around, and I knew we were on part of the Akrotiri site.

"This could have been a smugglers' path at one time, and someone thought it was a cool find," I said. It didn't seem practical for any other use.

Michael took in the surroundings. "This path had a use, and it was to sneak in and out of the ancient city. I don't think it was for smuggling though...not what you are thinking of, at least."

"Then what?" Jax asked.

"Someone pretending to be a god would use it to make random appearances is where my brother is going with that," Barachiel said. That made more sense than my smuggler theory.

"So, Adam?" Jax said. "It had to be him. Who else would it be with the Hypnos temple and using the cover of darkness?"

Michael crossed his arms over his chest. "I'm becoming more convinced with every step we take that it is, indeed, the work of Adam."

I reached out to sense Adam, but I found no trace. We all saw Eve deal with him in the throne room. It shouldn't be him. He shouldn't be able to recover that fast, but every cell in my body said it was him. "He doesn't appear to have been here as far as I can tell."

"No, it could be his followers, but I would be surprised if he wasn't somewhere close." Michael walked a few steps down the path and turned. "Aren't the rest of you coming?"

"Are you familiar with this area?"

"Enough," Michael said. "I was here a sufficient number of times to get us through the ruins."

His words should have been comforting, but my senses were on high alert. The tingling at the base of my neck sent small shocks out across my arms, causing goose-bumps. We were either going to run into Adam or some insane followers of his. Either way, it wasn't going to be a reunion I wanted. If his followers were killing people to try to bring him back, that could be part of Armageddon. Everything we were trying to stop could come down to whatever we found in an ancient city of ruins, albeit well-preserved ones.

Michael led us through what once must have been

prosperous streets. The remains of many shops lined the avenue, and the frescoes had been safeguarded under layers of volcanic ash. Since being uncovered, the artwork revealed depicted a rich society. Many of the scenes reminded me of dreams. Huge chunks of rock from volcanic pyroclasts were a reminder of the destruction that took place, but no bodies had been found during excavation, despite the area having been very densely populated. A jinn, especially Adam, would have had his own feast here. But was he hiding among the ruins, or were his followers performing nefarious acts in his name? Had Adam been here when the volcano erupted?

"Rena?" Jax jarred me from my thoughts.

"Hmm?"

"Do you think we'll win?"

"Armageddon? I'm not sure if one wins, but I believe we can stop it." And I did believe we could stop it, but there was a very real chance we wouldn't either. My chest ached with the heaviness of dread. Some of us, my family, might not make it. Stassi might be lost in the events of Armageddon. Not only could she still be a target, but she'd be at risk as Armageddon manifested. I'd kept my distance from her out of respect for her new relationship and mine with Jax, but I had checked in on her through scouts. She'd settled into life with her vampire. And Jax...if something were to happen to him, I'd willingly sacrifice myself after I made sure the others were safe. The heaviness melded on me as if I was encased with lead, and my movements slowed.

"Are you okay?" Jax took my hand, and even the simple act was weighted.

"Fine." I forced a smile.

He returned it with a frown. "Do you need to rest?"

Rest wouldn't release the force pressing down on me. I knew it. Jax probably knew it as well. He drew my hand to his mouth until his lips were a delicate caress against my palm.

"My life and yours, my love, they are one. I can sense the pain festering in you."

Michael jogged back to us. "Are you unwell, Morena?"

"No," I said, but I was anything except well.

"Are you lethargic?" Aunt B asked, stopping beside Michael. "The energy in this place is draining if you don't have your walls in place." Their concern was appreciated, but I wanted to keep moving forward.

"That's not it. I built my mental walls before we stepped on the temple grounds. They should still be intact. I just feel...encumbered and heavy."

"How long?" Michael asked. "How long have you been feeling that way?"

"Since we started walking through the city," I said. "The further we go, the heavier it feels." I glanced at Jax, and he seemed to be fine. Whatever affected me wasn't doing the same to him. *Is this how he felt when the vampires were massacred at Gothica?* "Jax?"

"I know what you're thinking," he said. "It was like my chest was squeezed so tight I would explode."

"It doesn't feel like that," I said. A small amount of

relief came to me. "It's more like a weighted blanket. A very weighted blanket."

"Maybe sit for a moment." Jax gestured to a large volcanic boulder.

I dropped onto it, but the pressure kept building. "Is this the burden of death here?"

Michael squatted down in front of me. "I don't think it's death. The source seems to be targeting you."

"No one else feels it?" They all shook their heads. It was aimed at me. Whatever it was.

Michael patted my knee. "It could be a protection on the city."

"Against me? I wasn't even a being when this was a living city."

"It could be against demons," Aunt B said.

"But Jax isn't impacted," I said. It hit me then what was different between Jax and me. "It's my blood. The protection is against my father."

"Lucifer's blood," Michael said. "For a protection like that to hold, they would need his blood."

"That sounds like something only Adam could and would do," I said.

"We don't know that, Morena. There is no evidence the enchantment was recent. It could be centuries old." Michael helped me to my feet. I'd caught my breath and could move a little easier. "But I think it's time to get back to Gothica."

Maybe he was right. This place was interesting, but I

was disappointed it didn't give us anything more than conspiracies.

"Jax, call our ride home," I said, ready to be free of the pressure of this place.

He formed the symbols with expertise, but no portals opened. *Unusual. I'm the one who can't call portals.* Jax nailed them nearly every time. He formed the symbols again, but nothing happened.

Fear flared like a stake in my spine. "Jax?"

His face flushed. "I can't do it. I'm doing the right sequence, but the portal isn't responding."

We're trapped.

Michael looked around, as did Aunt B. He wrapped his fingers around my elbow. "Maybe we should make our way down to the hidden room since we teleported there."

My birthmark itched. It could just be an itch, but my senses went on alert. Something wasn't as it should be here.

CHAPTER 36

JAX

I stared at the ground as we made our way back. "Fuck." I rubbed my nose from the abrupt stop. A wall, nearly invisible, stood between me and the entrance. We were trapped. I looked over my shoulder at the others. "What is this?"

"A spell," Barachiel said, her tone cautionary. "A strong one from an ancient being."

"It looks like a dome," Rena said. I peered in the same direction to see the translucent shimmer over us. *Fuck. We're trapped.*

"The question is who?" Michael put a hand against the barrier. It rippled in response but didn't break or show any weakness.

"It was me," a female voice said from behind us. *That bitch. She's supposed to be Lilith's replacement for Alessia, who died during an attack on Gothica.*

"Selene?" Rena said, her tone bitter with betrayal.

"You were next in line to be second-in-command of the Night Children," I said.

"She is no Night Child," Barachiel said.

"No, she used spells to conceal her true origin," Michael said, drawing his sword. "We will not allow you to harm the balance."

"Or the scale." Selene gestured to me. *How did she know?*

Barachiel and Michael moved to position themselves between Selene and Rena and me. I positioned myself at Rena's side in my fighting stance.

"Put your sword away, Michael," Selene said. "I'm not here to harm anyone. I just require Morena's help. I don't need any of the rest of you, and you may all go if she stays."

I growled. "Not going to happen."

"Is it not her choice? She is the crown princess of Hell. Is she not?"

"She is," Michael said. "Which is why we will not let you near her."

"You archangels are always so dramatic." Selene rolled her eyes.

Rena snorted under her breath. "Welcome to my dysfunctional family. What is it my help is vital for?"

"I have no desire to bring Adam back, as you were musing. Many centuries ago, my one true love had a spell cast on him, and he has slumbered since that time. I've waited for the right one to come along to break that spell." The sadness in Selene's voice twisted inside me. I couldn't imagine centuries without Rena, but I wouldn't allow Selene alone time with her either.

"Can you tell your mate to relax? His energy is unsettling."

Mate...I hated when angelic beings reduced Rena and me to mates. We were many things, and the sum of those was more than mates.

"Jax, it's fine. She's not going to hurt me. She needs my help." Rena's voice was soft and smooth like silk skimming over me. The caress was gentle, and some of my tension cascaded away.

"Morena, you are living your life with your love, and if our time is short or long, I'd like to do the same with mine," Selene said, her tone pleading. "I apologize for manufacturing a story so serious to get you here, but I hope you will understand."

The story was fake. This was a trap from the beginning. *How can we believe anything Selene says?* I moved closer to Rena, but she held up a hand. Dread doused my hopes as I watched Rena shift her weight.

"Let them go. I'll stay." Rena closed the distance to Selene. Selene twisted her hand, and the invisible wall slammed down between us.

RENA

I froze my features in neutral and shoved my emotions far away as the barrier between me and my loved ones rippled. Jax's confused expression turned to anger. I held his stare. He balled his fists, and the wall shimmered with each punch inflicted. He pounded it until blood ran down the barrier. I tightened down on my sadness and met my uncle's stare. I mentally pleaded with him to take Jax away, not sure if I was able to let enough of my expression show. If I'd let any emotion to the surface, I would have crumbled to the ground to match my insides.

Michael must have understood. He looped his arm around Jax's waist, and he and Aunt B rocketed away no longer bound by the barrier.

"He will come back, so whatever you need me for, let's get it done," I said.

"I told you. It's not to bring back Adam," Selene said.

"But I do need to bring your grandmother, Eve, back to this realm."

"Because she can awaken your one true love?" I asked, even though I thought an act like that was damn near impossible.

"Yes." Selene's face lit up. "And then you can go back to yours."

I wanted to judge her, but I couldn't. I'd taken great steps to save Jax, and I knew I'd do it again if the situation required it. And wasn't that exactly what she was doing?

"What part do I play in this?" I asked. "I'm a demon."

"Adam granted Endy's wish to remain youthful by putting him in a stasis of sleep. Now that Adam is gone, I need the balance to restore him."

"I'm the balance now that Eve is gone, but I don't know how to bring him out of the slumber."

"Eve will know," Selene insisted.

"My grandmother sacrificed herself to prevent any more of Adam's cruelty in the world. If I had the power to bring her back to this realm or any realm I inhabit, don't you think I would have done so already?" I asked, fighting the frustration. "I never got to know her as my grand-mother, and she sacrificed herself for me and my love and humanity."

"That is why we need her. She is goodness and love personified. Her sacrifices have been many in the past millennium and then some."

The one thing I knew for sure about Eve was that she wanted to help people. She believed in life being lived.

"Do you have a ritual that will bring her here, and will she have a choice? Given all her sacrifices, especially the one she made for me, I do not want her forced into this if she is at peace and wants to remain so," I said, firm with my words.

Selene's voice softened into a gentle tone. "The choice will be hers, and I have a ritual that will allow us to connect to her. If she agrees, she will be able to pass through in a way similar to how a portal works."

I nodded. I didn't like it, but Eve wanted to help people, so the decision would be hers not mine. "And where do we perform this ritual?"

"In Endy's room," Selene said like I should know where that is. "The room you found that led you here."

"There wasn't anyone in that room," I said, confused.

"Oh, he's there. He was on the bed. You just couldn't see him because of Adam's spell. I can fix that once we're in the room."

I followed Selene down the steps. My skin crawled like it had when we entered through the cave. The room hadn't changed from before until she waved her hand. A man deep in sleep appeared on the bed.

The sight brought back unsettling memories of my father after the battle caused by the Ascendant. A tremor shook through me. This man was here by choice. My father hadn't been.

"You're sure he would want to be woken?" I asked.

"He never wanted to sleep. He just wanted to stay young to live with me, even though I told him I'd love him no matter his outward appearance," she said, her voice wistful with longing.

The man was handsome. He had thick, dark hair that appeared to be in a style from his century. His skin was sun-kissed but not damaged like he'd found the perfect balance of time with the sun. He must be tall. He was propped up on pillows, and his feet still almost hung off the bed. His facial features were symmetrical and his jawline chiseled. I would be surprised if he wasn't thought of as a god in his time.

"Do you have everything we need for this ritual?" I assumed she did, but she hadn't offered up any materials.

"Yes, in the drawers of the desk," Selene said.

She took one side, and I sifted through the other, opening a drawer and setting items out. I mentally noted the inventory of the items and realized this was a summoning spell. Not what I expected. I'd assumed it would be a higher celestial incantation to open a doorway. What she did, though... It was the exact summoning spell that was used on me when I took human lives, a moment I regretted and only recently found some peace for my rash actions with Uriel's help. My knees went weak, and I gripped the desk for balance. Uriel might have given me forgiveness for my deeds, but I didn't forget. The night played back vividly in my mind. My ass landed on a hard surface, but I barely felt it. The memories of the deaths I inflicted, and the aftermath, consumed me. The only thing that had stopped how it haunted me and my dreams was Uriel's offer of forgiveness. *Uriel.*

White flashed in the room. I heard my name, but it sounded so distant. Until it was almost a yell. The blur in front of me came into focus. My uncle. He'd been able to get through the barrier. *Is this real? Am I having a mental breakdown?*

"Uriel...How?" I stumbled over my words. "How are you here?"

He bent at the waist and offered me a hand. "I've always told you I'd be here if you called."

"But I didn't..." *Did I?* "Sorry. I was just...this is the spell." I wasn't making any sense.

He raised an eyebrow.

"Hello?" Selene waved. "That was a panic attack, and why is there an archangel that is supposed to be sleeping in here?"

"A panic attack," I repeated. It made more sense now. "This is my Uncle Uriel."

"I'm aware of who he is," Selene said, her voice a mix of anger laced with confusion. "What I don't understand is why he is here?"

"I recognize you. You are Selene from Gothica," Uriel said. "But you are the Selene from the tragic love of Selene and Endymion. Why did you pretend to be a vampire?"

"That is Endymion on the bed. She wants to wake him up," I said. "I understand her desire, but the spell she planned was the same as the one the group of humans used to summon me. The same one you helped me find forgiveness for." I cringed, saying it out loud. My past actions were shameful, and I wasn't sure I was able to get past that to perform a ritual.

"Why would you need forgiveness for a summoning spell?" Selene asked, her eyes widening. "Oh...you killed the humans."

"I did." I didn't elaborate. While I understood her desire to be reunited with her love, I owed her nothing of myself. "Uriel, you can go. I'm sorry I brought you into the middle of this, but I have it covered." I absolutely did not have it covered, and I didn't want him to go. It wasn't fair to ask him to be a witness to whatever happened when we summoned my grandmother. He'd seen many of her sacrifices. *I can't ask him to stay for what could turn into a shitshow.*

Uriel took a seat in one of the chairs, dwarfing it. "I believe I'll stay and supervise. You do realize Endymion cannot be summoned from this state?"

"I do," Selene said with immense confidence. "That's why we're summoning Eve."

My uncle's expression hardened. "She should not be disturbed. What right do you claim to summon her?"

"Because she was the balance when Adam put Endy in this slumber, and she is the only one who can restore him." Selene's confidence evaporated. Her tone became exasperated.

"Eve will have the choice to answer the summons," I said, hearing the flatness in my voice. I didn't believe it, and I wouldn't blame Uriel if he judged me for it.

"The reason Selene wants you to help her do the spell

is because Eve will not refuse her blood, especially one who is the balance as she once was."

Selene left that part out of her recap. My anger spiked because I knew it was true. It was the same reason Father gifted me his dagger. *How have I not realized this before?* Because I was distracted. *Fuck.*

"I can summon her anyway," Selene said. "It's just easier if you are here to connect with her."

The desire to ditch her to do it herself was strong, but I wouldn't risk Eve's peace.

"If you wish to leave, Rena, her boundary cannot hold me," Uriel said.

His ability to pass through the barrier was a discussion for another day. Right now, I had questions for Selene. "Not yet," I said to Uriel and turned to Selene. "Why didn't you tell me the whole truth? I'd already agreed to stay and help you."

"I was about to when you said you wanted to make sure Eve had a choice. And she does. Anyone does in a summons." *Not true. Those older, stronger, and trained to resist them can, but for most of us, it's almost impossible to refuse it.* Selene's strong facade caved. She sank onto the bed beside her love and took his hand. "I just wanted to hold Endy one last time before the end times came."

I shouldn't have let her grief pierce my emotional armor, but I let it in. All of it. I rested a hand on her shoulder. "I'll help you, but if my grandmother is harmed, both you and Endy will pay for it."

Selene's eyes glistened. "She will not be harmed. I give you my word."

I turned to Uriel, who stood far too close to me. "You can stay, or you can go, but Selene and I are doing this summons."

Uriel didn't say a word and retreated to the chair he'd occupied earlier. He was protective of me and my grandmother. His presence comforted me, but I wished he would leave at the same time.

I let Selene lead the setup, but I knew the proper placements for all the ritual artifacts. They were embedded in my memories like a hot poker.

"Ready?" I asked.

Selene took my hands in hers. Her face relaxed, and her voice was a hushed tone. "Thank you."

"Thank me when it's done and everyone is where they are supposed to be." I placed too much trust in her, and I had little doubt it would come back on me. She'd betray me, and I had to stay alert to protect my family when the time came. Eve wouldn't deny me, and Endy had been tricked by Adam. Eve would want to set that right. One of us would have to sacrifice, and it was my turn. There was no way this would end well.

CHAPTER 38

RENA

Selene stood on one side, her stance strong with determination. I'd positioned myself on the other per her instructions. Candles were arranged precisely and lit to represent some kind of intersection I didn't comprehend but Selene told me I didn't have to understand, so there we were. I repeated the words with her she'd had me memorize. We'd been at it for what seemed like a long time, but it could have only been a few minutes.

Blue light shimmered across the room, and a figure formed at the foot of the bed. The long, dark hair was as unmistakable as her beauty. She was my grandmother.

"Eve," I whispered through the knot in my throat, happy to see her looking well.

"Hello, Morena," she said. "Selene."

She was gentle with her words, and her face was soft. Not a hint of anger or tension. Kindness and love radiated from her and filled the room with a faint, warm glow. Her gaze dropped to Endymion. "I know why you two have called me here."

A bright light flashed. Uriel left, and it seemed like a judgment of my choice.

"Can you help free him?" I asked, in awe of the sense of calm she brought to the room. I'd never noticed it when Mother and I visited her.

"I can, but I'll need you two to remain where you are. I do not have the ability to complete the reversal of this spell, but I can wake him." Eve began moving her fingers through the air as if she were writing a letter.

"But he will wake up?" Selene asked, and the excitement in her voice was electric.

"Yes, he will wake up," Eve said. The way she didn't elaborate made me wonder just how awake he would be, but we were about to see.

She continued making gestures in the air and reciting words from a language I didn't know.

"You two need to take each other's hands. Both of them."

Selene held her hands out to me, and I placed mine in hers, ignoring the warning in my head of what would come after.

"Now, I need you both to reposition a hand on his chest."

We did as she instructed. He was cool to the touch, and his chest rose and fell in shallow breaths. Selene stifled a sob.

"Good. Now, you both release the other hand and put it on his head. Then, you will repeat his name as evenly as you can until I tell you to stop."

"Endymion," Selene and I said in unison. I counted to seven repetitions.

"You can stop now," Eve said.

"Now what?" Selene asked.

"He should wake up at any moment," Eve said. "But he has to want to be awake and here with you. He's been asleep for a very long time. He might not choose to come back to reality."

"Is there anything else I can do?" Selene's tone was one of pure panic.

If Selene waited all these years and Endy didn't choose to come back to her, I could only imagine what would come next. I'd want to destroy everything in my path if it was me and suspected something similar from her. I glanced toward Uriel, but he was focused on Eve with an intent, almost painful look. *Would he help me end Selene if it came to it, or would I be on my own?* I didn't want to end her, because I understood the kind of love she held for Endymion. If it had to be done, I would take the task on my own.

"You can sit close to him and talk. Try to coax him toward you," Eve said.

Selene took the seat beside Endymion's bed and leaned in close to his ear. She didn't want the sweet words she whispered to be known by others. I wanted my private life to remain so as well, but it was hard with the way our lives were. It was something else Selene and I had in common. I watched Eve. She observed the couple with a deep sadness on her ethereal face.

A gasp came from the bed, and it was Selene's. Endymion was sitting up. He looked groggy but very much awake. I smiled that they would be given a second chance, and I readied myself to get the fuck out of the cell and back to Jax.

"Endy," Selene repeated and cried into Endymion's shoulder. This was the kind of reunion of hearts written about in mythical stories. The kind that gave hope that love would triumph overall, and I hoped that Jax and I had a love that would fall into the same category.

"Endy is as free as I can make him," Eve said. "For now. But this is only a brief reprieve. I cannot permanently lift Adam's weaving as it is tied to his jinn. His dream walking."

Adam was rotten to the core, and a bitter taste formed in my mouth at the thought of what he'd done. I'd suspected there was no breaking his spell. Powerful rituals are rarely able to be undone, at least not fully, by someone other than the original caster. "How long will they have?"

"It's hard to say," Eve said. "If Adam has other strong tethers, they might get years. If Endymion is Adam's only one, it will happen far quicker."

The tragedy of it all tugged on my heart until it ripped open a river of inquietude. Jax and I might end up with a similar story of separation in time, and it was unthinkable for me to live a life apart from him. If examples of the past were any indication, it wouldn't be avoidable, and it frightened me to think of the future.

"You have to send me back, Morena," Eve said. "The balance will unravel with both of us in the same planes now."

My eyes burned with tears I wouldn't let fall both for saying goodbye to her and the hole she would leave behind here. "I can't."

She pushed the hair back from my face. "I lived for thousands of years as the balance. You have only just begun your journey. There is still so much left for you to do. I will never refuse your summons. If there is a time you need me, you know what to do."

"Thank you," I said around the knot in my throat.

"Send me back, Granddaughter, with the knowledge that my love lives in you."

I closed my eyes and whispered the words to send her back from which she came. It was a ritual I'd learned after I'd killed four humans, and I'd practiced it dozens of times. Not once had I messed it up. It was part of my commitment to not take innocent lives, and I couldn't let it fail. Ever. My hands chilled in her absence. They no longer rested on her arms. "Goodbye, Grandmother."

A dizzying wave of power hit me. I stumbled and caught myself with the back of the chair. Another one stronger than the first hit me. "Selene? Do you feel that?"

She looked up from Endymion. "Feel what? The shield is down now. You can leave whenever you wish, but you are welcome to stay and celebrate with us."

The kind of catching up they were bound to do was not something for others to witness.

"I'll go." I forced the words out over the wooziness. "You two need some time alone."

"Thank you, Rena," she said.

I nodded and partially crawled up the stairs. In fact, I crawled the last few steps. A third wave rumbled through me, and my body shuddered, fighting against the intensity. I understood what this was. I hadn't felt the power in years. I inhaled and breathed through it. There was no way to resist the force forever without snuffing out my own existence. This was a fucking summons at the worst possible time. Summoning my grandmother or sending her back must have used so much energy that my block against them fell apart. My family could get through it. They wouldn't be the ones using this spell. Another wave came, and this one shook me. My body burned with pain. *Fuck.*

I closed my eyes to think. *If I give into the call, I don't know where I'll go or when I'll be able to return to my family. To Jax.*

I needed someone to help, but I couldn't summon Jax. He wasn't summonable by anyone other than Lucifer. Aunt Jophiel was wise, but she didn't like to bend the rules much.

A throb scattered through my body before the last wave. "Uriel," I whispered. I began the angel's call for him. He was one of the few strong enough to tell a summons to fuck off.

I opened my eyes to watch for him, but another wave hit, and the excruciating torment turned the corners of my vision black. Vomit shot out of my mouth, and I was forced to lie in it. *Disgusting.* I surrendered to the darkness rather than allow the summons to take me.

CHAPTER 39
JAX

Uriel handed Rena's unconscious body to me. As much as it disquieted me to see her like this, she looked peaceful in my arms as I carried her to our room. She resembled an angel, not a demon, but then again, she carried angel blood in her.

I laid her on the bed and covered her with a blanket. Lilith came through the door in a rush. "How is she?"

"She'll be fine." I was sure of it. This wasn't completely uncommon, but most demons didn't have it in them to resist like she did. "I asked one of your ladies to bring blood to her. Uriel said fighting the summons drained her, both emotionally and physically, along with sending Eve back. But someone tried to summon her, and her fight against that knocked her unconscious."

My love was tougher than maybe even Lucifer, and I was proud of her. I would hunt down and dismember whoever had tried to trap her as soon as she was better.

"She had protections in place against a summons. It's been in place since..." I trailed off, not wanting to recount something so sensitive to her in case she could hear us in this state.

Lilith gave me a side hug. "Morena always keeps so much inside. I'd hoped that would change when you two were finally together, but she thinks she must do everything on her own instead of asking for help." She smiled at me. "You are one the few she trusts with...well, anything."

"I want to marry her, Lilith," I said in a rush. "In a grand ceremony fit for the future queen of Hell." I longed to steal her away and marry her in a field with just us and her family, but she deserved the big wedding. The people would expect a spectacle, and it would be her duty to give it to them. My duty would be to stand by her side afterward, and that was the place I most wished to be.

"I expected an announcement soon." Lilith clasped her hands together and brought them to her chest. "She won't need or want a grand ceremony, but the people will. You'll need to help her see that."

"Rena might surprise you by how much she already understands about politics. She is more in tune with it than she lets others see." Lucifer and Lilith saw Rena was an adult, but they saw their little girl there too. Rena was capable of so much, and ruling Hell was one thing on that list.

"But you see it." Lilith smiled, but it faded. "She will not accept the proposal until she stops Armageddon. You know this, though."

"I do." My heart dropped because Armageddon hung over us like a neon sign flashing at us to stop here. But we didn't know exactly what we were supposed to be stopping. "I do."

A soft knock came from the door, and it opened. Lilith's maid, Tilly, brought in a carafe of blood and glasses. She set them on the table. "Is there anything else I can get?"

"Bacon," I said. "A lot of it. That's one of her favorites."

"I'll bring it right away."

"Thank you." I felt Lilith's eyes on me. "It's the one thing I can always get her to eat, even when she claims to not be hungry."

"It was the same when she was a child," Lilith said. "You'd cook bacon for her despite her assigned staff being there."

I smiled at the memories. Rena stirred on the bed, and I pulled a chair close so I could hold her hand. Lilith sat on the side of the bed. "Lucifer will be here soon. If she's not awake when he gets here..."

"She will be," I assured Lilith. "Lucifer will not be the start of Armageddon on my watch."

Lilith laughed. "He would be impressed to hear you say that."

"I don't think I've ever dazzled your husband," I said. My suspicion from my interactions with him was that he knew what went on in our bedroom and didn't like it despite the fact we were both consenting adults. I guessed that was how a dad was supposed to be.

Lilith laughed a high, tinkling laugh. "You most certainly have, and I think he respects you most for the way you never seek to overshadow his daughter. You support her decisions and stand beside her."

She made it sound like some great feat, but I wanted Rena to live her life with me at her side. "It is her world. I'm just a passenger."

"You are a copilot," Rena rasped out. Her voice was rough like a smoker's, but it was her.

Thank Lucifer. She's with us. My pulse thrummed, and I needed to be closer to her. To touch her. I leaned over and smashed my lips to her forehead. "You're awake, my love."

"Don't ever forget you're my fucking equal." She sounded hoarse, but her voice evened out.

I kissed the knuckles of her hand. "There is no equal for you."

She opened her eyes. They were demon red but a beautiful sight. "You are as valuable as anyone in any realm and more so to me."

She meant her declaration, but it would take a great deal for me to believe I was that important. I was content being the passenger.

Lilith held a glass in front of Rena. "I know you don't like the taste, but you need to drink to the last drop."

Rena didn't argue and guzzled the blood as if she'd been in a desert for days without water. "More."

Unusual for her to drink more than a glass, but she was weak when Uriel brought her to me. Lilith refilled the glass and Rena held this one on her own.

"Bacon is on the way too."

Rena smiled. Blood coated her lips and teeth, and I'd never wanted blood so much as I wanted to lick it off her.

"How are you feeling?" Lilith asked.

"Better," Rena answered, and her voice sounded closer to her normal tone. "I smell the bacon."

The scent carried through the room before the knock came. Tilly carried a tray in with what looked like a full pound of bacon on it. She had included some toast and fruit in what little space was left.

Tilly set the tray over Rena's lap. "Do you need anything else?"

"No, thank you. This is good." Rena's eyes bugged out as she looked at the pile of bacon and snatched a piece.

"I'll be outside should you need anything," Tilly said and closed the door.

"You two eat up on the bacon. I'm going to take my leave, or she'll stand outside your chamber door all night." Lilith kissed the top of Rena's head and patted my shoulder.

Rena grabbed Lilith's hand. "Stay and help me eat this bacon. Then we can go back to Gothica."

"Rest, Morena," Lilith said. "Gothica isn't going anywhere."

Rena and I were alone, and I grabbed a slice of bacon. "I'll help you eat it."

Rena laughed, and the sound vibrated in my chest.

"I was really hungry," she said.

"Uriel said you were spent mentally and physically."

Her recovery was quick even for a demon, so Uriel must have done something to stop the summoning. I just hoped he didn't kill the bastard doing it. I wanted that honor.

She put down the half-eaten slice. "It's coming back to me slowly, but there are still blank spots. Where is Selene? Did she come back with us?"

"Eat," I coaxed and waited until she picked up the bacon. "She wasn't with you, so I don't know where Selene is. Gabriel told us to meet Uriel in Hell, so Lilith and I portaled here. Uriel showed up with you in his arms moments after we got here."

"I don't remember Gabriel anywhere near me, but I remember Uriel being in that secret room with me and Selene," I said. "Her love was there. Endymion. Adam had put him in a slumber, and he'd been in it for centuries."

Uriel said she summoned Eve, and she didn't appear to remember it. Rena still needed to recover. "We can talk about it after you eat. Don't rush," I said.

"I really am fine now. Just trying to piece together the memories," she said. She froze for a moment. "I remember. Selene needed to summon Eve to wake Endy. Since Adam was the one who put him under, it had to be my grandmother. I had a panic attack because the summoning spell was the same one used to summon me when I..." Her voice trailed off.

"The humans when you were a teenager," I filled in the blank for her, but I despised doing so knowing how much the memory hurt her.

She nodded. "In the panic attack, I thought about how Uriel had helped me release the guilt. The memories never go away, but at least I wasn't haunted constantly. Somehow, I called out to Uriel. I'm still not sure how."

I sat still. *Was I happy she called Uriel? No. Was I thankful she was safe? Yes.*

"Don't be mad, Jax." She rested a hand on my knee. "I didn't mean to call him."

"I'm not mad at you, Rena. How could I be? He brought you to me," I said. *Do I want to strangle Uriel? Yes. The events of his damn Ascendant that set all this in motion. Do I want to burn away every part of him that touched Rena? Yes. Will I do it? No, because that will hurt my love.*

Rena rubbed the place between my eyebrows. My skin heated under her touch. "It's you, Jax. It's always going to be you. You are my choice."

I picked up the tray and sat it on the floor. Rena leaned over and snatched one last piece of bacon. She offered me a bite, and I ripped off the end.

She dropped the rest of it at the side of the bed. Her arms winding around my neck, she smiled. "I'm glad you ate some of the bacon."

I chuckled. "Why is that?"

"When I kiss you, we won't know whose bacon breath it is." Her mouth covered mine, and she pulled me down on top of her. I propped myself up, so the bulk of my weight was suspended, but hovered close enough our bodies grazed. My dick hardened in anticipation from the little contact we had.

"There is a promise I made to you in Picher that I need to make good on."

I slid my hand up her side and my thumb over her nipple. The peak stiffened through her bra. My cock twitched, and I nudged against her apex. A moan escaped her lips. I dropped my mouth to hers and staked my claim.

"Too many clothes," Rena whispered against my lips.

I smiled against hers. "Way too many."

I stood from the bed and pulled her with me. She reached for my shirt and lifted it over my head. I reached for hers, but it didn't budge.

"Zipper," she said, her tone hurried.

"Where?"

"On the back." She spun around and lifted her hair to expose the metal.

I unzipped it from her neck to her waist, but it was like I couldn't move fast enough. "Fuck."

She shuffled out of the top, and I worked the clasp of her bra. She dropped her arms, letting it fall. Her bra landed right on the tray of bacon. I smirked. "Lucky bacon."

She laughed, and I hauled her back against my chest. My hands roamed her stomach. I found the button of her pants and undid it with one hand. I dipped down until I found the bundle of nerves. She groaned, and my dick throbbed. A tremor ran through me.

I stroked two fingers over her and moved faster with every swirl.

Rena shuddered against me. My cock strained against

my zipper. I flattened my palm against her mound and dipped my fingers inside. She ground against me, riding my hand.

A low sound rumbled from my chest. "Are you ready for me?"

She rewarded my question with damp heat, and I ground my hardness against her. I wanted to fuck Uriel's touch and the memories of the day away for her. But mostly, I wanted to worship her with the pleasure she deserved.

She removed the rest of her clothes, and I fumbled mine off. I picked her up and sat her on the bed, positioning her at the edge. "You know what comes next?"

A wicked smile grew on her face. "What?"

"You," I said and buried my face between her legs.

She shuddered and let out a moan that I was sure any guard nearby heard, but I didn't give a fuck. If it still bothered Rena later, we'd find someone to wipe their memories. I sucked on her clit and drove my fingers in and out. Her soft sounds grew louder. I wanted to bury my dick inside her, but I wanted to taste her come on my tongue first.

"Jax," she murmured with a sigh.

I nearly lost my control at the way she said my name. She would come first.

I worked my tongue in circles around her and listened for her breath to increase. It came in small pants, and she clenched on my fingers.

"Yes," I said. "Give it all to me."

I continued to move my fingers as her body jerked around my hand in waves. Her lids fluttered, and the sight was like a miracle of beauty. The pleasure in her eyes and her body's reaction was for me, and I wanted to give her every bit of it to show her how I revered her. She was my queen, whether she sat on a throne or not.

Her body relaxed, and I moved over the top of her. A lazy smile drew across her face, and I kissed her with the hunger of a starved man. My tongue found hers, and I slid my dick inside her. She moaned, but the sound was trapped in my mouth.

I stroked deep and fast, and her head fell back.

"You are so wet. My cock slipped right in, and you can feel how easy it's sliding in and out. Fuck, it feels good."

"Yes," she said. "So good."

I moved my hips in slow circles to make it last, but it wasn't going to take much for me to find my release after seeing her come so hard on my mouth and fingers. I climbed higher with each little gasp and moan Rena made.

"Jax," she gasped out, and her muscles clenched again. There was no sound more erotic than hearing my name on her lips as she came undone.

I met her release with my own. Rena's body trembled under me, and my cock throbbed inside her, spilling my seed. I waited for her eyes to open. "I love you, Rena. You are the only one for me."

"And you are for me, Jax. I love you," she said, her voice breathless.

I slid myself out of her and rolled over where I could gather her against my side. The closeness of holding her against me was almost as good as what we had just done. She was all the realms for me. Everything.

The hallway outside our bedroom was devoid of the usual noise. I figured Jax threatened death to anyone who disturbed us. He slept so hard that I didn't want to wake him. I moved in slow motion out of the bed and closed the bathroom door as gently as possible. A hot shower wouldn't fix all my problems, but it couldn't hurt, and there was a conversation on my agenda with my mother.

I dressed and checked on Jax to find him still out. He'd earned that rest after taking care of me in more ways than one. I left the chamber to find guards waiting at the end of the hall instead of closer to the door. They stood at attention as soon as they saw me.

"Do you know if my mother is still in her room? Or where she might be"

The shorter of the two nodded. "She's in Lucifer's office."

"My father is here?" I asked. A tiny twinge of hurt skated over me. He hadn't been by, but he hadn't ventured close to the room since Jax moved in with me while I ruled during Father's recovery. Besides, Mother might have encouraged him to stay away for a while.

"He is, Princess."

I held back a gag at the title that was no longer a nickname. I detoured down the familiar hallway.

I opened the door to Father's office without knocking. It was a bad habit my family had, and we all needed an etiquette lesson on knocking before entering. Mother and Father sat opposite each other in the sitting area.

"Morena," Father said, his voice full of surprise. He stood and opened his arms. I relished in the hug before turning to Mother's warm embrace. My parents loved me unconditionally, and for years, I didn't see it. I thought their rules were too harsh and even called them crazy. As an adult, I understood everything that seemed over-the-to was done in love, and my actions would speak the same language going forward.

"We didn't expect to see you for a few more hours," she said. "Where's Jax?"

"He's still sleeping. He's been through a lot lately. I wanted to let him sleep as long as he needed," I said.

"He might not be happy about that when he does wake up. He takes your protection very seriously," Father said.

I smiled. Jax's protection wasn't out of some stupid oath. It was out of love. "I know."

Mother sat down in the oversized chair that was her favorite in Father's study. "I'm glad you are feeling better." Her eyes flicked to Father and back to me. "You called for Uriel when you were in trouble?"

"Yes, it was a panic attack," I said and filled them in on the details. I woke up with the overwhelming urge for transparency. Our family had another bad habit of keeping secrets, and I didn't want that anymore.

"How did Jax take not being the one you reached out to?" Mother asked.

"I believe he understood." We hadn't actually talked about it, though. I told him, and we had sex. I kept that information to myself. Telling my parents Jax and I fucked over the topic seemed an inappropriate, if not embarrassing, answer.

"As long as you two talk through things, you will always be fine," Father said. "The few times your mother and I have had issues, it has always been because we didn't communicate well."

He didn't say it specifically, but I knew one of those was the time Mother used his dagger on Gabriel when we didn't know he was affected by the Ascendant. Father had been under the Ascendant's influence either then or soon after. Aunt B had channeled a lightning bolt into him, and his coma afterward reminded me a lot of Selene's love, Endymion.

"Morena, did we lose you?" Mother said.

"No. Sorry. I was listening. I just had a thought about Endymion," I said. "All that to free him, and it will only be temporary. What if we used lightning to break him free of Adam's spell?"

"It'd be more likely to kill him than break the spell," Mother said. "He was given a long life, but he is still somewhat mortal...a human."

"There has to be a way," I said, disappointed there wasn't more we could do.

"You and Jax are not Selene and Endy," Mother said. "Your situations are completely different. Don't hinge your hopes for happiness on the actions of others."

The words sounded wise. *They are wise.* My brain refused to accept them, though. *Saving them saves us.* The phrase repeated through my head. I couldn't ignore the parallels or the chant. I didn't know if their journey was meant to be part of my destiny, but helping them was part of my story. I'd given back to them what Adam had cruelly taken away, but it wouldn't last. Eve told me so. *Is it a metaphor for Jax and me? Temporary happiness. Is that all we get?* I studied Mother and Father. They were happy and had been for a long time, but they had to become someone else to do it. I didn't want to be anyone else, and I damn sure didn't want to become a different person. I thought coming to talk to my parents would give me clarity, but it gave me more questions. The conversation I needed to be having was with Jax.

JAX

Rena snuck out of bed while I slept. I wasn't sure which bothered me more--that my slumber was sound enough she was able to do so without disturbing me or that I woke after dreaming about her without her there. The massive hard-on deflated when my fear took over for her safety. I thought the worst before I had the good sense to ask a guard where she was. I knocked on the door to Lucifer's office.

"Come in," Lucifer called. I didn't hear any other voices, and it was going to be awkward as fuck if it was just the two of us staring at each other.

I entered to see Lilith and Lucifer in the sitting area while Rena paced. *Always pacing when she is in thought.* I wouldn't have to ask what occupied her thoughts today. It was on all our minds. *Armageddon. Adam's misdeeds. Survival.*

Rena came to greet me. Her eyes were full of love, and

I couldn't decide if I liked her better like this or the way I had her last night. She ran her fingers over the locket from her parents. The stress lines between her brows were tight, and I denied myself from rubbing them in front of her parents. "I hope you don't mind that I let you sleep."

I brushed my lips against her temple and leaned in close to her ear. "Next time, I would prefer a different kind of wake-up."

Rena's cheeks glowed a rosy pink. "Noted," she whispered back and kissed the corner of my mouth.

"Lilith. Lucifer." I swallowed hard. Lucifer was her dad and the king of Hell. He could wipe my existence from the realm, but he wouldn't. It would hurt Rena too much.

An uncomfortable expression crossed Lucifer's face. Lilith patted his hand, and he went back to neutral. "Jax, I trust you are rested up."

I nearly choked. If he knew the things I'd done to his daughter, he wouldn't be making any references to that. "Yes, thank you."

"We'll leave you two alone to talk," Lilith said, a mischievous grin on her face. "Lucifer? Coming?"

"Oh, yes." He stood and joined her. This was his office, and Lilith ushered him out of it so Rena and I could have a moment. *Odd.* "Communication. It is key to all relationships."

Rena covered her eyes. Lilith and Lucifer made the most awkward exit I'd seen in my lifetime, especially given how graceful the two were together.

I tugged Rena's hands from her face and kissed her fingertips. "What was all that about?"

"Just my family being weird per the usual," she said, exasperation in her tone. "You should be used to it after all these years."

"That was awkward." I smirked.

"Very," Rena said. "But they suggested I need to talk to you about the ritual to clear the air between us."

Ahh. It's the ritual on her mind. I tucked the stray hair across her face behind her ear. "I told you I understood, and I meant it. I'm fine because you are safe. My wish is for you to be safe and happy."

"You are far more understanding than I remember you being when we were teenagers," Rena said.

"Well, we're no longer underage hormonal beings." I caressed her cheek with my thumb. "I know your love for me is as true as mine is for you."

"Then we're good?" She studied me with her shrewd scrutiny. I didn't attempt to avoid the assessment.

My love for her outweighed any discomfort I had. "Yes, we are more than good." I kissed the sensitive place just under her ear.

Her gasp was my reward. My need for Rena was more powerful than any hunger I ever experienced.

"Do you think your father would know if we — "

"Yes." She leaned back. "And I want to talk through a plan with you."

"Oh." I sat back on the couch next to her. Lucifer would know for sure if I took her in here, and I had every intention of my existence lasting long enough to propose to her officially and properly. "Tell me what's on your mind."

Rena ran through her idea to free Endymion from Adam's spell, and I was with her until the "Barachiel's harnessing of lightning like she'd done for Lucifer" came into the discussion. "Could Endymion survive a lightning bolt? He's not an angelic being like your father. Isn't Endymion mortal?"

"He was human when Selene fell in love with him. I don't think he's considered human anymore. He's slept through many lifetimes. My thought is he might be more immortal than mortal."

She seemed almost desperate to save him, and it had to be coming from a source. "Is it your gut telling you to do this or something else?"

Her brows furrowed with uncertainty. "It's like I just know."

She was driven to this exactly as I was driven to step in front of Gabriel's sword. I'd set all of this in motion with my mistake. I'd follow her regardless, but damn, I wanted to sweep her away from this destiny. "Then maybe it is the role of balance telling you what to do."

Rena resumed the pacing she had been doing when I first walked into Lucifer's office. "I believe it is. I know that this is what needs to be done."

"If the idea is fighting this hard to be heard, then you shouldn't ignore it. I wouldn't." As it was, I hadn't several times when it came to her.

"Thank you." She crossed by me. "For not dismissing my idea."

I drew her close and wrapped my hands around her waist. "I'm here for you. You never have to question that."

"You always have been." She studied me as if she needed to see the confirmation. "But it means a lot to me for you to say it."

"There's something I've been wanting to talk to you about," I said, my voice cracking like a teenager's. I hadn't planned to bring this up now or here. *Fuck. Why did I say that?*

"What's that?" She looked up, concern in her eyes.

"Nothing bad." I cleared my throat. "It's...I..." My throat was dry, and it was hard to form words. My palms were sweaty. We'd already talked about marriage. *Why am I struggling now? Idiot.*

"You can tell me anything, Jax."

"It can wait," I said. "We've got important things to do."

"Are you sure?"

I nodded, chickening out like a dickhead. "Who makes better bacon, me or the chef in the kitchen?"

Rena laughed. It was from her belly and the real kind that vibrated through my body. It reminded me to make her laugh more.

"You, of course," she said. "I can't believe you have to even ask."

I smiled at her and took her mouth with mine. I devoured her with my passion until we were both breathless, letting her enjoy a happy, light moment as long as I could.

"We better go find the others," she said when we broke apart.

"Lead the way," I said, taking her hand. "But let's stop by the kitchen for bacon first."

CHAPTER 42

RENA

My belly was full of bacon, and my heart was full of Jax. Even with those few moments of happiness, the task ahead sat heavily in my thoughts. The group assembled in the meeting room surprised me. I hadn't expected so many archangels to come to Hell, but there they sat around the table along with my mother and father. Jax squeezed my hand for reassurance before letting it go.

Mother sat next to Father, but on the other side was Gabriel, followed by Michael, Barachiel, and Jophiel. On Mother's side sat Uriel and Zadkiel. The head of the table and the seat to the right of it were open. I glanced around the table for another open seat because I sure as shit wasn't sitting at the head. That was Father's seat. But there were only those two seats. Sweet angel's ass. I had to take it.

"Is there news?" I asked as I moved to the head seat.

Jax took the other open seat between me and Zadkiel. Father was directly across from me.

"We're seeing spikes in violence across the world," Michael said. "It's difficult to identify what could be related."

"What about the mass death in Greece? Did we confirm Selene planted the story, and no one actually died there?"

"We did," Aunt Jophiel said. "It was pretty easy to track it down once we got on her computer."

"Thank you for confirming," I said, relieved that more than two hundred people hadn't died there. "Now that we have validated her story. I'd like to move forward with assisting Endymion in a permanent solution."

Uriel shook his head. "You can't do that without—"

The door to the room swung open. "Me."

Adam. I couldn't speak. My lungs seized. He looked like he was perfectly restored to the picture of health. Jax jumped up, and his chair slammed against the floor. He shoved me behind him.

"Stop. He has no power," Father said. "He is here to share knowledge."

Mother's hand went to her chest, and she stared at Father. The shock on her face reflected my own. Her mouth gaped open. Despite his recent advice to me, Father clearly hadn't communicated to her Adam would be here. If I didn't kill Adam, she might.

I took a few breaths to compose myself and stepped around Jax. He would follow my lead, so I had to get it together for whatever Father had planned but failed to tell me. "Well, this is certainly a surprise to many of us."

"Yes, that is my fault," Adam said. "I didn't think any of you would come if Lucifer told you in advance."

Father listened to Adam. What was he thinking? "If you have no power, how will you help us remove the spell you cast on Endymion?"

"Someone will need to channel their power through me." Adam studied Jax. He would have to kill me before he got anywhere near Jax. I swallowed down the profanities on the tip of my tongue.

Jax tensed beside me. He'd barely recovered from their last encounter.

"Absolutely not," I said. "You will not use Jax again."

Jax settled a hand over mine. "It's fine, Rena. I know giving Selene and Endymion a second chance is important to you. I can do this."

Running away with Jax sounded better at the moment, but Jax was the best one at calling portals. Not me. I inhaled a breath. "It's not more important than you are to me."

He caressed my cheek. "I know that, but maybe releasing him is one of the keys to stopping Armageddon. You're drawn to them for a reason. Let's trust that feeling."

I turned to the rest of them. "Do the rest of you think this will work, or do you object?"

"The decision is yours, Morena, and we will support that decision. I do believe you are following the right path," Zadkiel said.

"Based on what we know of the spell and the power used to create it, I do believe it will work," Jophiel said.

There was a moment of silence. No one offered an alternative, and my lightning idea was more likely to kill Endy than save him. I did not want Jax to be anywhere near Adam, but I was backed into a corner. My hands shook, and I clasped them in my lap. "Anyone else?"

Not only was my lightning theory just a dangerous theory, but we all knew that Adam had been powerful when he tricked Endy. A similar power would be required to reverse it. Like that of the scale...Jax. He was the only scenario that made sense. I sat still for a few moments, willing my brain to come up with something else. When I slid my hand into Jax's, he squeezed it. He'd known and accepted his role.

I shut down all my mixed emotions and focused on being a blank slate in front of Adam. He didn't deserve to see how affected I was by sending Jax into a viper's den. "The decision is made, then. We will channel Jax's power through Adam to release Endymion. Gabriel, will you carry the message to Selene that we will arrive tomorrow to perform the ritual?"

"Uriel, will you help Adam identify what we need? I'll join you in the lab where we tested the Ascendant later to finalize the details of the ritual. I trust you remember how to get there?"

"I do, and we'll see you there." He grabbed Adam's shirt collar and hauled him from the room. Gabriel followed them, and they were gone based on the two flashes of light bleeding in from the hallway. Adam's absence was a relief, like lifting lava from bare skin. It still burned and festered but wasn't as bad.

"Aunt Jophiel and Aunt B, can you help me research any precedent for this type of spell?"

"Of course," Aunt B said.

I went around assigning everyone tasks, including sending some people, like Mother, back to the command center in Gothica. The room had cleared, but my father and Jax remained.

"What about me?" Father asked. "What shall I do to help?"

"Go apologize to Mother for one thing. Regardless of what Adam asked, you should have told Mother you were bringing him here. Especially after your talk about transparency earlier."

"You're right," he said, taking me by surprise. "I should have. I didn't want to jeopardize getting him here, and I knew you needed him."

"Then you should have spoken to Mother and me first," I said.

"I'm not arguing with you, daughter." He patted my shoulder. "You are right."

"That was far too easy. What's up with you?"

"Even the Devil can admit when he is wrong, Morena."

"Or maybe you are hanging out with me, so you don't have to deal with Mother's wrath," I added. "Go talk to her. You know the longer you leave it the madder she will be."

He opened the door and waited for me. "Do you talk to your mother about me like this?"

I laughed. "Maybe. I'll be in the library with Aunt B and Aunt Jophiel if you need a shoulder to cry on after she whips your ass."

Father laughed, but there was fear in his eyes as he went to find Mother.

I held my hand out for Jax and waited for him to take it. His palm was warm but damp as I laced my fingers through his. I waited until we were near the library to speak. "You don't have to do this, Jax. No one expects you to endure anything else from Adam. You nearly died by his trickery. I'll gladly take the blame and tell them I changed my mind." It was important for him to always have a choice, despite my decisions.

He stopped and cupped my cheeks. "I love you more than the fires of Hell, and I fear nothing as long as you are by my side. I will do it."

Jax drew me into his arms and held me close. *How did he fear nothing?* I feared losing him more than my own life.

JAX

I flipped the pages of the book I was skimming for answers in the library, but the memories of Adam's control over me were fucking with my head. The ache in my muscles seemed real as if I were still there. I rolled my head around, but my neck refused to let go of the tension. Adam had been a few feet away. A cold shiver crawled over me. I wanted him dead with every fiber of my demon body. The son of a bitch shouldn't be walking around and especially not in the same realm as Rena.

"Jax?" Rena rested her hand on my arm. I looked into her troubled eyes. "Are you okay?"

The worry she had was over my safety, not the ritual we were going to perform or Adam, and she couldn't do what she needed to do and worry about me. I covered her hand with mine and lied. "I'm fine."

She glanced across the library to Barachiel and Jophiel,

who were engrossed in a discussion of their own. "Like you're really fine or you're ready to fight kind of fine?"

"You know me too well." I smiled at her. She wouldn't let it go. That was just who she was, so I gave her a bit of the truth. "I have this intense inclination to rip Adam to pieces, but I won't."

She grimaced and bit down on her lip. "I meant what I said, Jax. If this is too hard for you, you can sit this one out. No one would hold it against you."

Her gesture was out of love, but I wouldn't deny her this opportunity to follow what she believed to be the right thing to do. Besides, there wasn't another option for us. "You know me better than that, Rena. I will not back down from a fight."

Rena's expression softened the way it did when she delivered bad news. "This is about giving Endymion his life back. Not your revenge on Adam, no matter how justified it would be."

"Afterward, though..." I thought of the ways I could torture him in the dungeons of Hell. Lucifer shut them down years ago, but the devices were there.

"Afterward, we'll send him back to where he was," Rena said, backing away.

"Where was he?"

Rena sighed. "I'm going to tell you, but I want you to promise me you will let him go."

I would let him go, but that didn't mean I couldn't follow him. "I promise to let him go."

She let out a breath. "He's been exiled to the dream realm."

"That doesn't seem like much of a punishment for a jinn," I said. "But then again, he's not much of a jinn anymore." Eve had seen to that by banishing him. I hated that place almost as much as I hated him. I'd nearly killed Rena there because of him, but she was a celestial being. Death wouldn't have taken her that way. At least I don't think it would have. Adam deserved death for risking her life apart from the other things he'd done, and the list was long. If he was killable, he was mine. "Do you want to go over the ritual?"

"That would be helpful," Rena said. She led me through each step she and her aunts laid out. "I hate to do this, but I need to get to the lab to meet Uriel and Adam. You don't have to go."

Does she think I'm fragile now? I'd jump in the fires of Hell before I let her meet Adam without me. I formed the symbols for a portal and held out my hand for her. "I told you I'm all in, my love, and I meant it."

RENA

I landed feet first on the floor of the lab with Jax's hand firmly in mine. Uriel was at a table, placing some items from the lab into a bag. He looked up and glanced from Jax to me. I gave him the slightest shake of my head as a signal to not say whatever he was thinking about Jax being there.

I peeked into the bag, and it was full of supplies. "Did you find everything?"

"Yes, this is the last of it." Uriel picked up a charm.

Jax growled next to me. "Where's Adam?"

Uriel pointed to the corner. Adam was curled up across a table with his eyes closed. I was surprised to see him resting. He looked perfectly harmless instead of the evil bastard he was.

"Why the fuck is he sleeping?" Jax's voice had that quiet fierceness in it like it did just before he punched someone.

Uriel shrugged. "Without his jinn powers, he tires easily."

Jax stalked over to the table. *This is a bad idea.* I moved to stop him, but his hand was already in the air. His fist slammed down on the table.

Adam startled awake. He was like a frightened feline, leaping into the air and scrambling like a cartoon character to get away from the noise.

I stifled a laugh. "Time to go, Adam." I could feel his heart pounding from across the room, and people did their worst when they were afraid.

The expression on Adam's face transformed into pure anger. "What the fuck, man?"

"Out of everyone in this room, you are the least deserving of a peaceful rest." Jax turned his back on Adam and crossed the room to where Uriel and I waited. My eyes were trained on Adam to make sure he didn't retaliate.

"That was petty, Jax," I said, giving him a small smile of approval.

"Petty AF and proud of it," Jax said, his eyes narrowed to slits at Adam.

I glanced at my uncle, expecting him to admonish us, but he was smiling. Adam's circle of potential friends appeared to be nonexistent.

"Jax, take us home," I said. "To the library."

He made the symbols, and the rug of the library came into view. Being able to see the library so clearly was a sign of how strong Jax's portals had become. He jerked Adam by the arm. Adam tried to pry loose of Jax's grasp, but he wasn't strong enough to break the hold. Jax tossed him through the portal. *That landing is going to hurt.*

Jophiel and Aunt B both eyed Adam. No one in my family cut him any slack, and I preferred it that way. He didn't deserve kindness. I turned to face him. "This one act, if you succeed, does not right all the wrongs and terrible deeds you have done."

"A lecture from the Devil's daughter on what is right. That's an interesting concept." Adam clasped his hands together.

He thought he could hurt me with his words, but nothing he said touched me. He was a waste of the energy to form words.

Jax brushed past me and lifted Adam by his shirt collar. "Do not speak to her in such a tone, or I will rip your tongue from your mouth. Do not speak to her again unless she speaks to you." Jax bared his teeth, and his legs were planted wide with Adam suspended in the air.

I laid my hand on his shoulder. "Jax, it's fine. I've heard much worse than that in my life."

He looked back at me. His nostrils flared with anger.

"Really," I said, my voice soft. "He's not worth it."

"She's right. You're not, but she is." Jax sat Adam on his feet, but instead of letting go, he drew his fist back and landed a punch square on Adam's nose.

A yelp like a hyena yip came from Adam. His hands flew to his face. "That fucking hurt."

"It was supposed to," Jax said, still in Adam's face.

"And I held back, so you're welcome." His anger was barely in check.

Uriel worked his way between them. Jax's fists were still balled at his side.

"We need him awake for this." Uriel pushed his hand against Jax's chest until he looked at him. "Then you may do as you wish."

Jax gave one nod and backed away. His anger escalated with each altercation. We either had to get this done or forget it, and I wasn't ready to give up on Selene and Endymion's future.

"You go lay down on the couch since you need so much sleep now." Uriel pointed Adam toward the library couch in one of the sitting areas.

Adam stalked toward it in silence and lay down on the furniture. I was grateful for the separation between him and Jax.

"Not having power hasn't humbled him," Aunt Jophiel said.

I snorted. "No, he's still a dick." My aunts both looked at me. "I'm not apologizing for speaking the truth. Any word from Gothica?"

"Yes," Aunt B said. "There has been seismic activity at Megiddo. People have gathered there to pray."

From the corner of my eye, I saw Adam sit up, but I trained my gaze on my aunts. "I thought that was a false lead planted for fear-mongering in the religious constructs of men."

Uriel cocked his head to the side. "There is usually some truth in their stories."

It warranted investigation. With Armageddon upon us, any potential large-scale disaster could be a clue. "Are you up for another portal?" I asked Jax. "Let's take our ritual items to Gothica. We can travel from there to Selene and Endymion."

Jax eagerly spun up another portal, and our group, plus Adam, stepped through to the command center at Gothica. Mother and Father were huddled in the corner in what appeared to be a spirited discussion.

I reached for the locket they had given me, a symbol of their love and support. They would get through this like they always did. Light flashed between us. It was the brilliant illumination of Gabriel's entrance.

"Gabriel, is everything okay?" I asked.

"Yes, it is, but Selene said we need to perform the ritual soon. Endymion is having a harder time staying awake."

I nodded. My breath hitched in my chest as the need of Selene and Endymion beckoned my empathy. Megiddo would have to wait because the force of the balance said to go to them.

"Jax, you'll stand behind Adam," Selene said. "I'll stand here. Rena there." She positioned each of us to make the ritual strong. Since Jax's power was channeled through Adam for the ceremony, the more power to hold the bond steady, the better the results. I had little doubt Adam was going to try something, and I'd done a poor job of anticipating his moves in the past. I wouldn't hesitate to end him if he hurt Jax again.

Selene and I chanted. Adam joined in. The blue essence responded as if it had been waiting. The azure light encapsulated the room. I tried to move, but the power locked me in place. I glanced around to see where the others were. The power coursed through us and into Jax, and he looked...not frozen in place like us. Adam repeated his chant, and the power, more cerulean now, tunneled through his back and out through his chest. I looked back at Jax, and it did the same to him. Panic pulsed in me. It was too close to what I'd witnessed in the throne room. Jax's face paled. He would not die here. I tried to pull loose, but I was still immobile.

CHAPTER 45
JAX

Blue essence exploded from the center of my chest. I fought against the weight of power, but it forced me to my knees. Pins and needles of pain pricked from between my shoulder blades, down my arms, and through my fingertips. A scream burned in my throat, but I gritted my teeth to hold it in. I wouldn't allow Adam to hear it.

For his part, he savored the power. He stood tall with his hands outstretched like he was a god. He brought the sides of his palms together like he was making a bowl for the essence. The blue light pooled in his hands, and he uttered the words for the ritual. Or at least I assumed they were those words. My ears rang with an electric hum, and I couldn't understand him. I focused on channeling the power to him. The strain stole my breath. My vision narrowed.

Selene clasped Endymion's hand in hers as she stood

beside the bed. A soft voice came from near me. Rena's maybe. Selene let go of Endymion's hand and patted it. She stepped back from him, and I took it as a sign we were almost done.

The cold agony magnified. I bit down the pain. "Mmmph." A low grunt found its way up my throat, but I held my position.

Adam recited the spell multiple times. The blue light flowed faster from me and grew around him. Light framed him and drowned out everything until Adam stepped forward. He was close enough to touch Endymion.

With his fingers spread wide, Adam laid his hands on Endymion's chest. Endymion's midsection propelled up like he was possessed. He dropped back onto the bed. Adam stepped back and muttered something.

Relief washed over me as the icy suffering was replaced by the throb of discomfort. I tipped forward but caught myself on the chilled stone floor. A hand rubbed soft circles on my back. I tipped my head to the side, and the only face I cared to see was there. *Rena.*

Her mouth moved to speak, but I leaned forward and took her face in my hands. My lips found hers. I devoured her as if she was the only meal that would satisfy me. And she was.

"How do you feel?" She pulled back, her voice breathless.

"I'm good." The discomfort in my chest dwindled, but my stomach gurgled with hunger. "Did it work?"

Rena's head tilted toward the bed. Uriel and Michael

flanked Adam. Adam's head would look better separated from his shoulders, but my revenge had to wait until my strength returned. I panned around the room to see Endymion seated on the bed. He'd buried his hands in Selene's dark hair, and he had a genuine smile on his face. Selene wore a smile matching his. She leaned her forehead against his and wrapped her hand around his wrist. It made me long to touch Rena in such a way. The moment was intimate, but I couldn't avert my stare. Not because I was a voyeur, but because I wondered if Rena and I would have a moment of such joy in our future.

After lifetimes, Selene and Endymion were reunited without limits. It should be an inspiration. "They look happy."

"They do." Her voice broke.

Tears welled in her eyes, and I wanted her to believe it could be within her grasp, so I would believe it too. "Don't you dare mourn happiness. It will be ours."

She blinked several times. "I hope you're right."

"Don't hope." I tilted her chin up toward me. "Promise."

"Promise." Her words filled me with tortured regret that destiny might force her to break the promise I asked her to make.

Jophiel rested a hand on Rena's shoulder. "We should give Selene and Endymion some privacy."

My chest throbbed, and I rubbed the ache. Hunger rumbled in my stomach, and the thing it wanted most was blood.

"Can you call a portal to take us to Gothica?" Rena asked.

I ignored the weakness in my body and nodded. "Because you asked so sweetly, yes."

Rena smiled and popped up to her feet.

I followed the lines of her legs up until I stared at her face between the swells of her breasts. "I like this view."

Her eyes widened. "Get up."

I chuckled and wobbled as I stood.

Rena slipped her arm around my waist to steady me. "You need rest."

I wagged my eyebrows at her. "I need something."

"Stop," she chastised me but smiled.

"Food would be good," I said. "I hope they restocked the kitchen at Gothica."

My hands were heavy as I formed the symbols. Each movement was like sinking into thick mud, but the portal responded. I'd get Rena somewhere safe.

Rena turned to Selene. "Live."

"Every single day," Selene said from Endymion's lap and waved. "Thank you."

I gripped Rena to me as we stepped through the portal.

CHAPTER 46
RENA

Jax slid down my side to the floor. My stomach knotted, and I dropped down with him in the command center at Gothica. His lids blinked like they were lead weighted. Every muscle in my body tensed. "Jax?"

Mother knelt beside me. "What happened?"

"He was fine. Hungry but fine." I recalled his bobble as he stood. "He was off balance a little after the spell."

"You and you move him upstairs to my apartment." Mother pointed to two vampires. "Gabriel, find Lucifer and tell him we need him."

My mouth went dry and made it hard to speak. "What's going on, Mother?"

"I don't know for sure," she said. "Go to the main kitchen and grab some extra blood bags. I'm not sure how much is upstairs."

"On it." I ran to the kitchen, not wanting to be apart

from Jax any longer than I had to be. The door banged against the wall and two vampires stared at me from the counter area. "Sorry. I just need to grab something."

I opened the refrigerator and scooped up as many bags as I could in my arms. The vampires were still staring at me, but neither asked any questions. "Could one of you get the door?"

They moved at vampire speed to open it for me.

"Thank you." I rushed past them.

I'd never wished for vampire agility before, but I couldn't get up the stairs fast enough, even though I took the steps two at a time. Mother's apartment door was open, and I dropped the blood haul onto the coffee table.

"That's a bit excessive, Morena. I meant a couple of bags," Mother said. She wasn't admonishing me, but she didn't help me either.

A couple of defiant bags slipped to the floor as if to punctuate her observation. I picked them up and a few more overflowed onto the floor. "Fuck."

"Leave a couple and put the rest in the refrigerator."

I glanced at Jax on the couch. He was resting, and he looked content.

"He's fine for now."

I nodded and scooped up the bags to do as she asked.

"Lilith?" Father called to her. "What's going on?"

"I'm fine. Morena is fine," she said. "Jax appears to be ill, though."

I joined them by the couch. My insides were jumbled, but I ordered my thoughts to explain to Father. "He was unsteady after the ritual, but he called a portal here without issue. Then, he collapsed."

"Have you given him blood yet?" Father glanced between me and Mother.

"Not yet," Lilith said. "We brought him up here first, away from the eyes below."

"Let's try it."

I ripped open a blood bag. "Can one of you lift his head?"

Mother slipped a pillow under Jax's head and then lifted it so his lips parted. I dribbled some blood into his mouth. His mouth moved as if he consumed it. My hands trembled as I poured more in there. He swallowed, and I held the bag against his mouth. Jax latched down on it and inhaled the rest of the bag. His eyes remained closed. I reached for another one and ripped it open. He sucked it down. My hope grew with every drink he took.

I felt for another bag on the table. Father laid his hand on mine.

"He's hemorrhaging, Morena."

"What do you mean?"

"Your father is right, Morena," Mother said. "I feel it too."

Demons healed from hemorrhaging, but Mother and Father sounded concerned. My legs were weak, but I was already sitting down. I gave Jax more blood. "How do we fix it? Do we need to hook up an IV?"

"It's his essence that's hemorrhaging, not his blood," Father said. "His hunger is a side effect."

The bag in my hand slid to the floor. "What do we do? How do we stop it? Can I give him some of mine?"

"No, you can't, but I can," Uriel said from the door. "May I come in?"

"Yes, yes," Mother said. "All of you come in."

Gabriel, Aunt B, Aunt Jophiel, and Michael followed Uriel into the living room. The somberness of our family was heavy in the room, and I tried to tune it out and focus on Jax.

"Close the door," Lucifer said. Gabriel took care of it.

"How are you able to share it and not me?" I asked.

"Because I have the knowledge," Uriel said.

A warm, bright light flashed in the room. "Trying to take over for me, Brother?"

"Raziel," Father roared. "You are neither welcome nor wanted here."

"But I'm the one you need to fix the little...ahh, he's not vampire anymore." Raziel stared at me as he inhaled. "You used the ankh on him as well."

I didn't answer. It was Jax's choice, but I wouldn't give that disgusting excuse for an archangel the details. Raziel might be my uncle, but he was the biggest asshole out of all the archangels.

"Why did you use such a fragile being as a conduit for Adam? I thought you were supposed to be the smart one, Uriel?"

How did he... The collective consciousness of the archangels.

Uriel's wings unfurled, and part of me wished he would let one of those unique metal feathers slice Raziel's vocal cords. He'd heal, but it would hurt like a mother-fucker. He obviously knew something about Jax's injury, though, so I didn't convey my request.

"Do you know how to stop the hemorrhage? Or are you guessing?" Raziel challenged Uriel. "In terms everyone here can understand, it requires a piece of essence to plug the leak."

Jax was dying, and he was comparing the injury to a broken pipe. I leaped into the air and planted my foot on his shoulder.

He flew backward, and Michael caught him.

"Fuck you, Raziel. I'll trust Uriel a thousand times over you."

"Then your mate will die," he said.

I rounded on him to plant another kick and stopped short of his head. "If you want to walk out of here, tell us what you know."

Raziel jerked against Michael's grasp. "Let me go, Michael. I'm vested in saving the balance and the scale as well."

I dropped my foot to the floor. He was here for the balance and the scale, not for me and Jax. He was sworn, as all the archangels were, to protect our roles.

"Only if you behave, little brother." Michael was the strongest, or so the stories went, but he never fought Father one-on-one. He could hold Raziel without breaking a sweat. "If you do not, I will make sure you are bound for centuries."

Raziel's face paled. "Fine."

Michael released him but hovered over Raziel as he moved closer to Jax.

"I need a piece of essence to stop the leakage," Raziel said. "Shall I use my own?"

"No," we all said in unison, and it sounded like a chant. Not even his siblings trusted him.

"Use a piece of mine," I said.

"It cannot be yours," Uriel said. "You are the balance and cannot heal the scale. Use mine."

"Brace yourself then, because it will hurt," Raziel said with a grin. He enjoyed inflicting pain as much as Adam. They deserved each other. I wouldn't doubt if they were friends or at least frenemies. "Because I'm not exaggerating."

I wanted to slap him with everything in me, but I wouldn't jeopardize Jax's safety. *Afterward...*

Raziel moved his hands in front of Uriel's chest as if he were tying knots...or perhaps untying them. Uriel balled his hands into fists, and a slight tremor ran through his body.

"Get it over with, Brother," Uriel said.

A thin thread of white light appeared from Uriel's sternum. The fiber wiggled like a worm, and Raziel pulled it. Uriel grunted. When Raziel had several inches of stringlike essence, he made a cutting motion in the air. The light separated. He planted a hand over Uriel's chest, and Uriel relaxed.

"You're all done. That was the easy part," Raziel said.

"Performing this healing ritual on a fragile little demon is the hard part."

"He's not fragile," I gritted out. "He's stronger than an asshole like you."

"You say that, but I'm literally about to make an incision in his soul." Raziel positioned the piece of Uriel's essence across Jax's stomach. He laid a hand over Jax's chest and turned an ear in that direction. He stayed in the position with his eyes closed for so long that I thought he might have fallen asleep.

"Should we shake him?" I asked Uriel.

"No, he's listening. It's similar to how the human doctors do a diagnostic test."

It bore zero resemblance to that kind of assessment. Raziel looked like he was wasting time or stalling, but I trusted Uriel, so I waited.

"The hemorrhage is small. This should not take long," Raziel said, sitting upright.

His hands moved in a similar fashion to what he had done in front of Uriel. He wove paths over Jax's chest for several minutes. Jax was out solid and had no response. Raziel picked up the strand of Uriel's essence and wove it into the invisible threads above Jax's sternum. Raziel stood and raised his palm flat. He slammed it down into Jax's chest.

I gasped and jumped forward. Uriel caught my arm. "What the actual fuck did he just do?"

"The proper response would be thank you," Raziel

said. "I saved your little mate's life. Now, it's your turn to save the rest of ours."

Light flashed, and Raziel disappeared before I could respond.

"He's such a douchebag," I said.

"He's the epitome of a jerk," Aunt B said. "But he did what needed to be done."

I faced Uriel and squeezed his hand. "Thank you, Uncle."

Uriel smiled and let go of me.

Jax stirred, and I sank to his side next to the couch. Relief loosened the tension in my body. "Are you awake?"

"Hmm." Jax's eyes opened and widened as he took in the audience in the room. He tried to sit up but grabbed his chest. "What's going on?"

I pushed down on his shoulder. "You were injured."

"Did I have a heart attack? It feels like my chest was cracked open." He rubbed the area around his sternum.

"Similar," Father said. "But the injury was to your essence."

Jax grimaced. "Like my soul?"

I'd almost lost him. He was going to hate having a part of Uriel's essence in him, but he'd get over it. He had to because I planned on showing him exactly how happy I was he didn't die and how much I loved him...once we were out of danger. I ran my hand over his arm in light strokes. "Yes, exactly."

"What happened?" he asked. "The last thing I

remember is calling a portal after we freed Endymion from Adam."

Aunt B put a hand on Jax's shoulder. "Are you hungry? It might be easier to take it all in on a full belly."

Jax reached for a blood bag on the table and winced.

"Let me do that." I handed him two.

"One of you talk while I drink." He must be hungry to drink blood without batting an eye.

"The ritual worked as expected, but something happened we didn't account for in the plan," Aunt Jophiel said.

Jax took a break from drinking. "How does that get us to my soul?"

"It made a tear, and your essence was leaking out," Mother said.

"So, I was dying?" Jax asked. "Again."

I stifled a hysterical laugh that bubbled up. It wasn't funny, but our near-existence-ending encounters were stacking up since everything started with Uriel's Ascendant. *Almost dying. Oh, just another Tuesday. Nothing to see.*

Jax's face settled in a confused expression. He stared at the window and asked no one in particular, "And I just healed this time?"

He wasn't going to take it well, and I didn't want to upset him. He wouldn't let it go.

"Not exactly," Michael said, saving me from answering. Then he looked at Gabriel as if this was a message he should deliver. Gabriel shook his head and looked at Uriel. *Seems we are all afraid to drop this truth bomb.*

Father cleared his throat. "Raziel is a great healer, and he was the only one that was capable of capping off the leak."

"That motherfucker touched me? Last time I saw him, I punched him square in the nose. How do you know he didn't do something worse?" Jax's harsh tone with Father surprised me, but it made me proud to see him have that kind of confidence too.

Uriel shifted from one foot to the other. So, this conversation was what it took to make an archangel feel self-conscious. "One. Because we all watched his every move. And two. Because he used a piece of my essence to repair yours."

Anger flashed across Jax's face, but he tempered it and drew it back. "Thank you, Uriel." His voice was gruff and kind at the same time. "I know that is a big deal for an angel to do so, and I appreciate your help."

Jax focused his intense stare on me. I could read all over it that he wanted to know why I let that happen, but he would wait until later for his answer. I'd be honest with him and deal with the anger because the alternative meant he wouldn't be here. And that wasn't an option. A part of me was a little afraid that he waited so easily to have the conversation.

"If you are all here, where the fuck is Adam?" Jax turned to Uriel.

CHAPTER 47
JAX

Alone with Rena in her mother's apartment at Gothica, I tried to reason out the events that led me to owe my life to the two archangels I despised most. "Of all the angels, why did it have to be Raziel and Uriel who saved me?" I asked out loud, but not expecting an answer. Uriel and Michael had left to follow a lead where they believed Adam was hiding without me because everyone thought I needed to heal. *Bullshit. Adam's head should be mine.*

"Because they were the only two with the knowledge and skill to do the patch," Rena answered. I was surprised by her frankness, but I shouldn't be. She'd never shied away from the truth, regardless of the consequences. It was one of the traits I loved about her, and why I didn't give two fucks if part of Uriel was in me as long as she was still mine.

I wrapped my arms around her and held her close.

"Thank you for fighting for me, because I know you did. Thank you for saving me."

She leaned into me. "It was everyone. Not just me."

"But they need me to live because I'm your scale. You wanted me to live because you love me." I dropped my forehead against hers. She wasn't the balance, and I wasn't the scale when it was us. We were two demons who loved each other, and she'd fought for that love. My heart swelled in my chest, knowing how much she loved me.

She skimmed her lips over mine in a soft dance. "I do love you."

"And I love you, and if Armageddon does come, I'll still love you."

Morena shuffled back a couple of steps. "I almost forgot."

"What?" My stomach, full of a dozen blood bags, roiled with dread.

"Megiddo," Rena said. "There was activity there. That's why we were coming here to Gothica."

I remembered. I laced my fingers through Rena's, feeling myself and ready to face the challenges bigger than the two of us. "Let's go find out what your family knows."

She stopped. "Our family, Jax. You are part of it, whether you know it or not."

My heart pounded in my chest. I wanted that. All the messiness of it. Anything the archangels dished out as long as I was able to be with her. "There's something I've been wanting to ask you. Maybe we can find some time later, just the two of us, to talk." *And hopefully, I can give her the real proposal she deserves.*

"You're not breaking up with me, are you?" She narrowed her eyes.

I grabbed her wrists and pinned her arms behind her back, so she was forced to look up.

"Never in a fucking millennium or Armageddon." I claimed her mouth to seal my promise. She wiggled to free her arms, but I held her tight against me. I wanted her to know what being near her did to me.

Her voice was breathless when I let her go. "Please say that's what you want to talk about later."

"That will come after we talk." I kissed the tip of her nose. "More than once if you're not tired."

She laughed and led me down the stairs to the command center.

Lilith looked up in surprise. "I didn't think you two would be down this evening."

"I wanted to hear more about the activity at Megiddo," Rena said.

Lucifer joined us. "It's not the first time we've seen this kind of activity at Megiddo."

If the seismic disruptions weren't new, I failed to see the concern. "Does that mean it's normal or angelic-being related?"

"It could be both in the area." Lilith pointed to the screen. "But why we think it's not is what you should be asking. The place where the activity is happening is what immediately got my and Lucifer's attention."

"What's special about that spot?" Rena asked.

"It's the exact spot I landed when I fell from Grace and the exact spot where your mother found me." Lucifer looked at Lilith like he needed her permission to continue.

"I made my transformation there as well," Lilith finished.

Am I dense? I wasn't connecting what they meant. *Are more archangels following? Another first, like Lilith?* "Do you think something from your experiences is about to happen again? As part of Armageddon?"

Lilith swallowed hard. "I think it's Adam. I'm not sure what he's doing, but I fear it will have something to do with my mother."

Were we ever going to be done with Adam? My blood heated with anger, and the very mention of his name made me spiral into waves of fury. I inhaled to the count of three in the same fashion I used with Rena and let the breath out. One...Two...Three...

Rena slid her hand around my waist. "Could he do anything there? Adam doesn't have any power. How would he get to Megiddo from the dream realm?"

Lilith studied the screen. "Megiddo is an intersection which can provide a path to and from other realms if someone knows the way."

Rena sucked in a breath. "And Adam knows the way?"

"No, but Eve does," Lucifer said.

This fucker doesn't give up. "But he can't get to her. Not yet. Adam can't find Eve without his power."

Lilith and Lucifer exchanged a knowing look. Lilith nodded.

Lucifer swiped a hand over his face. "Eve created the intersection so that Lilith and I could be together. It had to be our decision, but Eve made it possible. Her spirit, her soul, is tied there and should remain there until she can walk the realms again."

"And Adam knows this," Rena said.

I'd deduced that too. Adam would attempt to disturb Eve's spirit to get what he wanted, and we couldn't let that happen. "How long until Eve is healed?"

"No one knows for sure, Jax," Lilith said. "Mother knew this could happen when binding herself there, but it's never come to this until now."

"Whatever Adam is doing, stopping him has to be the key to stopping Armageddon," Rena said. "Saving Endymion might have been a step in reversing it, but I think I can speak for all of us in knowing it hasn't stopped."

Lucifer rubbed his chin between his thumb and forefinger. "That could be it."

"Lucifer and I both thought there could be a connection between Adam and Armageddon when we saw the activity at Megiddo," Lilith added.

"If Eve is bound in the mountain, then her power is grounded there," Rena said.

"He could try to siphon her power." A sickness pitted in my stomach and twisted. "Do you think his love for her would outweigh his desire for power?"

Lilith shook her head. "Based on what I've witnessed, I would say his warped love would never eclipse his desire for power."

"We need to go and go now to protect Eve," Rena said.

I agreed. Adam was probably already inside and up to some kind of fuckery.

"Jax, are you up to calling a portal?" Lucifer asked.

"I've got it covered." My hands shook as they formed the symbols, but it wasn't from weakness.

Rena's surprised gaze fell on me. "You've been to Megiddo?"

I glanced at Lucifer, not for permission but so he knew I wasn't going to lie. "A few times during training."

The portal developed in front of us, and we were on a stone path at the edge of the ancient city.

"If this is where you began your path together, why did you never bring me here?" Rena asked, her voice low.

"Our story didn't start here, Morena." Lilith took Rena's hand in hers. "It was reborn here. While there is a lot of love here, there is almost as much pain."

Lilith and Lucifer's retelling for Rena summarized and simplified what they experienced. During a trip alone with Lucifer, he'd told me he lay at the base of the mountain for days while his body healed. Every bone in his body had been broken. He lay in the dirt in torment while he heard Lilith screaming as she writhed for the same number of days. Their old lives died, and they were indeed reborn here. Together. Lucifer never divulged Eve's involvement in the process. Rena's parents wanted to spare her from their pain but hadn't she and I experienced something similar? I'd lost count of the number of times I'd nearly died. And the things Rena had been required to do...I swallowed against a knot in my throat.

Rena's stare burned a hole in my heart. The fear in her eyes almost broke me. I nearly told her everything Lucifer shared on previous trips about this mountain, but it wasn't my story to tell. Her parents should be the ones to explain their journey, but the irony that a half-human half-demon knew before her wasn't lost on me.

I took her hand. "Let's go save your grandmother."

CHAPTER 48
RENA

The uneven stone path brought a heightened awareness to my senses as we wound through the ancient city, now an archeological site. No active digs were in process, and it wasn't tourist season. We had the place to ourselves.

Jax gripped my hand, and I appreciated the support. His reaction to what Mother said about my parents' tie to this land convinced me he was privy to more than training exercises. He'd tell me when he was ready. I trusted him even if I didn't like being on the outside of a secret.

"The entrance will be shielded with protections, but it is straight ahead," Mother said. "Lucifer and I can open it."

"It takes both of us," Father added.

"Both of you?" Jax asked. "Why both of you?"

"You'll understand in a moment," Mother said.

The path ended, and we traversed the gritty dirt. "I thought there was a mountain here."

Mother and Father smiled at each other.

"May I borrow the dagger I gifted you, Daughter?"

I pulled the dagger from the sheath at my waist and handed it to Father. Mother drew a circle on the ground and a symbol within I didn't recognize. *Oh.* Two epsilon characters and one beta entwined. Together they were the Greek letters for Eve.

Father sliced the dagger across his palm and flipped it in his hand so he held the hilt toward Mother. She took it and made the same cut on her hand. They knelt in front of the symbol and placed their bleeding palms, their hands touching, onto the symbol.

Blood ran through the indentions of the letters and around the circle. Mother and Father lifted their hands, and the blood sizzled to life. My birthmark burned in response, and I jammed my hand against it. I glanced around for signs of Nephilim, but there was nothing. It was triggered by the symbol. *Am I connected here too?*

"Look," Jax whispered, his voice full of amazement. He pointed up to the sky.

The moon traveled into the path of the sun. The bright blue sky dimmed to a dark blue mingled with rich, reddish golds. The eclipse cast shadows over us. This particular event occurred when the moon was at the furthest point from Earth and closest to the sun. The proximity meant it didn't fully block out the sun, and the effect mesmerized me. An orangish-golden circle encased the moon with what appeared to be flames blazing off of it.

"I've never seen one like this." Jax's tone was full of

wonder. "With the band around it."

"Ring of Fire," I whispered. "They are pretty rare, and this opportunity is a gift."

"Is this an omen?" Jax asked, head turned upward. "And am I going to go blind from staring at this?"

"If you were human, maybe." I watched the moon move from full annularity, which was not quite totality for this type of eclipse, and across the other half of the sun. The lack of totality was why the ring of fire was visible.

Mother inhaled, and I refocused on her. She rested her hand on her chest. "It's a beautiful omen. We are welcome."

Father touched my arm. "Watch over here."

The world shimmered before my eyes. The mountain came into view as the scene stilled. A door appeared at the base a few feet from us. I recognized the entrance.

"Mother," I said. "Is that the same door as your library at home?"

"They were fashioned by the same person." She smiled at Lucifer.

Father let out an almost wistful sigh. "I did it as a reminder of our sacrifices and undying love."

"Very romantic." I patted Father's arm. "Shall we?"

Jax was glancing between the waning eclipse and the mountain. He seemed lost in it all, and I couldn't blame him. The site was special.

"Hey." I moved closer to him. "Is something bothering you?"

"No, I'm taking it all in. When we will see something

like this again?"

If we were human, probably never, but in our lives, an event like this was a normal Saturday afternoon. I loved that he took the time to appreciate it and be in awe of the opportunity. My body liked to see the curious side of him, too, and this was not the place for that. I cleared my throat and tugged on his hand toward the entrance.

Father opened the door and let Mother enter first. Jax and I followed her into the tunnel. Father snapped his fingers. Flames spread along the side like path lights.

Mother's steps quickened the further we went. "She'll be deep in the cavern."

We wound into the mountain. Despite the depth, it didn't smell musty or dank. The earth scented the air, of course, but there was something else. A sweetness so soft it came in gentle waves over me. *An apple orchard.* "Does anyone else smell apples?"

"There is an intersection to all realms here," Mother said. "Even—"

"The angelic realm."

"Are we walking back to Hell?" Jax quipped. We had walked deep into the mountain, but there wasn't a way to reach Hell without a portal or falling or an intersection.

Father chuckled as if it hit him subtly at first that Jax cracked a joke. His chuckle turned into a full laugh. It was such a rare sight. I joined in, as did Jax. Mother turned around with a broad smile on her face. "Really, Jax." She shook her head like he had farted instead of making a wisecrack.

"There is an intersection to Hell here, but that's not where we're going," Father said through his belly laughs.

I wrapped my arm around Jax's waist. "Come on. We can't let Mother get too far ahead. She's already walking at vampire speed."

Jax laughed again.

"I heard that," Mother said. "And we're here."

A doorless archway was in front of us, but it wasn't empty. Blue light filled the space like a window shade. I could see into the room, and there, on what looked like an altar, was my grandmother. She appeared to be in a stasis similar to what Father had been in after the last battle. It made me uncomfortable with the memories and seeing another important person in my life in need of healing. Adam would be stopped, and I'd use everything in my arsenal to end him before another one of my family members had to be healed because of him.

"Eve," Jax whispered.

"Is this jinn essence?" I asked, my hand close but not touching the blue light.

"Not essence like a soul, but it is jinn," Father answered.

Jax reached out to touch it like it called to him.

Mother threw her arm out. "I know you feel connected, but we don't know what will happen if you touch it. Lucifer and I can remove it."

He stepped back. His face twisted in equal parts embarrassment and confusion. "I had the strongest urge to connect with it."

"Let my parents handle this one." I looped my arm through his. He'd had enough close calls with Adam's jinn magic. I wasn't ready for him to take another chance when he was just healed.

Mother and Father each went to an opposite side of the opening and situated their hands against the wall. The blue sheen flickered and disappeared.

"It kind of feels wrong entering Eve's resting place like this," I said, unable to shake the notion this was an intrusion.

Mother nodded. "You are not alone in that feeling. Normally, it would be a terrible trespass, but she needs our help."

Father looked over his shoulder and entered the room with us. "I never thought I would witness this."

"Neither did I." Mother wiped under her eyes. Father rested a hand on her lower back, and she leaned against him.

My grandmother looked better than when she and Adam disappeared, and she appeared more corporeal than when she appeared for the ritual with Selene. Her hair was partially turned back to the dark locks she'd worn since I could remember, but heavy grey streaks lined it. She didn't look younger than Mother like she had the other times I saw her. Wrinkles creased both her forehead and where her dimples usually were. She was beautiful, maybe even more so than her younger version. Her face was relaxed, and she looked peaceful. This might be the first peace she'd ever known from Adam's terror. The thought twisted my stomach in knots. Despite all he'd put her through, she maintained kindness and love in the world. She was a gift none of us deserved. I looked away and wiped my eyes, not wanting to upset Mother more.

"I don't think we should wake her." My voice broke, and I swallowed against the ache there. I'd summoned her against my better judgment but had felt sure it was the right thing, yet I wasn't so sure anymore. "She's earned this time of rest a thousand times over. We shouldn't disturb her."

Jax hugged me to his side. Hot tears rolled down my face, and I didn't bother swiping them away this time.

Mother smashed her lips together and nodded. Her eyes were misty with tears that did not fall.

"Then we shall make sure she is guarded at all times from Adam," Father said.

"Now that we know she is undisturbed, can we reinforce the protections?" Jax asked. He tactfully shifted his view of the situation based on my needs. "I know we assume Adam doesn't have power yet, but he could be lurking around here. He's fucking resourceful."

Mother's jaw was set with determination. "He needs her conscious, and she's not near that time. He can't awaken her without me and Lucifer."

"And I'm so glad you are here."

My stomach sank before I saw him, and I turned around to see the one responsible for everything that brought us here. *Adam.*

CHAPTER 49

JAX

Motherfucker. I dove at Adam. He tumbled backward on the floor, and I landed on top of him with my hands wrapped around his throat. "Your presence is not welcome here."

Adam gasped like he needed air, but I was pretty sure the bastard didn't breathe. I loosened my grip, hoping he would say something that would give me cause to yank his heart from his chest. He probably didn't have one.

He wheezed. "I have as much right as the rest of you to pay my respects."

"Let him up, Jax," Rena said with little energy. "He's harmless."

This asshole proved he was as toxic as poison, and I was not in a hurry to let him go. "I kind of like my hands squeezing his worthless neck."

"Jax," Rena said. Nothing else. Just my name.

I stood over and stared down at Adam. "You are lucky Rena is here, or I'd dim your light permanently."

Adam shook with a humorless laugh. "If only you could."

He was a celestial being, so I probably couldn't end his existence, but I'd take pleasure in multiple attempts.

Lucifer wore his devil face and squatted down next to Adam. "If you do not leave here, I'll give the young demon the okay to rip you apart until he tires of it. Given his age and strength, that could be years."

"But I brought friends," Adam said. Selene and Endymion entered and stood behind him along with two grey wings. They were made to look like angels, but their wings were a mottled grey like they were dirty. The angel-like creatures resembled monsters from children's nightmares more than celestial beings. The archangels had worked to end them since the battle with Lucifer. Seeing their emotionless pale asses with Adam was the least shocking thing to happen in recent days. They didn't attack, and their eyes were on Selene and Endymion.

"I'm sorry," Selene mouthed to Rena. *Why are they here with Adam?* He had no power on his own, and only Lucifer and Lilith could wake Eve before her natural time.

"You are choosing wrong," Lilith said. Concern and warning laced her voice, and her eyes locked with Selene's.

Sadness marred Selene's face. She didn't want to be here. *Why is she?*

"We will not let you take her," Lucifer roared.

"I don't intend to take her," Adam said. "I just need a little of her power."

Adam took a step forward, and I blocked his path.

I glanced over my shoulder to see Rena had positioned herself to defend Eve. She assumed her fighting stance. Lilith took up the space beside her. Lucifer guided me back with his hand and faced Adam.

"How dare you bring those things into Eve's sacred space?" Lucifer's voice echoed off the walls. To their credit, the grey wings did flinch. Something inside them registered the threat. Lucifer's voice grew louder, and a tremor ran through the ground. "You are the reason she is like this. Can you not let her have peace? Have you fallen so far from your origins to disrupt her?" Lucifer was so close to Adam's face that I swear I saw spittle splatter.

"That's rich coming from the Devil. Someone who thrives on torturing souls." Adam sneered.

Lucifer's jaw tightened, and he let out a disgusted snort. "I do not pretend to be good, Adam, but I do respect the Mother of Life."

"Mother, what does he mean, mother of life?" Rena asked Lilith.

"Later," Lilith said. The ground under us shook with another mild tremor.

"Yes, you even protect her abominations and make some of your own," Adam said.

I'd cut him down where he stood, but Lucifer remained calm.

"By your own definition, you are one of those abominations." Lucifer tsked. "You wouldn't still walk this world, or any realm for that matter, without her."

"Which is why I need to wake her," Adam said. "Among other things."

"If it is passage to your precious dream realm you need, I can assist you there," Lucifer said.

Adam rolled his eyes. "Selene could do that."

Selene shoved Endymion behind her.

A stronger quake shook hard enough dust fell from the ceiling. The tremors increased like a warning.

"Why are Selene and Endymion here?" I asked.

"I can show you," Adam smiled. "If you let me pass."

"Selene," Rena said. "We helped you reunite with Endymion. Why would you do this?"

"I had no choice," Selene said. "Adam tied his soul to Endy's during the ritual."

"That's impossible," Lilith said. "He wasn't in control of the ritual."

"But I did." Adam smiled like a lunatic. "I ripped a small space in the ritual spell to do it."

It made sense. Why I'd nearly died. The leak in my essence. He ripped me open while trying to get his way. Another casualty in the long line of people he had hurt. I pulled my double fighting swords from their holsters and leaped. Endymion shielded Adam. I couldn't stop. The sword slid into the soft flesh of Endymion's sides.

Blood covered his white shirt. He staggered backward. *No. Fuck.* I replayed it in my head. *Fuck.*

A scream came from behind him. "Noooo..." Selene's

tormented expression shattered into agony. She dropped down to catch him and cradled him in her arms. "Do not leave me. We waited all this time. I forbid you to go, Endy."

The shaking of the floor started again and lasted longer.

"I'll be waiting for you in the moonlight." Endymion reached for Selene's face. His bloody hand caressed her cheek. "My only regret is not living our life the first time."

Endymion's mouth went slack, and his eyes dulled.

I killed him. *What have I done? Why did he protect Adam?* I murdered him.

"Endy..." Selene sobbed over and over.

I flashed hot and then cold. Blood pounded in my ears.

Adam flicked his hand. The grey wings reached under her arms and hauled her to her feet.

"Look at me, Selene. If Eve were awakened, she could bring him back," Adam said, his tone callous. "Or if Lucifer could keep his little demons under control."

Adam deserved death, but I'd failed. Numbness crept over me. I sheathed my swords and swiped my hands over my face. Endymion's body still lay in the crimson pool of his blood. I shook my head. My rash actions resulted in a wrong I could not take back.

"What is happening here?" *Was that Rena?* I turned around to see Eve sitting up. She could fix this.

Eve stood and surveyed the scene. Her gaze landed on Endymion and Selene. She crossed the room and knelt beside them. Her white gown soaked up Endymion's blood.

"Let her go," Eve said to the grey wings in a firm voice.

The creatures complied as if they had taken their commands from her. Selene knelt next to Endymion's lifeless body. Her shoulders shook as she sobbed for the loss.

"Your time together was short now and then, but this was not meant to be," Eve said, her voice warm like honey. She laid one hand on Selene and one on Endymion. "You were entwined long ago."

"Yes," Selene said, her tone mournful.

Blue light encircled the three of them. Eve closed her eyes. Her mouth moved, but I couldn't hear the words. The blood from the floor and Eve's gown retreated as if Endymion reabsorbed it. His eyes blinked and opened. My chest loosened. I couldn't believe it. Eve reversed my mistake, and I was thankful Endy was alive. She hadn't rewound time, but she'd restored him to what he was before I killed him. The blue light looked like jinn essence. I shuddered, remembering what it was like seeing my very being sucked out by Adam.

"Thank you, Mother," Selene said.

Mother as in actual mother? Mother of life? I glanced at Rena, and she gaped at Lilith. She heard it too.

Eve's hair lightened. The areas that had returned to dark were salt-and-pepper grey now. She looked tired and needed to return to stasis.

"My turn," Adam said with the giddiness of a kid waiting for a new toy.

"You need to find yourself. I have nothing to offer you." Eve turned her back on him.

"She is exhausted, Adam. Can you not see that?" Lilith said, her tone pleading.

"Eve can sleep as long as she wants after she helps me."

Rena stepped forward, her eyes narrowed on Adam. "No."

"What?"

"I said no. You're done. Go figure out what you want to do away from all of us." Hell's fire erupted between us and him. I rested my hand on Rena's lower back for support. She didn't need my strength, but it was hers as always. A path remained open for Adam in one direction. Out of the room. The grey wings jumped back and past the barrier of the entryway. They might be smarter than Adam, who held his ground.

Rena turned her hand so the flames climbed higher. "If you don't want to know what it feels like to burn in the fires of Hell, you should leave now."

"I will return for Eve." Adam glowered at her.

"Careful," Rena said, and the flame grew as her tone dropped. Adam retreated.

Eve wobbled on her feet, and I moved fast to catch her under the arms. She was too weak to stand, so I cradled her to my chest. Selene helped Endymion to his feet, and I carried Eve back to the altar.

"Thank you," I said to her through my tightened throat.

"You have sacrificed so much for Rena. Just as Lilith and Lucifer have. Find your comfort in your love." She laid her hand over mine and blue light wrapped threaded through our fingers. A warmth spread from the touch. Her kindness was unending, even in a vulnerable moment.

I nodded. The burden of the scale was mine. Alone. Rena was my solace.

"Mother, what do you need us to do?" Lilith asked. Rena slipped her arm through her mother's.

"You need to all join hands around the altar, and I can do the rest."

I took Rena's hand in mine and she took Lilith's and so on until a circle formed.

Eve chanted in a language I didn't recognize, but blue light wrapped around her like a blanket of energy. Her eyes were heavy. "I love you all."

"She is back at rest," Lilith said. "We can't leave her, though, in case Adam comes back."

Hands released around the circle, but I held Rena's.

"He was only able to get in because Mother had given me the knowledge of how to get in with Endy. That's why Adam helped with the ritual. He needed Endy and I to get him here."

"If we reseal the entrances, then he can't reach her," Lilith said.

"Wait. Did you say 'mother'? I thought that's what you said earlier too. You are my aunt?" Rena asked Selene.

"I am," Selene said.

"Until recently, Selene and I hadn't seen each other in centuries," Lilith said. "To keep Mother safe."

"I have so many questions," Rena said, letting go of my hand to move closer to Selene.

Lilith reached for Rena and caught her elbow. "Which we'll answer at home."

"Are we not going to talk about the grey wings?" A shiver ran through me. They served no real master and had no conscience as far as I'd seen.

"When we get home, Jax." Lucifer squeezed my shoulder.

Our group moved outside of the room. Lilith, Lucifer, and Selene sealed and reinforced the spells protecting Eve. Rena was quiet. Too quiet. I was disgusted with myself for what I'd done to Endymion, and I wondered if she was too. Once they were done, I called the portal to take us to Gothica.

RENA

Jax wore his guilt wrapped around him like a blanket, and I wanted to take it away from him. Mother and the rest of the group left us alone in her apartment so we could talk. The heaviness was uncomfortable, but I wouldn't leave Jax's side. We sat on the couch that had seen many of our worst moments. He stared at the stained glass rendering of my parents, but I didn't think he was seeing it.

"I know what it is like to take an innocent life. It will be with you, but in time, you must forgive yourself, Jax."

"Your situation was different, Rena," he said, his voice low and defeated.

"Yes, you only killed one innocent. I took four. And my grandmother saved yours. Mine are still dead."

"But I did kill him," Jax said. "He died. The only reason he is walking around in the room below us is because your grandmother gave him his life back. The life I took."

Uriel could give him the same peace he had me, but he'd said the person had to be ready to accept it. I didn't think Jax was there yet. He was still trying to compare and rationalize. He might have even still been in shock, given it had only been a few hours.

"Go get your questions answered from your family," Jax said, his gaze still fixed on the window.

I set my hand on his thigh with the palm up. "You are part of that family too."

Jax studied my hand. His hesitation hurt, but I reminded myself what it was like for me. It shredded me inside, and I tried to shove it into a neat little box to not deal with it. My parents and Jax had shown me patience. I moved on, but I didn't find peace with it until Uriel helped me across that threshold.

I rose from the couch and stood in front of Jax with my arm still outstretched. He slipped his hand into mine. The depth of self-torture in his eyes spasmed my heart.

"Don't look at me like that, or I can't do this."

"Like what?" I asked.

Jax pulled me into his arms. "Like you need to fix me. Just give me time."

"Okay." I wanted to say so much more like how I was here for him and loved him, but he didn't need to hear my words of comfort. He told me what he wanted. *Time.* I kissed his cheek. "Take what you need."

He tilted my chin up. "Careful. What I need right now and what you need to do are two different things."

"Maybe they are the same thing," I said, muscles tensing in my lower belly.

Jax's mouth covered mine in a rough, demanding dance. He pulled back. "Trust me when I say they are not."

Desire pooled in my core, and I wanted more.

"Trust me when I say I'm quite sure they are."

He smiled, but it wasn't the warm smile he normally wore. It wasn't exactly cold, but it wasn't his usual either. "No, my love, not now. Not like this."

No wasn't a word he used with me often, and it stung in my chest. I understood. I had to. He needed time. I kept reminding myself.

He led me downstairs to where the others gathered around my desk, off to the side of the command center.

"What's everyone looking at?"

Selene regarded Jax before landing on me. There was another conversation to be had there, but I don't think any of us were ready for that one.

"Adam hasn't left Megiddo. He's wandering around the area with those nasty grey wing things in tow." Selene's nose wrinkled in disgust.

"He can't get in though. We made sure of it." I reached for the locket Mother and Father had given me and rubbed my fingers on it like a jinn would pop out with the answers.

"No, he can't get in without our blood," Mother said. Something unsaid in her words unsettled me.

Jax cocked his head to the side. "Does he have blood for any of you?"

"He has mine," Selene said. "It was one of the conditions of his help with Endy."

He couldn't do anything with half a... heart. "But he doesn't have Endymion's blood."

Jax let out a low, almost feral growl. "Yes, he does."

"Damn," Lucifer said.

Mother gasped. "Endymion's blood from the chamber floor."

"It's my fault." Jax bowed his head. "I spilled Endymion's blood."

I rubbed his arm. The guilt Jax ridiculed himself for belonged to Adam.

"The culpability is not yours alone, Jax," Endymion said. "Had I not asked Adam for help so long ago, none of us would be here."

"I could say the same about asking for Adam's help as well," Selene said. "While seeing Endymion die was traumatic, I do not blame you, Jax. Nor do I blame anyone in this room for Adam's nefarious doings. I have my own misdeeds to judge."

"Adam likely doesn't know the symbol is Mother's name," my mother said.

"He could figure it out, because unfortunately for us, he's smart. Like evil genius smart." I said. "That's not a risk we should take. She's too special. Since he cannot use my blood, I'll be the one to go. The rest of you should stay. We don't know what he might do to you to gain access again." Adam was intelligent, but he was also a narcissist. I could use that to my advantage to take him down.

"I'll accompany you, my love." Jax slipped his hand around my waist. "I appreciate everyone wanting to share the blame, but this one is on me."

His affliction was written on his face. If going with me to Megiddo helped him resolve his internal suffering, I wouldn't deny him the opportunity.

"Morena, we can't let you two go alone to face him," Mother said, her voice somber. "He's had centuries to refine his manipulation tactics. It is unwise to believe he wouldn't be prepared for you and Jax."

I believed he would be ready for us, which was why we had to do something so unexpected he wouldn't think of it. Bright white light flashed in the room. Michael and Uriel arrived together.

"We will travel with them," Michael said. He wore his full battle gear, including his helmet that I'd never seen him in. He was prepared for the worst, and Jax and I should be too.

Another blinding white illumination filled the room. When it dimmed, Aunt B and Aunt Jophiel were in the room.

"As will we," Aunt B said.

Father's eyebrow quirked up. "Should we expect any more of my siblings for this trip?"

Aunt B grinned. "No, we're it. You know how the others can be."

Gabriel's absence was the one I noticed. As the messenger, he should remain neutral, but he and Father were close. It surprised me he wasn't here in solidarity with the others.

"I'm trusting you all with my daughter," Father said to his siblings. "Her life is more valuable than all of ours. Protect her as such."

It wasn't true. My family was worth more than me. They were my treasure.

"You do not need to remind us, Brother. We are aware of our duty to her." Uriel took a knee in front of me. Michael, Aunt Jophiel, and Aunt B followed his lead.

The support of my family was all the strength I needed to keep going. Respect and promise of duty were what their actions represented, but what a spectacle. It made everything heavier than it needed to be. "Not this again. Why is this family so flipping dramatic? Just stand already."

Jax chuckled. I elbowed him in the ribs. "Ouch," he said, laughing.

I shot him a fake scowl, glad my attempt to lighten the weight worked. "Call our ride, portal boy."

"Boy?" He feigned offense. "I'm your portal man."

It was good to see him being normal, but I knew this was a distraction for him. I played my part, though. "Oh, geez." I sighed. "Let's just go."

He formed the symbols. "Portal for Rena, party of six."

JAX

The symbols came easily, and the portal opened. The group of six stepped through, but it wasn't the cobblestone steps of Megiddo, as I expected. The room was dark. My heart raced. My eyes weren't adjusting like they should. I could hear the others in the room, but I couldn't see anyone. The scent of earth drifted around us, but it wasn't where I meant for us to go. *Where the fuck are we?*

Most demons had perfect vision in the dark, but I couldn't see shit. I reached for my love but couldn't find her. My pulse sped up. *Where is she?* "Rena? A little light?"

"Hell's fire." Flames glowed from her hands.

"Are we inside the mountain?" Michael asked in disbelief.

"I believe so," Barachiel answered.

"But I directed us to the stone path outside." I tried to reason through what could have happened. The stone path Lucifer and I traveled to several times was clear in my mind. We should have been there.

"Could Adam have done this?" Rena found a torch and lit it, passing the light to Uriel. She snuffed out the flames on her hands.

"I don't see how he could," Uriel said. "Locking us inside the mountain doesn't help him if he isn't able to gain entry."

"True." Rena paced the circle. "But I don't see a door in here. It seems like a prison. Jax, maybe try the portal again?"

I made the symbols and held the stone path firm in my mind. "I'm locked on the stone path."

All six of us walked through together. I could see it through the portal, but all of us ended up right back in the room. It wasn't possible. I'd never witnessed a stable portal do this. "What the…"

"I don't understand what's happening." Rena glanced around like she was looking for answers.

I lost focus the first two times. That had to be it. One more time, and I'd dial in so tight there would be no room for error. "I'll try again," I said.

I formed the symbols. We all went through the portal, and much to my disappointment, I was still in the fucking little prison room. "Rena, I don't know what's wrong with it."

She didn't respond.

"Rena?" I spun around, looking for her. My panic rose as I thought Adam might have her.

"Rena?"

"She's not in here," Jophiel whispered. "Where is she?"

"There must be a door here," Uriel said.

I felt my way around the room, and Michael was moving in the opposite direction of me. I kicked the wall a few times. The force reverberated back on me. We were sealed inside the fucking prison room while Rena was out there on her own. Adam was a sadistic, deranged maniac, and I wanted to rip my own heart out at the thought of him near her.

"I don't think that will work, Jax," Michael said.

"No shit," I retorted. "If only there were archangels who could travel in the flash of Heaven's light."

Uriel stared at me. "It's worth a try. Whoever set the trap might not have expected us or been capable of building a trap strong enough to hold us."

"Well, one of you angel people give it a try," I said, my frustration mounting while they stared at each other. I kicked another place in the wall and gritted through the vibration. "Are you afraid you're going to explode or something?"

"No, nothing like that. We're debating who is needed least for the mission, so should one of us happen to be lost, the others carry on," Uriel said as if that was an obvious answer.

The angelic connection of their thoughts... "How about you discuss it out loud for my benefit?"

"No need. We've decided it will be me." There was no emotion in Jophiel's voice. It was like their decision was transactional. Warm white light engulfed the room, and she was gone.

"How do we know it worked?" I asked.

"It did," Barachiel answered. "She is in the main hallway."

"I'll go next." Michael was gone in the bright flash of Heaven's light.

I looked between Uriel and Barachiel. "And he's fine?"

"Yes," Uriel said. "He's with Jophiel."

I sighed. "I'm going to have to go with one of you."

Uriel held out his arm. I considered it and turned to Barachiel.

She smiled. "I told you he would choose me."

I let her tug me against her side. Their casual approach had me two seconds away from losing it. "Let's just get out of here and find Rena, and I'll choose you over Uriel every time, Barachiel."

Uriel was gone in the same flash of light as the others. Barachiel and I joined them in the hallway. There was no sign of Rena, and I growled, stopping myself from punching the wall.

"This is where we were before," I said. There was only one place Adam would take Rena if this was his doing, and I was confident it was. "I think checking Eve's chamber is our best bet. If Adam has Rena, it's to get Eve's power."

"I agree," Uriel said. "Lead the way, Jax."

I didn't need his permission. I narrowed my eyes at him and walked down the same corridor we used with

Lilith and Lucifer. "I wonder if we could portal from here. It'd be faster."

"I wouldn't chance it," Barachiel said.

"You're right. I don't want to have to start over from that prison room. We have no idea what Rena's dealing with right now."

The walk was quiet, and I figured the rest of them were doing their mind-talking. It pissed me off that they excluded me, but I kept my temper in check. A fight would delay us finding Rena, and she was the most important thing right now.

"It should be down the next turn," I said, anticipation and concern mixing in my broken voice. "She might be able to hear us now."

CHAPTER 52
RENA

The blue light in the chamber told me the location. My grandmother rested peacefully, encased in the steady stream of blue. I let out a breath, relieved to see her undisturbed. *Why am I here and no one else is? Are they on the path outside the mountain trying to get in?*

The door with the same blue light that encompassed Eve was in front of me. I walked over to the opening and flattened my hand against it. Zzzp. "Fuuucck."

There were no other entrances to the room, and it seemed I was stuck until the others found me. Since I was stuck and I didn't know if yelling would wake Eve, I sat down beside my grandmother and talked to her. It might be the only chance I get to talk to her.

"I'm not sure why I'm here, but if Adam comes for you, I will defend you. Something tells me you would like Jax. I hope you get to know him one day. Really know him.

Maybe when we..." My thoughts spiraled into what-ifs for Jax and the others. *Does Adam have them? Are they okay?* I fiddled with the hem of my white T-shirt. "If Adam does anything to my family, I'll give up my soul to make him pay."

Footsteps came from a distance, and I scoured the room for weapons as fast as I could. Not one damn thing to use to defend me and Eve. *Is it Adam?* I leaned as flat against one side of the opening as I could. "Hell's fire," I whispered and held out my hand.

"Rena?" Jax called my name. I relaxed into the wall.

"I'm here, but I can't get out," I snuffed out the flames in my hand and moved in front of the doorway. My heart fluttered with relief.

"Portaling isn't an option." He reached forward. His hand was close to the blue field.

"Stop. It will shock you."

His hand met the light, and it shimmered and opened. I opened my mouth but closed it. I hadn't imagined it would shock me but not Jax. He looked at his hand and then at me.

"How did you..." I trailed off. "Never mind. Let's just seal it up and then we can find Adam."

"No need to look any further. I'm already here." Adam stood behind Selene and Endymion. *How did they get past the puzzle to enter?* The grey wings were not with him, which left me wondering where they were.

There would be no repeat of earlier. I'd focus Hell's fire

on Adam and annihilate him in a way only the heir to Hell could. My hands flamed in response.

"You wouldn't kill a father in front of his own daughter."

I blinked, processing what he said. It was another one of his delusional statements. "You have no daughter here."

He turned to Selene. "Oh, but I do, and she owes me lots of favors."

I stared between Adam and Selene. It couldn't be the literal meaning. Could it? "Selene? Is it true?"

"Don't blame her. She didn't know until she sought me out to help wake Endy. Eve hid her from me. Can you believe a mother would hide a child from the father?"

"If you were the father, yes," I said without hesitation.

"It's true," Selene said, her voice flat. "But like he said, I didn't know, and I don't consider him my parent. The man who raised me was my father."

"Selene." Jax lowered his voice. "Are you a jinn?"

"No," she said, a little sadness in her tone. "Not anymore. I don't have the powers of jinn."

"You were the one. The first jinn who fell in love with a human." I glanced at the once-human man beside her. "Endymion."

Adam strolled into the room. "It's a disappointment, but we can work with that."

Jax took a big step toward Adam. "No one is working on anything except how to end your existence."

Selene looked disconnected as if she were engulfed in

a memory. "I am the first child of Adam when he became jinn." Her voice hardened with hatred.

How is that possible? "But Eve and Adam hadn't been together in centuries when he became jinn."

Selene's lips curled up in a snarl. Her eyes narrowed at Adam. The sheer abhorrence in her stare convinced me she wanted a piece of Adam as much as I did. "No, they hadn't been together, nor were they together when I was conceived." Her glower fell back on me. Guilt and pain stared at me from her dark eyes. "Ask yourself how I came to be if they were not together?"

The word landed in my mind, and the weight of it was crippling. I looked at Eve resting peacefully here and back to Adam, who conversed in whispers with the grey wings.

"Say it, Morena," Selene said. "Make it real."

I let out a shaky breath. Mother protected Eve from him because of his brutality, and it was clear there were no bounds. I wiped away the tears seeping from my eyes with a renewed conviction Adam would be ended by any means necessary. "He raped her. Your mother. My grand-mother. He took what he wanted from her without permission."

Selene stared at Eve as if she wanted to hug her. "But she still found it in her heart to love me, because as awful as he is, she is the epitome of goodness."

"He will not see another century, another year, not even another day."

Adam clapped his hand, and the two grey wings from earlier entered the room.

I studied how the grey wings submitted to Adam. "Are you their creator?"

The grey wings watched him as if they wanted to know the answer too.

"I am," Adam said. "With one of my ribs."

Jax huffed. "You created a species that is an abomination under your own definition of abominations."

Adam smiled. "But they serve a purpose."

"What?" Jax sneered. "Only listening to you?"

"Exactly." Adam looked at one. "Take her."

I moved to defend Eve, as did Jax, Uriel, Michael, Jophiel, and Barachiel. Everyone except Selene. She blocked the view of Endy with her own body. The rest of us encircled Eve's altar. "Did you know exactly what he did to her?" I scanned my aunts' and uncles' faces. No response was a response. *They knew.* My rage burned inside me they let him live this long under their no interference rule. Another scale could have been chosen. Adam would never come near Eve again after this day ended.

One grey wing went for those to my side, while the other came straight at me. The grey wing tried to grab me, and I ducked away. Right into the clutches of the other one. His arms caged me. I tried to kick out, but I couldn't. The grey wing dragged me across the room to Adam. The others were consumed with fighting the remaining one. It retreated, and Jax spun until he locked on me.

"Rena," he said with a growl, and it was the sound of a beast, not a man.

Jax and Uriel advanced toward us, but I caught sight of

what was in Adam's hand. He tossed it to the grey wing, and it flamed to life.

"Stop. Stay back. It's Jophiel's sword."

"It can't be. My sword is locked away in—"

"The Library of Knowledge." Adam shot her a wicked smile. "Not anymore."

The grey wing backed up to me. It turned and held the sword close to my throat. To be kissed by the flame of the sword was said to drive you mad before you died. Being impaled by it was a quicker death but more painful.

"Selene, let's get to work," Adam said, motioning for her to follow him to the altar. "The rest of you go stand on the far side of the room or I'll order my friend to burn a trail across Rena."

Why don't they just stop him? Because of me. They wanted my life to be spared, but I wasn't the most important person in this room. That honor belonged to my grandmother.

Selene and I studied each other. Her eyes said she wasn't the traitor I thought her to be. I gave a single nod, and she returned it. She asked Adam a question, and I didn't listen for his answers.

I hurled my head back against the grey wing holding me and heard that satisfying crunch when it connected. Flames from the sword grazed my arm. "Ugh." I stifled my grunt against the pain. Those consequences would be dealt with later.

Selene kicked for Adam's head, and I saw the grey wing raise Jophiel's sword. Selene wouldn't be able to move fast enough to avoid it, and my fate was already sealed. I dove in front of the sword as the grey wing hurled it toward Selene. *This is going to hurt.* The flames went out, but it buried several inches into my chest. The ache started with a throb before moving into full-on torment. My vision darkened from the agony. I hit my knees against the base of Eve's altar. Red coated my white shirt as I pulled the sword from my chest and dropped it to the ground. Adam darted out of the room, but I couldn't stop him. A glimpse of Jax came into view in my narrowing field of vision. His mouth moved, but there was no sound except for the intense pounding of blood slowing in my ears. My arm was too heavy to lift to Jax's face one last time, but I tried to channel my love to him. I gave in to the pain, and everything turned to black.

JAX

Rena's blood seeped through her clothes and ran to the base of Eve's altar. I retrieved my dual fighting swords, now soaked in deep crimson. Her blood. Adam had fled, but I relieved both grey wings of their heads. I sunk to the floor next to Rena. My hands shook even as I put pressure against the wound in the middle of her chest. She wasn't moving. Her pale skin dulled. "Why isn't she healing?"

Uriel knelt beside me. He put his hand over mine on the wound. "You know why, Jax."

"Angelic artifact."

"Yes," Uriel said, his voice low.

"Is she..." I stopped, afraid to say it aloud because it might make it real. "Is she gone?"

"No, but she will not last long. Such a brave act." Uriel rested a hand against her cheek. "The blade takes its captives quickly."

"Can we turn her like she did for me?" It could work. There had to be a way to save her.

Uriel's arms hung down to his side. He wasn't even trying to help her. "There's not enough time. Your injury was just a knick. Hers is internal. I'm not even sure she can be turned into a Night Child. Say your goodbyes for now. You will see her again."

I looked at the slick red liquid on my hands. *Rena's blood.* My anger painted everyone and everything in the shade of her lifeblood.

"We could try to wake Eve," Uriel offered.

"She would never forgive me for using the last of Eve's essence. At least they will be together this way." I grasped the altar and pulled myself up. "Adam will be nothing but pieces spread across the ends of the Earth." Light erupted around us.

Pins and needles pricked my hand. I jerked it back. Eve stood at the foot of the altar.

"Jax, I didn't expect to see you so soon." *She expected to see me?* Her stare fell to Rena's lifeless body. "The balance must always exist." She raised her head to look at me. "Just as the scale must."

"I don't want to be the scale without her. I don't want to exist without her." My eyes burned like the fires of Hell. "Can you send me where she is?"

"I cannot, Jax. I am the Mother of Life. Not death." She rested a hand on my cheek. "I can do something else to restore the balance, but I'll need your help."

I nodded. I'd cut out my heart if she told me it would

save Rena. "Whatever it is. Tell me what you need me to do."

"All of you form a circle around us and think of your favorite memory of Rena. A time she made you happy. A time she made you look at something in a new way. A time she made you laugh. A time she made you feel loved." Eve's soft lilt filled the room and soothed enough of my rage that I was able to focus.

Rena's death would be my greatest regret. I inhaled, holding back the tears and anger to honor Rena's life properly with her grandmother.

Eve positioned herself to the side of Rena. "Jax, you sit on the opposite side."

I did as she said. Rena's face looked pale. I brushed the back of my fingers over her cold cheek, leaving a streak of red. Blood coated the ends of her silver-blonde hair. I thought of the first time Rena handed my ass to me while sparring and of the first time I kissed her. I thought of how soft her lips were and how I could never get enough of her. I thought of her bravery on the battlefield to save her father and how she restored me to myself. I thought of what a badass she was and how proud I was to be hers.

Eve positioned her hand over the wound. "Put your hand on top of mine. When I lift up, you push back down. Do it until I tell you to stop."

I placed my hand over hers. Eve chanted as she raised her hand, and I pushed it back down. Our hands moved like a heartbeat. Blue light flowed from her into Rena. *The essence of life.*

"Keep going," she said.

The wound closed. *Come back to me, Rena.*

"Keep going, Jax."

Rena's chest moved like she'd taken a breath, and I held my own to make sure I hadn't imagined the rise and fall.

"We need to continue, Jax."

I followed her instructions.

Rena's eyes fluttered under the lids like she was in a deep sleep. "Rena, I'm here, my love. We're all here waiting for you."

"We can stop now." Eve touched my cheek. "You did exactly as you should, Jax. This was how it was meant to be, so be patient with her. She might be a little different for a while."

I pressed the heel of my palms against my eyes. Relief overwhelmed me. Rena was alive. Eve saved her. I didn't deserve such a gift, but Rena, sure as Lucifer, did. *How does one thank the Mother of Life for giving life back to the only person who has ever mattered in my abomination of a life?* "Thank you. I—"

"No need to thank me. You both have the burden of being the intersection now, but you will be together as the balance and scale should be." Her skin shimmered, and she disappeared into what I could only describe as starlight. I scooted under Rena to lift her.

"When will Eve reappear on the altar?" I asked as I studied Rena to see the moment she would wake up.

"She will not," Michael said. I glanced up at him and

took in the room. Uriel consoled Jophiel and Barachiel. Selene sobbed into Endymion's shoulder.

"What do you mean? She did last time."

"When she banished Adam, she did so at great expense. What she did for Rena—" Michael's voice broke.

"She gave all of herself to save Rena, Jax. She will not return from Heaven this time," Uriel finished.

My heart was like a grenade of gratitude about to explode that she saved Rena, but sadness for the fact Eve was lost to this world. "When she said we were the intersection now?"

"You and Rena are the key to the entry of the realms here," Uriel said. "And Morena will be the Mother of Life."

No. Can she be? My love, the heir to the throne of Hell, be the Mother of Life? Confused how the Mother of Life and a demon could be the same, I studied Rena. Eve did say she would be different. Perhaps that is what she meant. "Will she still be a demon?"

Uriel knelt next to me. "She will still be Rena, Jax. That's what is important."

He didn't answer my question. Well, he did, but not in the precise nature I'd wanted.

"I'm still going to end him," I said, tearing my eyes away from Rena's face to meet Uriel's scowl. "Adam's existence will come to an end."

"I'd help you if I could," Uriel said, his face turning cold and stonelike for a flash of a moment.

Rena stirred in my arms. I cupped her cheek in my hand. "My love, are you with me?"

Her eyes opened. "Why do I feel sick?" Her voice was scratchy, but it was a fucking perfect song for me. "My whole body hurts."

I kissed her forehead, barely letting my lips touch her. "There was a fight with Adam, and you were injured. You're better now. Do you remember any of it?"

"No," she said. "Where am I?"

"You are in a chamber of your ancestors." Uriel squatted down so Rena didn't have to strain to see him. "Let's take it slow."

"Uriel? You're here?" She sat up. "Aunt B, Jophiel, Michael. Why are you all in this place?"

The traumatic part of dying wasn't in her memory. Part of me thought we should leave it that way as long as possible, but she wouldn't like that. Rena fought for her family, and she deserved to know the events of the day, even if they were painful.

"Do you know these two people?" Uriel pointed to Selene and Endymion.

"Yes, that is my Aunt Selene and Endy," she said, giving Uriel a what-the-fuck look.

That's my love. She is Rena. I let out a sigh of relief. She was there.

"Why are my clothes covered in blood?" she asked, her voice confused and shaky. "And you, Jax. Whose blood is that?"

"It's yours, my love," I said, keeping my tone as gentle as possible. "You were injured, as I mentioned earlier."

Rena rubbed at the base of her neck until her fingers

wound around her locket. She rubbed the gift from Lilith and Lucifer as if for comfort. "This looks like more blood than a single injury could cause. It looks like an entire body's worth of blood."

I glanced at Uriel, looking for guidance. He gave one shake of his head.

"Oh, no you don't." Rena pointed between Uriel and me. "Both of you know something, and you know I don't like secrets. Just tell me and get it over with."

"It's a bit of a long story," I said.

"Jaxon, I want the truth now." She used my real name. She must be feeling better, but I wasn't sure better meant she was strong enough to hear about Eve. Her emotions were strong and wild right now, and Hell's fire responded to her like a well-behaved dog. She needed to be in control when we told her. I wasn't even sure I could say the words when the time came.

"Wouldn't you prefer talking about this after you washed the blood out of your hair?"

She clenched her jaw. "What are you afraid to tell me? Have I ever not been able to handle anything thrown my way?"

"This is different," Uriel said.

She leveled a glare at him that would frighten most. "You stay out of this. I'm speaking to Jax."

Shit. "Rena..."

She spun around. "I know this room." She tried to stand, but it was difficult for her to get her balance. I stood, wrapping my arm around her waist. I lifted her to her feet with me. She stared in contemplation at the empty altar. "This is the chamber for Eve to recoup." Rena took in everyone in the room, one by one. "Where is she? She woke up, right?"

She was going to fall apart when I told her, and I didn't know how to be fucking gentle with the explanation. I didn't want her to suffer any more than she already had.

I placed a firm but gentle hand against her shoulder to angle her away from the altar. "Your injury was from an angelic artifact."

She shrugged as if an angelic artifact injury was an everyday event. "What does that have to do with my grandmother? Am I a vampire now, and she can't see me or what?"

I took Rena's hands in mine. My heart pounded. I was about to hurt her, and I'd sworn myself to protect her. "No, you're not a Night Child."

She looked frantic. "Just tell me, Jax. Spit it out."

I cleared my throat and swallowed. "Eve used her essence to heal you. She did so in a way that is not recover-able. You and I are still the balance and the scale, but we are the Megiddo intersection now too. She passed it to us."

"She's gone?" Rena's knees buckled, and I caught her, supporting her until she got her bearings back. "But she was the Mother of Life."

Uriel came closer. "We believe you possess that now as well."

"I'm the heir to Hell. How can I fulfill that role? It's not my role to give life." Rena took a couple of steps back. I didn't move toward her, even though I wanted to wrap her up in my arms. She needed space to work through the news.

"We should tell Lilith," Selene said, her voice thick with tears.

Rena shook as she nodded her head. "She might already know, but we should tell her."

I looked at Uriel. "And where the fuck is Adam? He needs to suffer for this."

CHAPTER 54
RENA

Mother was inconsolable. Several days had passed since we returned, but I couldn't cry. I left Selene and Mother with their grief in the apartment and walked around Gothica. Everything felt wrong to me. *Why can't I grieve or even be angry?*

I settled on one of the stools at the bar in the kitchen alone, because it was the only unoccupied room I could find. The silence offered me some relief. Not peace. But the heaviness when I was around others dissipated in the quietude. I plotted revenge on Adam in the few silent moments I got.

"Hey," Jax said from behind me.

I turned on the stool. He'd done everything I'd asked since we returned. I wanted him close, but I didn't want to talk to anyone. It was easier to send him away than to keep putting him through my selfish pissiness. I tried to sound normal with him, but I didn't even know what that was anymore. "Hey. I don't feel much like talking."

He nodded. A grimace formed on his chiseled face. "I figured. I came to tell you I'm going after Adam. Uriel and Michael are going with me. It's time to end this before he does something else."

Our entire family deserved vengeance on Adam, but I was the one who died. It was my grandmother who paid the sacrifice to reverse what Adam had done. Jax had been punished and nearly died at Adam's hands too. He was owed some retribution, but I wanted to be there to end the psychopath. I couldn't do that until Mother was in a better state. "Jax, I don't think you should."

I met his eyes and saw the rage and anguish I should feel. His determination was etched across his face. "I'm doing it, Rena, and I'm going to be the one to deliver the blow."

A death blow. Adam had dealt one to me. A tremor shook through me.

Jax rubbed my forearm but stayed at arm's length. "Are you okay?"

"I'm fine," I said. I wanted to tell him I loved him, but the words wouldn't come forward.

"I'll see you soon." He didn't try to kiss me and walked away without looking back.

"Come home safe," I said. He was giving me time and space. Something he once asked of me but didn't get the chance to have. I should be going with them. This was my death blow to deal, not his. The fight left me, and I didn't know if that part of me was coming back. I wasn't sure if I wanted it to.

I looked across the bar at my reflection in the stainless-steel refrigerator door. It was me looking back, but I didn't recognize that person. The woman reflected on the metal surface was tired and unhappy, and I didn't know her. "Who are you?"

The blood bag in front of me wasn't what I was hungry for. I wanted fried bacon made by Jax and the strength of his arms around me. I wanted the happy person I'd been. I tossed the blood bag in the trash and went to my desk in the command center. There were only a couple of Night Children working. They glanced up when I walked in but went right back to whatever they had been doing on their computers. I went straight to my desk, which sat a good distance from them.

The sophisticated equipment we'd installed could access spy cameras. It was how we'd monitored a lot of activity, but the seismic activity was telling too. It's what led us to Megiddo.

I pulled up the seismic activity for the last week, wondering if there had been any changes. There were peaks, but there were two close together on that day. "That must be it."

"This is the moment you died, and this is the moment she saved you." Selene pointed to the screen. "She knew what she was doing, Rena. She never made a rash move. Ever."

"One is for her, but the first one is for me?" I understood why a force like Eve, Mother of Life, might cause a seismic disruption when she woke up and saved me. What confused me was why my death would cause one.

"Yes, she either knew or calculated somehow what needed to be done for survival. Not hers. Not yours. But the world's. If that meant saving you to see all realms continue, she would do it."

"It wasn't just because I'm her granddaughter?" Deeper relief than I'd gathered from my solitude washed over me. She made the choice for a bigger reason than just my life. While most people might not find comfort there, I did. The decision wasn't based on a familial bond.

"No, I'm not saying she wouldn't have tried anyway because you were, but that wasn't her purpose in the chamber. She did it for the greater good."

Some of the guilt weighing on me lifted. "Thank you."

Selene blew off my reply. "For what? Adam is my father. I should probably receive the same fate you dole out to him."

I didn't know if she knew Jax, Michael, and Uriel were hunting Adam, and I didn't tell her. I wasn't sure if I trusted her, but she was part of Eve, just like Mother, so I had hope for her. "No, you shouldn't. You are my aunt and my mother's sister. There is good in you too. Look how long your love for Endymion survived."

Selene had dark circles under her eyes, and that wasn't a normal thing for a celestial being. "It drove me a little mad, though. My love for Endy made me agree to things with Adam that went against my moral code. That is hard to reconcile. It's almost like I was a different version of me."

Her words resonated with me. For the first time since Eve brought me back, I connected with something someone said. "I feel like a different person too. Like I'm in here, but I can't find me."

"I understand." Selene sat on the edge of the desk. "It does get easier, Rena. Be patient."

An ache formed in my gut for the first time since I died. "I can't even tell Jax I love him. I do. I know I do deep down, but the words will not come out."

"He's a good man, Rena. He's backing off to give you the space you need. How do you feel physically?"

"Fine. I could fight without any issue. I was thinking about sparring to take my mind off everything. Want to join me?" I wanted to focus my mind away from whether Jax and my uncles were okay. I knew it was unlikely they would report in until it was done.

Selene fell into step with me. "Sure. Are you going to take it easy on me?"

"Absolutely not," I said.

"Then count me in."

I LANDED a roundhouse kick on Selene, and she hit me in the jaw so hard I saw stars. The pain woke me up, and I was happy to not feel like I was in a fog.

Selene ran at me and flew into a drop kick. Her feet were aimed right at my chest. She pulled back at the last second, and there was no impact.

"Why did you pull your kick?" I threw the helmet on the mat. "I thought we agreed to go hard."

"I was worried it might be a trigger for you," she said, her tone apologetic.

"It wouldn't, and I don't like to be coddled. I want to feel it all. The laughter. The pain. Everything."

The memory of the strike Adam had dealt swallowed me. I'd jumped in front of Selene, and the sword pierced right through me. I pulled it out of my chest. Adam snatched it up when he slinked away. "The fucking bastard."

Selene came to my side. "Sit down and take some deep breaths. You're okay now."

I closed my eyes, drawing the lids tightly together. "I remember how Adam killed me."

She let out a breath slowly. "It was cowardly of him, and I'm sorry you will be forced to relive his spineless act as one of your memories."

My breath hung in my chest like it was stuck. "What does it say about me that Eve gave me this tremendous gift, and all I want is to see Adam destroyed?" My fight returned a little as I talked through my experience.

"It's called normal," Selene said. "Which is what your reactions are. Normal."

A guard stepped through the door. "Princess, your mother has asked to see you in the command center."

"On my way," I said, standing. "Come with me. I'm sure she could use us both."

We made our way to the room, but Mother wasn't there yet. Two Night Children were working at the desks near the door.

I sat down in the chair at my desk, but Selene did a double take and screamed.

"What?" I asked, scanning the room but seeing nothing.

She pointed to a little white blur dashing toward us.

"Aaah!" I hopped up on my desk and pulled her up with me. "Aaah!"

We looked at each other and screamed some more. I searched the room for the two Night Children, and they were crouched by the door like they were ready to fight.

The white blur stopped in front of my desk and sat on its haunches watching us watch it. *Little asshole.*

"Aaah!"

Mother came through the door at vampire speed. "What is all this commotion?"

Selene and I pointed to the rodent. "Aaah!"

"Is that a..." The white blur beelined for her. She leaped onto the closest desk. "Aaah!"

Father entered the room. "What is happening? Those screams could be heard in Hell."

Mother pointed to the creature in front of her. Father reached for it, but the furry blur was fast. It darted back in Selene's and my direction.

"Aaah!"

"Stop screaming," Father said. "You are scaring it."

"Get that thing out of here," Mother said, her voice stern.

Father crouched close to the rodent and held his hand out. It worked a path closer to him, and he caught it. He held it up for us to see, but none of us wanted a closer look.

"Aaah!"

"Good grief. It's a mouse. You have all charged into battles where your life was in danger, and all they needed to do was send a mouse in to defeat you. Imagine if it got out that the Mother of Night Children, the heir to Hell, and the Moon Goddess were all scared of such a small thing." Father carried the mouse out of the room.

"Fuck that mouse." Selene laughed.

"We showed it." I burst out laughing, and it felt good.

Mother joined in. "I figured Lucifer would turn into a snake and eat it." Our laughter was the first real emotion I'd felt in days, and I realized I was going to be me again... in time.

CHAPTER 55

JAX

I found Michael and Uriel in Lilith's apartment on the top floor of Gothica. The two archangels were seated on the couch I planned to burn at some point. They lifted their heads, and I saw anger in their eyes.

"I'm hoping that hatred is for the same person I'm planning to go end."

"We'll have to hunt him down," Michael said.

"How do we kill him? I want to end him permanently so he can never touch Rena again. He can't be allowed to go where Eve is either. Rena wouldn't forgive me for that."

"There is a way, but it's brutal." Michael paused, holding up a handful of spikes. "These will prevent him from healing, but it requires dismembering him while he's alive."

"We can handle this one, Jax," Uriel said. "He is a

threat to the balance and the scale. We can take care of him without our actions being interference."

I wasn't sure if he was giving me an option for an out or a justification for himself, but it didn't matter. My decision was made. Adam's death would come at my hands. "No, I want to do it. I want him to beg me for mercy, so I can remind him of the lack of mercy he has shown to this family, especially to Rena."

"Rena will want to go," Uriel said.

I'd told her we were going without her, and that plan hadn't changed. "We can't let her. She's still struggling with what he did to her and what that cost her grandmother."

"Agreed," Uriel said.

"She will be angry with us," Michael said.

"That's a risk I'll take to stop the fucking piece of shit, Adam." I clenched my fist until my nails dug into my palm.

"When do we leave then?" Uriel asked, his determination equal to mine.

"Now." I patted my double-fighting swords in their sheaths.

Michael, Uriel, and I had tracked Adam for seven days across the human realm, and we'd closed in on his location. *Picher, Oklahoma.* Rena had summoned Michael and Uriel at different times. Neither of them answered so she had to know we were together as I told her we would be. Adam had to be taken down tonight, or Rena was going to come looking for us.

I leaned against the wall of the tunnel, watching the sheets of rain coming down.

Michael shifted. "There he is."

"Remember the plan," Uriel said.

Michael went in one direction while Uriel moved in another. I strolled out into the dampness with deliberate steps toward Adam.

The son of a bitch smiled as he appraised me in the dim light.

"Jax, you cannot take me on your own."

He thought I wanted him as a prisoner. "Oh, I don't want to take you." I paused, finding the two archangels in position behind him. "And I'm not alone."

Adam shrieked when Michael and Uriel seized his arms. He was weak and couldn't put up much of a fight. I hated myself for how badly I wanted to make him scream in pain, but I planned to make him pay with every drop of his blood.

Michael and Uriel stretched Adam's arms out against the wall of the tunnel. I picked the mallet up from the ground and stalked toward Adam as if I was a predator and he the prey.

"Don't pierce your skin with the spikes," Uriel said.

I slipped one of the spikes from my jacket pocket, and I moved fast, driving the metal through Adam's palm in a single swift motion. Adam's guttural scream reverberated down the shaft of the tunnel. Uriel's fingers flexed. Heavenly fire shot out and heated the spike until it glowed red. A smile crossed my lips. "How does it feel?"

Adam spat on me. I'd hoped he would do that. My hand already balled at my side, I landed an uppercut to his chin. His teeth jammed together in a crunch as his head snapped back. The satisfaction of the sound spurred me on, and I drove another spike through the hand Michael had pinned against the wall.

"Solid hit, Jax," Michael said, something akin to pride in his voice. He patted my shoulder.

"You call this a fair fight?" Adam wheezed, blood trickling from his mouth.

"Fair?" I smirked. "Was it fair what you did to this family? What you did to Rena?" I gripped his chin in my hand and stared him in the eyes. "You have mistaken me for the fair one between Rena and me. She is good at her core. So much better than the rest of us. But you...you are nothing but evil, and I will enjoy torturing you tonight for every single time you hurt her." My vision reddened. The demon side burned to take over. I shut my conscience off. Shoved it in a box to deal with later.

"Jax, all spikes must be placed," Uriel said.

"On it." I retrieved another one from my pocket and hammered it through Adam's knee.

"Ugh."

I repeated the actions on the other knee.

"Stop," Adam pleaded, his blood running down his legs. "I'll do anything."

"There is nothing you can do to make it stop," I said, lapping up the terror in his eyes. Despite all she'd been through, Rena had never shown she was afraid for herself. She'd shown dread for others, but not for what might happen to her. Adam feared only for himself. He was a piece of shit.

I held the last spike in my hand. The one meant for his heart. "You made me put my hands on Rena's throat. Let me show you how that feels."

"Uriel? Michael? You are archangels. How can you allow this?" Adam looked between them.

"You are a threat to the balance," Michael said.

"And so, you must be eliminated," Uriel said.

"Destroyed," I said, my voice coming out in a growl. An emptiness formed in my chest as I unleashed the final bit of fury I'd been holding back. I wrapped my hands around Adam's throat and squeezed, pushing my thumbs into the soft flesh. His body writhed under my hands, but the spikes held him against the wall. The fucker tricked me into hurting Rena. I could have killed her, thinking she was him. He caused her death and took away her chance to know her grandmother. Adam's eyes bugged out. "You will never be near her again."

Uriel hooked his arm under mine and pulled back. "If he passes out, it is a mercy he does not deserve."

I inhaled and forced myself to let go. Adam gasped for air.

"Don't lose yourself in it, Jax," Michael said. "This is vengeance, but you are not the same as him."

I positioned the final spike over Adam's heart and drove it in. Blood spattered across my face. The fleshy sound turned my stomach, but I ignored the feeling.

"Time is short. We need to complete the process by dividing his body and placing it in multiple realms. Here in the human realm, an archangel's vault at the Library, and Eden. The head and heart should go to Eden," Uriel said, drawing his sword.

I unsheathed my swords. "The head is mine."

Michael's sword flamed to life. "Then you must take it to Eden."

"I know the way," I said. The three of us struck simultaneously. The sickening, fleshy sound consumed me as we struck again and again in unison until unrecognizable pieces were left. I swallowed against the bile rising.

Lightning flashed and illuminated the three of us against the ruins of the vacant town of Picher. Rain pelted down on my face in the darkness, but it wasn't enough to wash the red hue off me. The deed was done, but the satisfaction I'd craved from it dissipated. Michael, Uriel, and I looked like a gruesome trio as we prepared to scatter the parts of Adam. "Why is there no relief from it?"

"It will come in time when you don't have to worry about Morena's safety." Michael gathered the remains of Adam, placed them in equal portions between three bags, and passed them to us. He handed me the bag that contained Adam's head, heart, and other pieces. "Scatter them around the garden, but the head and heart should be left at the base of the tree in the center."

"It doesn't feel that way. The relief doesn't even seem to want to come." My bloody hands were reminiscent of the way they looked when he impaled Rena. "I feel...hollow."

"Maybe you need a sabbatical," Uriel said. "Some time to sojourn in order to reconcile the events. You and Rena have been through a lot of upheaval in a short amount of time."

"We have, but I'm not sure how she would feel about me taking off without telling her. She might welcome it though. She couldn't even tell me she loved me when I left." It hurt, and even saying it to Michael and Uriel revived the ache in my chest. I didn't resent her, but it stung.

Uriel let out a deep sigh and looked in the direction of the tunnel where we ended Adam. "She does love you, and she will understand your choice, as you will hers."

Fatigue wound deep into my bones, and my limbs were heavy. "Yes, I think she needs some time to reconnect with herself, and I think I do too."

"Will you go back to tell her?" Michael asked.

If I went back, I wouldn't be able to give her or myself the space we both needed to heal these wounds. "No, I think we need the time apart if we want to be together in the future. I understand neither of you are messengers, but would you mind doing something for me?"

I faced Uriel and rested a hand on his shoulder. It made me a hypocrite for the promises I'd made to Rena, but I needed some time to get myself realigned. I hoped she understood I was always with her. Always hers. Always by her side. "Will you watch over her while I'm gone? She trusts you."

"She doesn't need my protection, Jax." Uriel mimicked my gesture and gripped my shoulder. "But I will do this for you."

"Thank you." My hate for Uriel turned to admiration and respect. He put the family first. He put Rena first more than once. I trusted him as Rena did, even if I still didn't like him.

I relayed my message to them, and we parted ways to scatter pieces of Adam across the world. I formed the symbols for the portal and stepped into the Garden of Eden. It was the beginning for Adam and Eve, and while I wanted to bury him in a giant pile of dinosaur shit, that wasn't an option since I couldn't time travel. Out of respect for the death that was his, I brought the remains I had here. I placed them in various parts of the maze. Adam's remains were destined to be fertilizer for the plants here.

Uriel confirmed Eve was in Heaven, and I wondered if Adam would be too. Not a chance in Heaven that Lucifer would grant Adam passage to Hell. My brain wouldn't stop assessing and processing the events. In my mind, I saw Adam set in motion the events that led to Rena's death over and over again.

The mirror side of Eden was a prison, so I couldn't go there. The silent room offered the quiet I desired most. I could go that far.

I wound through the network of paths until I reached the hidden door. The silence blanketed over me. On previous trips, the pressure was awkward, but I welcomed it into me. The stark, white, pass-through had an avocado-green couch. I stretched out on it and closed my eyes. The room quieted my mind, which was what I was hoping for. Sleep called me, but concern for what might be lurking in this respite made it hard to fully relax for a deep rest.

I let my eyes fall shut, and I slept for the first time since Rena died.

RENA

The bed invited me with the lure of sleep, but I couldn't go back. I needed to get up, get dressed, and face the day. No one was sure if we had stopped Armageddon, but the seismic activities had quieted. It was a good sign and a welcome reprieve, but it meant nothing without confirmation.

Jax had been gone for a week, and it wasn't a long time given how long our lives could be. Worry festered in my gut that they were in trouble. I'd scried for him and my uncles, using the lesser magic in an attempt to find where they all were. Michael was at Megiddo, which triggered flashbacks to a sword in my chest, but Jax and Uriel weren't found. *Where are they?*

I swung the door open, and instead of finding my guards, Uriel leaned against the wall. Alone. I glanced up and down the hall, but no Jax.

He shot me an awkward, uncomfortable smile. "He's

not with me. I thought today would be a good day to go to the Library of Knowledge."

I wanted to sink to the floor that Jax wasn't with him, but I straightened my spine instead of deflating. "Where's Jax?"

"Come with me, and I'll tell you what I can. I remembered some texts about Armageddon I thought might be useful to you." He held out a hand to me.

Where is Jax, and what does Uriel know? "Why not just relay them to me?"

"You prefer to learn things firsthand." He smiled.

He spoke the truth, and it irked me how well he understood me. "Any chance Jax will come back while we're gone?"

"No."

"Is he safe?"

"You have my word."

I sighed and took Uriel's hand. He pulled me to his chest and wrapped his arms around me. It was weirdly secure, but not the warm shelter Jax's embrace provided. Jax wouldn't like it. But Jax wasn't fucking here. Light flashed around us, and when it cleared, we stood at the entrance of the ultimate library.

I inhaled the light scent. The amber, floral, and musky aroma relaxed me. They welcomed visitors in like a decadent but sweet invitation. The marble walls, floor, and pillars glistened as pristinely as they did the last time I was here.

"You like it here," Uriel said softly.

"I do," I admitted. "It's peaceful, and the solitude gives me energy, as strange as that sounds."

Uriel's posture relaxed. "It's not strange at all. I often came here for a similar reason."

I studied him and saw sincerity in his eyes. Uriel was more complex than the other archangels. The others seemed mission-driven, but Uriel assessed everything and redirected from those evaluations. His siblings often called him the smartest of them all, and he was cerebral, as was made evident by his serious nature. He kept his emotions so far below the surface they seemed lost. Even after facing the loss of his family, he still chose solitude most of the time. He'd slept for centuries. I guess time was what we all needed to reconcile our pain, and that definition of time was different for everyone.

"Come." He held out his elbow like we were going to a society party in the human world.

I took the offered elbow and slipped my arm through. Jax wouldn't like this, either, but he left.

Uriel led me through several hallways until we reached a gilded entranceway. A hum buzzed in my veins. "I know this entrance. You led me away from it before."

"I did. Do you remember what I said?" He plucked one of his feathers from his wing and positioned it in the center of the door. The feather glowed and melted into the gold. The lock clicked and the large slab of metal swung open, granting us entry.

"You said I wasn't ready for it that day, but there would be a day." My palms were sweaty, and I tingled all over with anticipation of what secrets this room would hold. "And today is the day."

"After you, Rena." Uriel held his arm out.

It wasn't the first time Uriel had used Jax's nickname for me, but it lashed across my heart with a sting this time. I blinked back tears and walked past him. "Interesting key."

The room was dimly lit, with only a desk in front of me. Uriel entered behind me, and the door closed. "Yes, this room is protected. Only archangels may cross the threshold."

I turned to face him. "I'm not an archangel."

"No, but you are the balance. There are exceptions to every rule."

"Are there any others allowed as exceptions?" My throat thickened.

"Only one," Uriel said.

"The scale," I whispered. My stomach twisted as I tried not to think of Jax because it hurt. I only succeeded in thinking about him more.

"Yes," he said. "Let me show you what I wanted you to see. The others know when the door has been opened, and they may come."

"You don't want them to know we're here?"

"They already know, but they might not agree with what I'm about to show you."

"You were the friend Aunt Jophiel had to see before she left that day." The archangels were much better at keeping secrets than I was. "The day I was drawn to this door, but she stayed behind when the rest of us left."

"Yes, she found me that day and agreed with my decision then, but she might not agree with the one today, so move."

Odd for Uriel to exclude the others. While it wasn't unusual for the archangels to disagree, it was unusual not to inform the others. Maybe he considered the notification they received when the door opened as informing them.

"Show me," I said.

He snapped his fingers, and light filled the dark room. The space seemed vast compared to my original appraisal. Books with golden spines lined the bookshelves along the wall. A circular couch framed a sitting area toward the back.

"What is this place?"

"Mostly musings of archangels, but there are prophecies and historical records that were deemed too sensitive for the world."

"You hid important shit from the humans?" I teased. "Imagine that."

"Not just the humans. All realms and beings."

I shook my head, but I wasn't surprised. "Gatekeep much?"

"Rena, you know how information in the wrong hands can have dire consequences." Uriel pulled a book, larger than most of the others, and led me to a nook area with a table and four chairs. He held one chair out. After I was seated, he took the one to the right. "This is the one I wanted you to see."

"Where do I start?" I took the volume from him. It was a little bulky in my hands.

"Open it. It will show you what you are meant to see."

I set the book down and opened it to the middle. The pages flipped back and forth until they settled about three-quarters of the way through.

"The balance and the scale are two halves of a whole." I glanced up at Uriel. "We know this."

"Keep reading," he said.

"One cannot exist without the other. They begin and end together. Their duties may lead them apart, but they must find their way back to each other. Should one become lost, the other can find the missing half by placing a hand over their heart and speaking the absent one's name." Tears pricked my eyes. "This was how Adam kept finding Eve."

"Yes," Uriel said.

"But what does this have to do with Armageddon?"

He tapped the page. "There's still more to read."

"Should the bond be broken between the two, Armageddon will be upon us." I gasped. "Uriel..."

"Eve knew the bond between her and Adam was irreparable. She could not save him. No one could. We've been in Armageddon waiting for you and Jax. None of the archangels knew, and I'd forgotten the text until Jax touched my shoulder and asked me to look out for you while he was gone."

Too much to process. "He what?"

"I promised I would tell you what I could. He's in a deep sleep in Eden."

Panic lanced through me. "Is he injured?"

"No, not physically. Like you, he needed time to process."

I searched Uriel's expression, but it was guarded. "Process what?"

"He should tell you in his way, but I will say we found Adam. He will no longer be a threat to you. Jax is reconciling his role in it."

"Role?" I understood. "He told me the three of you were going together to take care of him." It sunk in what Uriel had said. "He's really gone for good? Adam?"

"He will never return," Uriel said.

Relief waved over me and evolved into guilt. How could I be relieved when Jax suffered because he wanted to free me of someone who would have haunted our entire lives? I closed my eyes and tried to breathe through the burn in my throat, but the tears fell. A sob exploded from me. Uriel wrapped an arm around my back, and I leaned into his shoulder.

"Let it out," he said. "Cleanse yourself of the pain you feel. Joy will be yours soon."

I cried until there were no more tears. Uriel's shoulder was wet, and my hair was too.

"There are other causes of Armageddon, but none more delicate than the balance and the scale. I want you to read this last paragraph." He pointed to the end of the section.

My eyes were blurry, but I could still read it. "Armageddon may come from any realm. Angels against man. Demons against angels. Any species who wages a war of extinction can start Armageddon, but only the balance and the scale, along with their army, can stop it."

"Our family," I said. "We're the army."

Uriel smiled. "Yes, and many of us have been responsible for starting Armageddon in the past, and many times, Eve stood alone without Adam to hold it at bay. She could never stop it. She knew her destiny was to wait for you. She held the balance until the day came when she could empower you. When you were ready."

A shaky breath escaped my lips. "I can never measure up to her."

"You don't have to. Your journey is yours."

I reached for the locket Mother and Father had given me. "What you said is close to the inscription on this gift from my parents."

I flipped it over and held it out for him to see. He read it out loud. "Your destiny is yours." He paused. "And it is, Rena. You will always have a duty, but your life is yours."

That remained to be seen, but time would tell if I got to have a life that was mine. "It hasn't always felt like that, but thank you for showing me these texts. For the first time, I feel like I understand my purpose."

Uriel inclined his head toward me. "Then maybe it's time to go see Jax."

"What if he's not ready?" I wasn't sure I was ready. The guilt I felt for his suffering to provide us a future without Adam was equally matched by my anger at him for not coming home.

"He's ready, Rena. He's waiting for you to be."

My heart beat faster in my chest. I stood up and laid my shaky hand over my heart. I pushed against my chest to stop the vibrations. "Jax…Jax…Jax…" A warm, incandescent light threaded around me until it encased me. I spun and closed my eyes against the dizziness. When it stopped, I found myself in the middle of tall stones. I'd seen these before. *Stonehenge. It can't be.*

"What the actual fuck is this?"

"It's Stonehenge." His voice washed over me like a tidal wave of warmth.

"Jax." I faced him. Love and anger battled in me to see which one would react first. Anger won. I threw a punch like when we sparred. Jax sidestepped it. Apparently, the cry with Uriel didn't get everything pent-up out.

I spun into a back kick aimed for his head. He ducked under it.

"Rena…" Jax warned.

"You left, Jax."

He moved close to me into his stance from the mat, but we'd sparred enough that I anticipated his move.

"You acted behind my back." I came down with my elbow and connected with his collarbone.

"Ugh." He stumbled back. "Fuck. Damn it. Would you stop and listen to me?"

"Why would I do that when this feels so good?" And it did. Sparring had been an outlet for us since we were pre-teens. Maybe younger. We'd settled our differences like this more often than I could count.

He moved forward and resumed his fighting stance. "Then we'll do it your way."

I readied myself. He inched forward, and I rounded to land a spinning back kick. Jax swept under me. I was already in motion and couldn't stop. His hit took me down to the ground. He landed on top of me, pinning my arms. I kicked my legs.

"Rena, stop. Let me explain."

CHAPTER 57

JAX

I laid on top of Rena, but she wouldn't stop. If she wasn't ready to talk, why had she called me here? Just to whip my ass while we sparred? This wasn't how I planned our reunion to go.

I held her there until she looked at me. Her eyes flashed red, and anger dominated them. I needed to give her an out if she wasn't up for this discussion. "Do you want to keep sparring with me? If you do, I'll stand up and be your punching bag until you are ready to converse."

Rena stilled. "I'm so pissed at you, Jax. And hurt. And worried. You didn't even tell me yourself. You didn't tell me you weren't coming back."

"I know, my love. I didn't know I wasn't. It was really messed up. I was messed up. I'm sorry."

She didn't say anything, and I let go of her wrists. I sat back on my heels and offered her a hand. She refused it but sat cross-legged across from me. Her posture was stiff.

Tension settled across her jaw and at the base of her neck. "Talk. I'm listening."

"We..." I inhaled. "Michael, Uriel, and I tortured Adam to death, but it was primarily me. I wanted him to suffer, and I made it happen." The details lived in my head. They didn't need to live in hers. "It fucked me up that I was capable of that. I've seen plenty of gruesome deaths, but I've never been the one to deal it out. Not like that."

Rena's shoulders relaxed as if the fight was gone from her. She was listening. That was a start.

"I didn't want you to see me like that. I wasn't the me you were used to, and I wasn't sure if I could ever be again."

Her gaze took me in, and I wanted to take her to the ground and burn that anger out. She needed words, not sex, so I forced my need away.

She sat in silence for a moment as if she considered my words. "And what about now?"

"I'm ready to come home if you'll have me." There wasn't anywhere else I wanted to be but with her. I'd hurt her again, and I'd done the right thing. Those two things weren't an either or, but I understood there would be consequences for my actions.

She sighed. "Do you know how I got here?"

"I suspect Uriel shared with you a special call between the balance and the scale."

She nodded. "It allows us to find the other when we are lost."

"He told me the story too." The temptation to use it

had wrecked me.

"But you didn't use the power?" The hurt on her face would have dropped me to my knees if I wasn't already on them.

I ached to touch her. To have her beneath me and on top of me, but she had to forgive me first. "No, I wanted it to be your choice to see me again. When you were ready."

"Really, Jax?"

Inhaled and let it out slowly. "You weren't ready to see me until now. Were you?"

"No," she admitted. "But I would have told you myself. Not hidden away."

"I sent a message with Uriel and asked him to stay with you. Would I have done that if I didn't plan on coming back?"

"I don't know." She stared up at the moon. "It hurt, Jax. I had to process everything without you, and I told myself to give you time because that is what you would do for me. And you did. But I'm so angry at the way you handled it."

"I'm not going to make excuses, but I can go if you want. I don't want to upset you if you aren't ready for me to come back with you." *I'll die inside if I leave her right now, but I'll do it if that is what she wants.* "You are my heartbeat, Rena. My everything. The reason I exist. And I love you."

She closed her eyes and inhaled deeply. "I love you too. So much it impairs my judgment. The space between us may have been uncomfortable, but it might be what we needed to keep a clear view of the world."

I tilted my head back, unable to look at her. My heart splintered in my chest, and I rubbed it against the ache. There had been an immense amount of suffering around us, and it was possible that was too much to repair what we had. At least for the moment. I stood and walked along the ley line at Stonehenge, drawing strength from it to keep moving forward.

"Jax?" Rena called.

I froze in place. A small bit of hope stirred in my fractured heart.

Rena looked at the stones as if she was drawing courage from them. "He raped her. Adam raped Eve to produce Selene."

"I know." It was one of the reasons I'd kill Adam all over again, even if it brought us back to this same situation. "But he's gone now, Rena. He's not coming back from what I did to him."

She bit down on her lip and nodded. "Thank you, Jax." She let out a breath. "Don't disappear. I'm furious with you. I need space, but I don't want you to disappear. Okay?"

The hope I'd gathered dropped into an abyss of darkness. She was the reason for...everything to me, and I had to let her go, not because of what I wanted, but because of what she needed.

"Okay." My voice cracked as I formed the symbols for a portal. I let myself fall backward into it, not caring how I landed.

CHAPTER 58
RENA

Jax was ready, but I couldn't forgive him. I couldn't put my finger on why. I wasn't there yet, and I hadn't reconciled that fact until I wanted to beat the shit out of him while he stood in front of me. The past week was tough. I'd chosen to go back to Hell instead of Gothica. For seven days I thought about him and the exchange at Stonehenge, and every night I dreamed of it in my sleep. I couldn't escape it. I drank until sleep came on its own, hoping I wouldn't dream, but the dreams found me.

His words echoed in my head. Adam's death at his hands confused him to his core. It resonated with me and my own experiences. I could forgive that, but I struggled with how we moved on from this disconnected space. That was the part I couldn't reason through.

A knock came from the door. "Come in."

"You're in here by yourself?" Mother asked like she

had every day when I retreated to the meeting room in the afternoon.

"Yes, like I have been for the last six days." I smiled at her.

"At least you're smiling today," she said. "Does that mean I can ask you about Jax?"

My heart dropped into my stomach at the sound of his name. "Sure, Mom."

She pulled a chair in front of me. "Do you miss him?"

The bluntness and directness of the question caught me off guard. "Of course, I do."

She nodded. "And do you want him to come back to Hell and be with you?"

"More than anything." I swallowed against the knot in my throat.

"Why are you letting life pass you by? You can be happy, Morena. You are not a victim in this scenario. Jax had to find his way, and so did you. Your circumstances are unique, but we all have pain we face in life and relationships. You can't avoid the pain, but you can choose to be happy. And you can do it with Jax."

I leaned back and let out a long breath to collect my thoughts. "I'm trying to be happy, Mother. He didn't even have the courtesy to tell me himself he wasn't coming home after they ended Adam."

"Give him some grace, Morena. He dealt a brutal death to a celestial being. One he was related to many generations back. He sent the archangel known for wisdom to you. He was thinking of you even as he was broken. You would be wise to show him leniency because you might need some from him one day. If I recall correctly, he was giving you space too."

"He's shown me grace many times over," I said, thinking of how he'd been there when I took four innocent souls. "You're right, but what if he doesn't want to see me after I sent him away?"

"I am positive he is waiting for you," she said, patting my knee.

Mother had a gift for observing, and she'd helped me see that I was being a stubborn ass. I made up my mind to go see Jax, and I knew exactly where and how I wanted to make it happen. "I need a lieutenant to call a portal for me."

Mother winked at me. "That's my daughter. I saw one in the corridor. I'll send him in."

THE AIR WAS damp and chilled, similar to the last time we were here. I laid my hand over my heart. "Jax...Jax...Jax."

"We meet here again." His voice was warm like his breath against my skin when we made love.

"Stonehenge, you know."

"I do." He smiled but kept his distance.

I held up my hands. "No sparring this time. I'm not going to elbow you or kick you."

He flashed a wicked grin. "Would it be awkward if I'd hoped you would?"

My core heated. "Would it be awkward if I said I liked hearing you say that?"

He reached a hand out to me. "You excite me when you say such things."

I took his hand, and mine warmed from his touch. He smelled of salt and sea instead of his usual scent. "I miss you, Jax."

"I miss you too, my love. I promise to never leave without telling of my own volition. You are the place where everything is safe for me, and I never want to violate that trust."

"Then don't. Be honest with me. Not that we can't have things that are our own, but trust me to accept you as you are." I took a deep breath. "Because I love you, Jax, and I want to spend the rest of whatever our lives are with you."

"That sounded an awful lot like a proposal, Rena."

I blushed. "Maybe I should."

He dropped to a knee in front of me. "No, my love. That is something I've already asked your parents' permission to do. You are not stealing my thunder."

I giggled and shook my head.

"Morena." Jax paused. It never sounded right when he used my given name. "Rena, will you run into the fire of life and burn through eternity with me? Even if we must stop Armageddon together to get to the altar, will you do me the distinct honor of being my wife?"

My stomach fluttered, and my heart hammered in my chest. I tried to speak, but I was breathless. If my shoes hadn't sunk into the wet grass, I'd think I was floating.

"I'm going to need you to say something, my love." Jax smiled until his laugh lines were visible.

"Yes," I said. "There is no other right answer than yes."

Jax rose to his feet in one motion and lifted me from the waist. He spun us around and lowered me down. I wrapped my arms around his neck and captured his mouth.

He pulled back. "I have a ring, by the way. I carried it around with me everywhere until the last time we were here. Then, I put it up for safekeeping, but I'll get it on your finger as soon as you let me come home."

"I wasn't expecting this since we'd already talked about getting married. How long have you been planning this proposal?"

"I hadn't planned to ask here but for a while."

"What's a while, Jaxon?"

He sat me down on my feet and pushed the hair out of my face. "Since before all the Armageddon stuff."

"That's a long time."

"Not for our lifetimes."

I'd seen how short our lifetimes could be. "I don't know. I did die."

"Shh," he said. "Let's put that in the past and focus on the present."

"And the future," I added. The subject would need

discussion later, but this was a time for celebration. "We need to tell my parents."

He glided his hands up my sides. "Maybe we could celebrate with just the two of us first."

"Mmmm," I said. "I don't know. We're standing on the grounds of an internationally protected landmark. We might get caught."

Jax nuzzled my neck and burned a trail of kisses up to my ear. He dragged his teeth over my earlobe. "Can I change your mind?"

A shiver ran through my body. My arousal was immediate. "I was going to say yes."

"That's my girl." He devoured my mouth, and I melted into him. He slipped his hands under my T-shirt and lifted it. He broke the kiss to lift the fabric over my head. I reached for his shirt and did the same. We removed the rest of our clothes in a frenzy of need and want.

Jax picked me up and leaned my back against one of the stones as he drove into me. His hard length glided in from how wet I was. I bit down on his shoulder adjusting to his thickness, and he groaned.

"I don't think we're supposed to touch the stones," I gasped out in between Jax's thrusts. His touch melted me inside, and I wanted his hands on every part of my body.

"I don't fucking care about the stones." His voice was ragged. "I care about feeling you sliding up and down my cock." He plunged his length deep hitting the spot that made my toes curl.

My core constricted. I buried my head in his neck and

moaned. He reached between us, rubbing my clit. "I'm not going to last long, but I won't go without you."

His words were like liquid fire and seeped in to tighten the tension building in my core. The stone dug into my back, but I welcomed the pain mixing with the pleasure. "Deeper, Jax. Faster." I shoved one hand against the stone for leverage so I could drive my hips to meet his. I shook as the first wave of ecstasy came, and Jax cried out. His mouth covered mine. The sun rose, and I took in the beauty as Jax and I found our release together.

His lips locked on mine as he sat on the grass with me still wrapped around him. He adjusted so I was sitting in his lap. I leaned my head against his shoulder. My hair was a total mess, and it was worth it to connect with him. I relished in the bliss of being so close to him again. "That was…"

"Fucking perfect," he said, kissing the top of my head.

"Something like that," I said, wishing we had time to bask in the afterglow before going again. We couldn't risk being caught here, though. "Better get us out of here quick or we'll be in the pictures of eager tourists."

"And I want to get you somewhere I can take my time with you." Jax echoed my thoughts.

"Then get us out of here." I paused. "Portal man."

CHAPTER 59
JAX

I portaled us to our room in Hell. While we were adults and Lilith and Lucifer were well aware of our living arrangement, appearing in front of them in grass-stained clothes after mind-blowing sex at Stonehenge until the sun rose didn't seem like the appropriate choice.

"We smell like..." Rena's melodic tone was relaxed and soft.

I chuckled. "Like we just fucked across an internationally protected landmark?"

Rena's cheeks reddened. "Yes, that. Maybe a shower?"

"Are you going to be blushing like that all day?"

"Shut up and get in the shower with me." Her voice lowered, and the breathy sound filled my veins with liquid fire.

I scooped her up in my arms and kicked open the bathroom door.

"Put me down, Jax." Rena laughed.

I sat her on her feet.

Rena stripped her clothes off and threw them in the hamper. I'd forgotten about my clothes, staring at every perfect curve of her body.

"Need help?" she asked.

"No, go ahead. I'll be right behind you." I watched the water flow over her beautiful body, and my dick hardened in response. I yanked off my clothes and joined her under the water. I took the shampoo bottle from her hair. "Let me."

I INHALED DEEPLY as we walked toward the room the guards indicated Lilith and Lucifer were in. The floral scent of the shampoo I'd washed Rena's hair with wafted around us. My cock twitched, reminding me how I'd fucked her against the shower wall and drove into her until she called my name. *Stop. You are about to see her parents, dumbass.* Her parents were in the same library where Rena fell from Hell for the first time and multiple times after that. It was the beginning of this journey but not the end.

"It's going to be fine," she said. "You already have their permission. We're just letting them know I didn't turn you down."

I chuckled. "I thought you were going to say no."

"You're stuck with me now." She smiled up at me. Our

arms swung as we walked down the hall. She was blissful, and her happiness and safety were the most important things to me.

"If that's your form of punishment, I welcome it." I kissed her cheek.

The door opened as we neared it. Lucifer filled the doorway and stepped aside for us to enter. His towering presence heightened my nerves. *Fuck. This is going to be harder than I thought.*

"We're delighted to see you are home, Jax." Lilith sipped her tea and glanced at Lucifer. She motioned for us to sit on the sofa. "Both of us. Aren't we, Lucifer?"

"Yes, things were off without you here," Lucifer said. "Was there something you wanted to talk to us about?"

Rena's eyes sparkled, and she smiled so big her cheeks were raised and prominent. She looked like an angel instead of a demon, but she'd always been more on the angelic side.

"Yes." I blinked a few times, and my mouth went dry. I cleared my throat. I had their permission, but that was before I'd done the official proposal. It was like I was starting over. "Last night, I asked Rena to do me the honor of becoming my wife."

"And I said yes," Rena said in a rush. She sat up straight with excitement.

"I see," Lucifer said, turning his attention to Lilith.

Lilith clasped her hands to her chest. "I was hoping a wedding was what we'd be discussing today." She spread her arms wide.

Rena hopped up and crossed the sitting area to hug her mother. The two of them were having a mother-and-daughter moment, which left Lucifer and me staring at each other. He scrutinized me, and I glanced at the distance to the door. It wasn't that far. I might have been able to make it before Lucifer reached me, but he was the devil. He'd eventually find me.

"She's happy," Lucifer said.

"Yes." My voice came out in a broken squeak.

"I like seeing her this way. Make sure your life is lived in a way to make that happen."

"Yes, Lucifer." *Why couldn't time move a little faster for once? Fuck me.*

"Rena?" Lucifer used her nickname and opened his arms for her. "Come here."

She embraced him. "You'll walk me down the aisle, right?"

"Of course," he said, his voice gentle with her. "I'm happy for you and to officially welcome Jax to the family." He looked at me. "Although I considered him family before."

I gave him a head nod, and he returned it. I hadn't known he felt that way, but I realized I was where I belonged in more than one way.

"Lilith and I have some business to take care of this morning, but I'm sure you two have things to do as well."

I was relieved to have that over and get Rena to myself again.

"Yes," Rena said. "We'll see you this evening."

I CALLED THE PORTAL. "Trust me, my love."

Rena looked hesitant. "I do trust you. It's portaling that makes me uneasy these days."

She had a right to feel that way. Adam's spell had portaled us into the trap where she died, and Eve brought her back. "You portaled to Stonehenge."

"That was a necessary evil."

"I can go without you and bring the ring back."

"No. No, I'll go." She inhaled and then breathed out.

I counted silently One...Two...Three... "Just imagine we are falling from Hell like we did on your birthday."

"Let's do it before I change my mind."

The first portal I called closed by the time she decided, so I formed the symbols again.

Rena's gaze met mine, and she was looking for something. I held out my hand. "I've got you."

She took my hand and made the first step through the portal. I squeezed her hand and welcomed the warmth of not only her touch but the trust she showed. Waves lapped at our feet.

"Where are we?" Rena looked from the beach to the ocean.

"This is our private island. Lilith gave it to me for us when I was planning our proposal."

"You were going to do it here?"

"Stonehenge is pretty memorable too," I said, smiling

at how she almost snuck in her proposal. My dick hardened at the memory of thrusting into her against the ancient stone, and I wanted to make a similar memory on our island.

Rena giggled. "We definitely left our mark on Stonehenge."

"The house is just over there." I pointed to the porch protruding from the palms.

"And the entire island is ours?"

"It is, and see that island on the horizon?"

Rena shielded her eyes. "Yes."

"That is the closest one, and it happens to be your parents'. Lilith said they haven't been in years, though.

"I remember going to the isle when I was a kid, but I can't remember the last time we went as a family. We need to make sure they get away soon."

I didn't want to think about her parents tonight, and I laced my fingers with hers and led her to the house.

"This is a beautiful island. It's like our own personal paradise."

"That's exactly what it is." I ushered her up the white steps of the porch and into the cottage.

She took in the sloped plank ceiling and ran her hand over the white couch.

"Wait here." I ran to the bedroom and grabbed the ring from the nightstand. When I returned to the living room, Rena held a picture of us in her hand.

I loved that picture. It was right before I left to train with the guard. I already knew I was in love with her but needed to be someone worthy of her. The phones couldn't flip the camera like the new ones, but I'd held it up and told her to lean in for the photo. She'd kissed my cheek as I snapped the pic.

"When was this taken? I don't even remember."

"We don't have many pictures of us. That needs to change." I took the framed photo and looked at it. "This was on one of those flip phones Lilith gave us. They were antiques, I think. We couldn't do anything but take pictures on them. When I was in the human realm, I found a demon posing as a shop owner who could enhance and print them off. This was my favorite, but there is an album of all of them on the coffee table." I'd been looking at them every day since I'd been here. I put the picture back in place.

Rena cradled my cheek. I closed my eyes and relished in the touch. "I'm sorry I sent you away."

"You have nothing to apologize for. I left first, and we're leaving all that in the past. Remember?"

"Focused on the present and the future." She smiled, and her eyes lit up. I took her hand and knelt. She deserved the proposal I had planned, and I'd do it a dozen times for her if that was what made her happy.

"I know I already proposed, but I want to ask you again with ring in hand."

"Okay." Her smile grew. I opened the small black box with the ring I'd had made inside.

"Rena, love of my existence, life is meaningless without you. With you, I found what it means to love and be loved back. I learned what it means to have a family, and most of all, I found my equal. Will you be my wife?"

"Yes." Tears filled her eyes, and I slid the ring onto her finger.

"I can't wait to do that again with a wedding band." I hugged her to me. "I love you."

CHAPTER 60

RENA

I froze for a heartbeat, overcome by the deep affection I had for him and the devotion he'd proclaimed for me twice now. "I love you," I said the three words he wanted to hear, but they weren't enough. He was a realm all to himself, and there would never be words to describe that. All the other parts of our world fell away when he looked at me or touched me. And it was his touch I desired most. "I need you, Jax. Around me. On me. Inside me."

He was on his feet in a blur, pushing me backward. My back slammed against the wall, and for a split second, my thoughts were wasted on whether or not the wall would hold. A gasp escaped from my lips. *Damn.* His mouth crashed down on mine. I ran my hands up his arms and cupped the base of his neck. A groan rumbled against my body, and it was guttural, letting me know he craved my touch as much as I did his.

"I'm sorry," I whispered against his lips.

He leaned away just far enough he could make eye contact with me. "For what?"

"For taking so long to call to you." My voice was breathless.

"Never apologize for taking what you need, my love." His lips explored in a soft dance against mine, claiming my mouth again.

His words could fill a tome on how to love the heir of Hell, but to him, I was Rena. My heart was full as the tension built in me. I arched my back, forcing my breasts into his chest.

"I want you, Jax. Only you. Always you." I nipped at his jawline.

His eyes flared and heated with something unhinged, and I welcomed it. Wanted it. Hot need unlike anything else I'd experienced spiked down my chest and into my core.

"Rena." His timbre was rough like a warning, but whatever opened in him, I wanted to expose.

"Jax, too many clothes." I reached for his shirt, but he caught my hands, pinning them above my head. His mouth burned a trail along my neck and down to the V-neck of my shirt. He grabbed the material between his teeth. "Jax..." He yanked the fabric, and my shirt was free of my body and thoroughly destroyed. Heat flooded my chest like a wave of fire.

I extracted my hands from his and grasped his navy blue crew neck.

"Rena, I'm already down several shirts."

I smiled. "We'll get more." I ripped his shirt off and tossed the remnants to the floor.

"I'll get my pants," he said, unbuckling his belt with speed. He worked the button and zipper, and his pants dropped.

I shuffled out of mine, dragging my eyes up his body to find his massive erection. I gripped his hip and moved closer. My fingers curled around his length. He growled. Our mouths collided, and the way we devoured each other was carnal.

Jax skimmed his hands down my back and over the curve of my ass until he reached my thighs. He lifted me, and I wound my legs around him, letting out a whimper. His tongue stroked in my mouth, and it was deliciously wicked. My back crashed into something hard, and it screeched along the floor until it hit the wall. Wood splintered behind me.

"Shit." Jax reached for something falling. He held it up like a prize. *Our photo.* He set it on a table. His eyes came back to mine, and they were like golden fire. He speared his fingers through my hair. I leaned forward and kissed him with a hunger greater than a new Night Child.

His mouth savored the sensitive spot on my neck as he fiddled with the clasp of my bra until it fell away. I pressed my chest against his, eager for skin-to-skin contact. He coaxed me to lounge against the couch and cupped my breasts while he drew a line with his tongue from the base of my throat to the valley of my breasts. I groaned and arched my back to get closer to him. He swirled his tongue around a peak, and the thumb of his other hand flicked across the turgid peak of the other.

My insides were liquid lava. His hands skated down over my stomach and kept going until he reached my inner thigh, squeezing it.

"Touch me, Jax. I need to feel you touch me."

"My pleasure," he said, his voice ragged. His eyes flared, and he tore my panties away. Those magic fingers of his stroked my slick core. I arched up toward his hand. He held me in place with his other hand, digging into my hip. I ran my fingers through his hair and down his neck to his shoulders. My fingernails scraped against his flesh drawing blood. He made tighter and tighter circles against my swollen clit. Pleasure coiled in my core, demanding release. His mouth found mine and captured the moan on my lips. He slid a finger into me, and I bucked against him.

"So soft and wet." His voice was rough like gravel. He slipped a second finger inside me. "I want you to come around me. My fingers and my cock."

I tilted my head, and my arm flew up and knocked something over—a lamp, I think. The sound crashed around me as I rode Jax's fingers. He curled them into my inner walls, and it undid me. I clamped down around his fingers while he stroked my clit with his thumb My back bowed, and my vision narrowed. The friction tipped me over the edge, and I spiraled into my orgasm. Everything we'd overcome brought us here, and our love heightened every single sensation. I shattered. Shuddering, I cried out, "Jax."

His tongue stroked into my mouth as my body continued to vibrate. "Beautiful," he whispered.

My breaths came in erratic pants. The grin on Jax's face looked like he'd reached his peak instead of me. I cradled his face with my hand. "I love you."

He slid his fingers from my body and reached underneath my thighs until he lifted me in his arms. He nibbled my earlobe as he carried me toward what I assumed was the bedroom. His woodsy scent filled the space, and I wanted him closer.

He spun us around and sat on the bed with me in his lap. His thick cock bumped against my belly. I reached between our bodies and stroked his warm, hard length. Jax pumped into my hand and groaned. "I need to feel you around me, Rena."

My pulse pounded at his raw hunger for me. It matched my need for him. I raised u onto my knees and slid the tip of his cock along my slickness, relishing how soft it felt against my core despite how hard he was.

"Rena, please."

I lined him up with my center and inched myself down on his head. I breathed in, adjusting to the fullness. Jax flipped me over onto my back. I gasped at the change in sensation.

"I need you now, Rena." Jax bit my shoulder.

"Then take me, Jaxon," I said.

He thrust into me. I screamed my pleasure.

"Never call me Jaxon. I'm Jax to you. You're Rena."

The lust built in me and was primal. I lifted my hips as he thrust again, and his cock drove deep inside me. "Jax."

My body heated, and I opened my eyes to see fire skimming over my skin. *Sweet angel's ass. What is happening?* The flames expanded out over Jax without burning us or the bedding.

"That's new." Jax pulled back and thrust into me again, his pace quickening. *Damn, he feels good.* Every stroke drove me closer to the edge.

"So is that," I said, seeing a blue cocoon around us that was Jax's essence. My breath came in rapid, shallow pants.

"Fuck." Jax groaned, grinding the base of his dick against my bundle of nerves.

I propelled my hips up to meet his next stroke. Pleasure built in me again, demanding release, and the flames over our skin flitted against the blue bubble.

"My love, you are beautiful." His lips caressed my jawline and claimed my mouth. I bucked my hips against him at my breaking point. "Let go."

He thrusted as if demanding my compliance, and the first wave of pleasure consumed me so powerfully I would explode. Jax shuddered and rode the waves with me through our mutual release. Every time we'd been together had been good, but that was on another level. It was like we were one. Our chests heaved against each other. Jax rested his forehead against mine.

"I missed you." His lips caressed both my temples. "All of you."

"I missed you, too, even when you pissed me off by giving me the space I needed." I brought my mouth to his in a soft dance.

Jax chuckled and rolled us over so I was nestled against his side. There was no safer place in any realm for me than in his arms. He made feather-light circles on my shoulder with his fingers. "What do you think the fire and essence meant when we…"

"Were fucking?" I laughed. "I think it was part of the balance and scale thing. Like maybe how connected we are from it."

He wrapped his other arm over me. "I thought something like that as well, but we don't need a sign like that to tell us how much we belong together."

Our connection was stronger. I'd sensed it even before the mind-blowing orgasms, but I wasn't sure if it was the balance and scale or us in general. I wasn't ready to talk about it yet, though. That would come soon enough. "Pretty sure we destroyed that shelf in the living room."

"It's replaceable, and I'm sure there will be other casualties," he said, his voice sleepy.

"I hope so," I said, yawning. "Mother is going to flip her lid."

"Over broken furniture? I know for a fact she and Lucifer—"

"Eww. If you bring up my parents' sex life in comparison to ours right now, we will never break furniture again."

"Point taken." Jax chuckled. "Then what did you mean?"

"She's been wanting to plan my wedding since I was a little girl." I sighed. "I'd rather it be small and intimate, but that is not going to be what we have. Are you okay with that?"

"I knew what I was signing up for when I asked you, Rena. You are the heir to Hell." He shifted, so I was up on his chest and forced to look into his eyes. "I love you, Rena. There are no conditions for it. I love the messiness as much as the good."

"I don't deserve you, Jax. Not one little bit."

"No, you deserve more, but you have me. All of me." He sunk his fingers into my hair and kissed me into a soft oblivion. Everything would change from here forward. We were the balance and the scale, but we were Jax and Rena too.

CHAPTER 61

RENA

S ix months later

MOTHER and I turned one of the meeting rooms we rarely used in Hell into a makeshift wedding planning area. Fabric swatches, flower samples, and various other wedding-related items were spread across the tables.

There was still a lot left to do, but Mother thrived on designing and planning. We were using part of my coronation dress in the design. I insisted on it since Mother's coronation was part of mine. She'd shed happy tears when I told her I wanted to repurpose it, and she got the seamstresses right on the work. My final fitting was scheduled for next week. I picked up the list of foods we planned to serve.

"Mother, do you think we should change the menu? I don't know if we have enough options for our human guests," I said. Planning a wedding where demons, archangels, vampires, and humans would all be in attendance proved rather challenging. The difference in etiquette among each of them was maddening.

"Morena, there is less than a month until the wedding. You must stop changing things. Besides, there will be a total of twelve humans at the ceremony, and most of the attendees will either not be eating or will partake of the human food. There should be plenty."

"Three weeks," I said. My stomach roiled. I let out a slow breath. A zip went through my birthmark. It'd been doing that for a month or so like it had short-circuited. At least that was my assumption since there hadn't been any threats, much less any Nephilim. Not one Nephilim had been sighted since they broke into Gothica and stole a statue for an obscure mythological god.

Mother pursed her lips. "What?

"Three weeks until the nuptials." A knock came at the door. I opened it to see Jax. His eyes were distant, and my stomach knotted at the sight. "Why are you knocking?"

He refocused on me. "This is your wedding space, and the door was closed." Dark circles were noticeable under his eyes, and he appeared to be in shock. Something happened. But what?

"Very polite, Jax," Mother said, looking up from the seating chart. "Have you come to go over details?"

"It looks like he needs to eat," I said, cupping his cheek

and skimming my thumb under his eye. "And I'm not talking about human food."

He was quiet. His demeanor was so serious I dropped my hand to my side. His eyes were filled with so much worry it made my throat close up. "We have an issue."

"What kind of issue?" Mother asked, crossing the room to stand close. She assessed Jax, and her worry mixed with mine.

My stomach sank to the floor. The look on Jax's face told me whatever he was about to say was bad. Very bad. *Nephilim?*

Jax ran a jerky hand through his hair. He swallowed like he had difficulty performing the simple action. "We were in a meeting, and all the archangels froze in place."

It was more than bad.

Mother clutched her stomach. "And Lucifer?"

"Frozen in place like the others."

"Our regular room?" I asked, mentally fortifying myself for what we would find. There was no maybe about it. This was an attack on my family, me, and Hell itself.

"They'll be vulnerable. We need to go now," Mother said.

I was already almost to the door. It took us less than a minute to get to the space, but it was empty.

I spun around trying to understand. "Jax? Are we in the right place?"

He looked around. Confusion etched across his face. "We were definitely in this room."

"Maybe they unfroze and went after who did it?"

"No," Mother said in an uneasy tone. "I sense a presence I haven't sensed in a thousand years."

"Who could have moved them that fast? It's not possible."

"It is if you are all-powerful." Mother's voice was barely a whisper. "Someone who hides in storms. The same being as the statue the Nephilim stole from Gothica."

"The weird statue of the mythological god?" I asked in disbelief it was a coincidence the Nephilim wanted that particular statue and the appearance of this new threat. Mother was being paranoid or maybe the wedding planning had taken its toll on her.

Thunder clapped. In Hell. That didn't happen. Lightning struck in the room, and I covered my eyes. Gabriel appeared directly in front of me, and I stumbled backward. Jax caught me. They all returned. *How? What just happened?* My relief and concern mixed as I tried to comprehend what I saw.

"What the fuck..." Jax whispered.

"Lilith?" Lucifer asked. "I thought you and Rena were working on wedding details today."

"Luce, you all were gone for several minutes and just came back." Mother's voice was even. Too even for the moment.

"Where's Uriel?" I asked. He was in the meeting, and Jax said he was one of the frozen ones.

"He was right here." Lucifer looked at the empty seat on his left. "What do you mean we came back?"

"You know what I mean," Lilith said, her voice remaining eerily calm. "He has returned."

"Are you suggesting a fabled god did this?" I asked. I couldn't fathom what being had this kind of power, but our fables had proved to be grounded in facts multiple times.

"I don't even want to speak his name." Mother's voice shook.

"Typhon," Father said, rage filling his voice. "His name is Typhon, and he is real. He was exiled from this realm for the devastation he caused."

"And he has our brother, Lucifer," Michael said.

"I know that." Father faced Michael. "Just as you know we can't approach a being like Typhon and will have to wait for him to appear."

Jax wrapped his arms around me, and I leaned against him. "I'm scared, and I don't say that often."

"I've got you," he whispered in my ear. "I've always got you."

"Who excited him, and how is he back?" I asked.

Gabriel paced the room. "We're just going to wait here for Uriel to reappear or for Typhon to do something else?"

"No," Father said. "We prepare for war."

Typhon was the nightmare of all realms. He was a being who cared nothing for life and would squash it without hesitation. Uriel told me once any being from any realm could be the catalyst. This was it. The start of Armageddon. The real Armageddon and not the trivial battles we'd had with Adam. Typhon would challenge everything we held in our hearts and destroy it just to conquer us.

As I took in the faces of everyone in this room, I wondered if we would get Uriel back and if the cost of our success would be the lives of some of those closest to me. We'd faced much death and overcame it together. It'd made us stronger, but it'd made us vulnerable too. Jax's face was the last one I found, and the fire in his eyes said he was there by my side. The balance and the scale would fight together and die together if that's what it required to defeat Typhon.

To be continued...

Acknowledgments

To my parents, although they have both passed on, I would have never pursued the writing journey I started over a decade ago without their encouragement. Their memories continue to inspire me to push forward in the toughest times and smile in others when I incorporate something they said or did into a character.

To my sister and my nieces, you continue to be my cheer squad, especially when I need it most. Thank you for being there and for always celebrating even the smallest wins with me. It means the world to me how much support you have thrown my way.

To my beta readers, ARC readers, and fans, your response to Rena and Jax's love story is what encouraged me to move forward with this series. As always, I want to recognize those who actively seek out indie authors to support whether that is on booktok, or bookstagram, or any other platform.

To my editors, Dawn and Lisa, thank you for asking provocative and thought provoking questions about my stories. Your honest input not only makes my stories better but makes me a better writer. I couldn't do it without you!

About the Author

Susan Person is a multi-contest finalist in the paranormal and dark paranormal romance categories. Recently, she returned to college to pursue a degree in anthropology and graduated in 2021. Susan enjoys meeting writers and readers alike at conferences and events. She knew at an early age she wanted to write powerful heroines and fulfills that dream by writing badass empowered heroines who take charge in their paranormal worlds.

Susan grew up on a thoroughbred horse farm before moving to the big city of Dallas. She considers herself a Texan but is loyal to her home state of Arkansas. A lover of travel, she has visited several countries with many more to go on her list. She particularly loved dowsing at Stonehenge and seeing the Parthenon in Athens. The outdoors is a place where Susan finds inspiration and can often be found in a park, at the lake, or on a road trip. She especially loves the mountains. Furry animals hold a special place in her heart, and dogs tend to seek her out as a friend.

Connect with her at susanperson.com

instagram.com/susanwritespnr

tiktok.com/@susanwritespnr

facebook.com/susanwritespnr

goodreads.com/susanperson

bookbub.com/authors/susan-person

WANT TO LEARN MORE ABOUT SUSAN PERSON?

Scan the QR code below to see where you find more of Susan's book or see what reader events she is attending.